IT IS WHAT IT IS

IT IS
WHAT IT IS

By
Maureen Edwards

Copyright: © Maureen Edwards

Copyright Front Page Image: © Elite Authors

Publisher: Sunflower Blooms Inc. 2020

ISBN: 978-1-69432-369-9

For Mom and Dad
who always encouraged me to keep diaries and journals.

CHAPTERS

CHAPTER 1

Georgie Nelson pulled into the desolate faculty parking lot singing Bon Jovi's "Livin' on a Prayer" at the top of her lungs. And why not? No one was around yet, and she was thrilled to be starting her new career in teaching! Beads of sweat rolled down her neck from the nerves, and the broken air conditioner in her old car. It had been impossible for her to pay for everything before starting work, so the air conditioning repair was on the back burner.

Her white linen dress stuck to her skin while her frizzy, curly auburn hair continued to expand with the humidity. Gathering her things, she left the car, jumping around, hoping the dress would stick a little less to her body. She wanted to look perfect but knew that was a delusion. Georgie was a hot mess, inside and out.

She threw everything she thought a proper teacher needed into her bag: paper, pencils, laptop, rubber bands, folders, even paper clips. Ever the perfectionist, Georgie had researched as many of "The Top Ten Things for New Teachers" websites as she could find. She needed to make this new career work out and was determined to become the rock star teacher she was hired to be. Finally, having gathered her things together, Georgie walked briskly toward the school. Eden Hills Middle School was a gigantic four-story brown brick building with large windows stretching for as far as she could see. Georgie could not help but focus on the cornerstone, which read January 2, 1895. The building had been around a long time. If she was honest, it looked as if it had.

"Can you hold the door for me, please?" someone called out.

Turning, Georgie saw a tall, fit, tanned woman who had obviously missed the dress code memo. She wore yoga pants with a big neon-orange T-shirt which read RELAX across it. Far from the motto on her shirt, the woman carrying a large bundle of full manila folders looked slightly frazzled. Georgie thought the size of the pile would have taken her at least four trips to move to and from the car.

"Can I help you with something else?" Georgie grabbed onto the railing tightly in order to keep her balance.

"If you could take the top one, they're slipping." And the determined, scattered woman walked into the building towards the main office, exactly where Georgie was heading.

Beating her to the door, Georgie held it open for her. The two secretaries sitting behind the desk jumped to their feet. "Julia, the superintendent's office called already. They need the building report for the next board meeting. And the shipments of supplies were just delivered downstairs finally!"

Georgie's eyes sparkled. "Oh! We've spoken on the phone a few times. Nice to finally meet you in person. I'm Georgie!"

Julia's face beamed. "It's Georgie Nelson, in the flesh. Come and let's chat in my office."

Turning, Georgie tried hard to keep pace with Julia, who walked at a fast pace across the room and into an office on the other side. Georgie wondered if Julia always maintained this type of speed. The baby blue room matched the sky in the large painting behind Julia's meticulously clean desk. Her educational degrees were placed proportionately around the art on the left and right sides. Glancing at the names of the schools listed, Georgie swallowed hard.

"Just gotta primp a little." Julia grabbed her suit and makeup case from the chair. "Central office loved you in the interviews, and once I saw our alma mater on top, I went from happiness to ecstasy in minutes! It's not every day we have the daughter of a Pulitzer Prize award-winning writer, but we'll keep that between you and me." And she winked. "So, I am currently knee-deep in dissertation research but would like to meet with you after the orientation so we can discuss your position further. Well, better get going, I wanted you to be aware, so if we only meet every once in a while, it isn't on you, it's me." Julia stood and held out a hand.

Georgie swiftly left the room, soon finding a woman in the outer office alone at her desk. In her sixties, she was a generously built Asian American woman with tight-fitting leggings and a baby blue T-shirt with white lettering saying Eden Hills across it. Looking up from the computer screen, she slowly stood and rubbed her eyes. It was hard for Georgie not to stare at the three pencils sticking out of her hair.

She focused on Georgie's face with a wide grin. "Hey, I'm Tiffany," she said as she bounced to the counter. "We're always crazy busy at this time of year. We have a full schedule." There were two stacks of papers on the long desk. She handed Georgie a piece of paper from both. "Here is the schedule, and here is a map. Oh, and turn around." Georgie did; whereupon Tiffany pointed to a wall of wooden mailboxes with names typed below each. "Your mailbox is over there. Alphabetical, of course." Then whispering she said, "Check it a few times a day if you can. Although Julia tends to use email, Jose sends information the old-fashioned way by snail mail."

Tiffany picked up a piece of paper from her desk, which Georgie noted contained a long list of names. Pulling one of the pencils from her hair, she quickly checked off Georgie's name.

"Georgie Nelson, eighth-grade English. Right! Orientation starts at eight-thirty in the cafeteria right across the hall." She pointed midair to somewhere unseen. "You'll get a load of information. This year we have twenty-two first-year teachers, so if you see other people looking for help, can you spread the word they have to be in the cafeteria by eight-thirty sharp? It's nice to see someone early, considering it's not yet seven-thirty." Tiffany abruptly moved back to her desk to answer the demands of the continually ringing phone.

"Err... Sounds great. I'll go and wait until it starts," Georgie said to no one in particular as Tiffany was otherwise engaged. Turning, she started to leave, holding the door for several staff members entering the office. Looking them in the eye, she received mixed reactions.

In the corridor, Georgie felt relief at being early as it meant she had missed the busy morning traffic. She'd only been to Eden Hills, New Jersey, once before, for her interview. She still had no idea how the job had landed in her lap! She had been sending out her résumé to hundreds of districts for months, without one phone call. As such, she had been amazed to hear last Monday from the assistant superintendent, calling her in for an interview. After what seemed like a grilling, she had then met Dr. Jonathan Salva, superintendent of schools. He seemed more interested in her favorite hockey team than about her educational pedagogy. At the time, Georgie was grateful she had had all the relevant documents, such as fingerprints, immunizations, and social security with her. It had been like a dream when he proclaimed those magic words some ten minutes later, "We are good to go, Georgie Nelson. You are hired."

Four days later, she was a full-time teacher for the first time in her life, especially considering she had been an editor for the previous ten years. The change was right for her as she had become tired of never feeling fulfilled. After the past few years, she was finally willing to rectify what should have been her first and only career - teaching. The teaching position was her big chance, especially after going to graduate school at night for all those years to try to make a difference in her life. To work with children was always a passion simmering beneath the surface. The minute she worked with students during her practicum, her heart sang a melodious song, one she could not stifle any longer working in an office.

It seemed the new people she passed on the way to the cafeteria were carrying more bags than she was. And they were dressed way more casually than she had expected. She was starting to get a little worried she might have missed some information. Georgie felt she stood out, and not in the right way. All she could hope for was to find a new friend to ask for help.

She sighed deeply. At least she'd arrived early and found the cafeteria without a problem. Entering the room, it smelled of potent cleaning fluids, which made the seafoam green tile floor glisten like a mirror. The air conditioning wasn't strong enough to cope, especially with the hot sun shining through the surrounding windows. However, Georgie noted the view off in the distance through the partially open windows. While there were trees and hills as far as she could see, at a closer look, Georgie saw factory chimneys to the west and, shooting along the vista, construction cranes to the east. Her eyebrows raised; Eden Hills seemed to be much more metropolitan than at first glance. Georgie's eyes drifted to the lumpy, uneven paint in the lower corners of the window ledge. The hard, brown substances seemed mixed in with a variety of white hues of color as if the paint was slopped on by someone in a rush.

Never one to sit in the front, she picked a table at the back which had a prime seat in case there was a PowerPoint presentation or a lecture. Muffled noises outside the room refocused her mind, as Georgie knew she would need all the help she could get.

Slowly staff began to trickle into the room, mostly in small groups. It seemed some people knew each other and were chatting in hushed tones. In contrast, others laughed hysterically about something secretly funny. Soon the tables filled, but Georgie was left alone at the back. She wasn't sure if it was due to sweat stains on the back of her dress or her massive curly hair. Or maybe because they'd all read the article on teacher orientation, which screamed, "Sit in the front row!"

She almost moved a little closer, but then a man, a good dozen years older than she, took her by surprise.

"Hello." He had spoken in a low, friendly tone as he joined her at the table. He wore shorts, an Eden Hills T-shirt, glasses, and sneakers. It looked as if he too, had a car with a broken air conditioner. "What are you in for? Let me guess… you're the new science teacher?" Georgie shook her head as he continued to guess. "Math? Special Ed? Guidance?"

By now, her head was hurting from smiling politely. Georgie was starting to get a bit of a complex. She was also wondering if he would only guess her specialty last. "Ah, English! That's it."

With relief, she pushed her shoulders back and sat straighter on the bench.

"Were you starting to get worried?" He smirked like a Cheshire cat and stifled a cough.

She laughed blushing. "I was starting to, yes!"

His light brown eyes glistened behind his glasses. "I was teasing you. As a mentor teacher, I sit in on most of the interview committees, but you were interviewed while I was on vacation. I knew who you were from a process of elimination. Congrats on the job! You nervous, excited, or what?"

Her stomach was churning. "Oh, everything. I feel so thankful to be part of the faculty and will work to the best of my ability to meet each child's needs."

He rubbed his black hands through his short tapered haircut. Georgie noticed he was attractive, even though he might not have showered today. She stared for another moment, thinking he could have passed for John Legend's older brother.

"Save the shtick for someone else. I'm sure you'll be great. You don't have to sell it to me."

She protested, "But I mean it! This is my dream to change a child's life! I'm sorry, I didn't get your name." Her face had turned red with embarrassment.

He tapped his feet on the floor. "Listen, trust me, here is the first tip of the day for orientation. Where is the school calendar?" He rustled through the folder he carried and placed the school calendar on the table. Leaning closer, he whispered, as if what he was about to say was top secret. "Look! The most critical thing you will learn today is... vacation days. Trust me, the first thing you need to do is mark off all the days you are off so you can plan vacations and fun things to do."

For a moment he looked off in the distance. "This is a burnout job, and you need something to look forward to. Beach, sun, snow, whatever."

Gobsmacked, Georgie gasped, "We haven't even started yet, and you're looking at the school calendar for days off? Winter vacation? April break? Is that what you mean?"

Dimples appeared on his cheeks and chin. "Now you're catching on! Look, we still have February break too! Woo-hoo!" He had whooped much louder than expected - most of the room was hushed and turned to look at the two of them.

Georgie suddenly felt slightly afraid to engage any more with this moron than she had to. How bad does this look? She thought, *I sat in the back row with a guy dressed like a bum counting the days until we are not working.* The image was putting knots in her stomach and making her face flush bright red. This was not the way to obtain tenure. It was also not the first impression she wanted to portray. Suddenly Georgie needed to get away from this guy before the administration came in and saw her as a bad apple! She started to move a little across the bench.

However, just then, the doors opened and the administrators walked into the room.

"Oh... my... God," Georgie whispered aloud. She was stuck at the back with the worst mentor teacher ever, corrupting her. "I'm screwed."

Glancing closer, Georgie saw Julia Bradley had changed into a navy-blue suit and high heels. She was carrying the massive pile of folders from earlier. An average-sized, middle-aged man with dark hair and brown skin, wearing too-tight khaki pants and a red polo T-shirt followed behind her. He made no attempt to help, even though the pile wobbled as she walked.

"What's wrong with you?" whispered her tablemate, snapping her back to reality. He was staring at Georgie as if he could see her panic.

"I... I... I..." She had nothing to say, so she shut her mouth.

The corruptible stranger pointed at her, and in a low voice said, "Listen, take a chill pill. Otherwise, if you can't handle this short introduction to 'teaching for the rest of your life' stuff, the kids will see right through you and eat you alive. As for me, I'm going to a beach in Bermuda at Christmas break... I hope. What do you want to do?" He knew he was confusing her every time he gave her some of his pearls of wisdom.

Clearing her throat, she leaned in and looked him in the eye. "I want to make my lesson plans and try to find my classroom so I can get things organized." She then tried to stop slouching and muster up some confidence.

"Good luck. I'm outta here before the administrators make me do something. See you at happy hour."

"Happy hour? It's only eight-thirty a.m.!" exclaimed Georgie in a whisper.

"When teacher orientation ends, happy hour begins. That's where you learn all the important information, so make sure you go. These guys will talk, which will only tell you one side of the school. Happy hour tells you the rest - trust me! You need to show up." And with that, the new stranger shuffled out of the room through the backdoor exit.

Once he had left her alone, Georgie felt much better, but she realized she better make some friends quickly. While the administrators organized themselves at the front of the room, Georgie moved to a closer table, glancing at her new colleagues sitting there. The three young female teachers acknowledged her briefly, introducing themselves by name and their subject specialties. Georgie was feeling a lot calmer meeting these new people, believing she'd made the right decision to sit with them. Better than staying with a crazy mentor teacher who, come to think of it, had not even told her his name. Tears began to well in her eyes as she felt hopeful about being in the right place at the right time in her life.

CHAPTER 2

Principal Julia Bradley began the orientation. "Today, I am privileged to welcome twenty-two new teachers to Eden Hills. I was once in your shoes; it seems like yesterday. You may hear people say, 'my door is always open.' Well, I'm the one who really means it!" It seemed as if she was taking a slight jab at the man next to her. "I love the first day of school activities since everyone should be refreshed and ready to go!"

Julia's face appeared to shine. "I've been working in this district my entire career. This year is my third one as principal, which is a thrill." She licked her lips with cautious hope. "Today, we have a packed schedule. Be sure to refer to the program you should have received. If you don't have a copy, although I already emailed it to you, there are hard copies here. After this, there is a technology portion. The veteran staff will join you for the training. We have a new district system for grades, progress reports, and remote learning portals everyone needs to learn. As some of you know, over the last few years, we had emergency closures, but we continue to work on our staff's technology skills to maintain the students' lessons remotely. After lunch, the superintendent will be here to meet you." Glancing at her watch, Julia gritted her teeth, "I'm pleased now to introduce Mr. Jose Gonzalez, our vice principal."

Jose was slightly overweight, with a belly falling over the belt of his wrinkled pants. He wore thin black-rimmed glasses with tinted frames which matched his short, curly black hair. It was hard for anyone to see precisely what or where he was looking. "It's a pleasure to see all of you today, and I welcome you to Eden Hills. You will each receive a folder with your class rosters and schedules in it for you to take home. It's the first step to getting you organized for the first day of school. Now, let's meet everyone, why don't we?"

One by one, the teachers stood, stated their names, hometown locations, and the reason why they had chosen to teach. Some added odd, obscure facts about their likes or dislikes.

As Georgie sat through the introductions, she tried to think of something witty or fascinating to say, but nothing came to mind. She couldn't believe how excited everyone was. Running out of time, she wanted to make a tremendous first impression. Finally, it was her turn to speak. With as much grace as possible, she slowly stood up. In a confident tone, she began. "My name is Georgie Nelson, and I will be teaching English to eighth-grade students. This is my first teaching job; it is a dream come true! I'm happy to meet all of you since I intend to learn something from everyone. If I ask a ton of questions, please don't mind me. I want to make a difference with kids and hope I can do so here at Eden Hills!"

Georgie had thought she would shrivel into a ball, but the unexpected happened. All at once, she heard the sound of applause. Looking around in shock, she saw everyone in the room grinning and clapping. However, she could not help but notice Jose scowling, and she wondered what had caused such a reaction, a total contrast to the others.

Jose opened his mouth to speak, but nothing came out. He walked back to the podium and murmured, "Back to Ms. Bradley." Placing the microphone in the holder, he walked away, cracking his knuckles.

Julia began the PowerPoint presentation, which had been Jose's job when she first became principal. Over the years and lack of cooperation from Jose, she had decided it was much easier for her to go through the information herself. Vital information about the mission, vision, and philosophy of the building was clarified. Finally, she summed up the hour-long presentation by saying, "I hope district and building goals are clear to you? Remember also that student attendance matters. High expectations for students are anticipated. State tests in the spring need to be a focus in your lesson plans, but they are not everything. It's a delicate balance to integrate test-taking skills throughout the year, so the students are prepared." Julia used excitable language as she made reliable eye contact. "Consult with one another along with your subject supervisors. There are some amazing tenured teachers who can troubleshoot with you if you're stuck."

With a deep sigh, she gazed around the room. "Finally, classroom management is the biggest challenge due to class size and the needs of the students. If there are discipline issues, address them immediately. Call the parents, send emails, Facetime; whatever it takes! Please consult with your colleagues, contact Jose or me. Are there any questions?" She paused to check to see if the group was still breathing. No one raised their hands.

"Thank you for your attention. That concludes the morning session. The second half of the day takes place in the computer lab with Mr. Williams. For lunch today you will be treated, by myself and Mr. Gonzalez, to pizza. It's the least we can do since we are packing three days of orientation into one. Before you break, please come to the front table and get your rosters and schedules. Remember, these will change, so check your email since the flow of information is constant. Enjoy your day."

Georgie's stomach was churning as she looked inside her folder and skimmed the names of her students. There were five long pages of names, too many to count. Referring to the building map, she still had no idea where her classroom was located. She had spent too much on items to decorate the room and had mistakenly left them in the car. She would have to run out to get them eventually. She closed her eyes for a moment feeling as if she was in information overload.

"Georgie!" someone called, causing her to jump. Turning around hastily Georgie dropped her folder, all the papers falling at her feet. Facing her was a twenty-something, golden brown-skinned woman dressed all in black with matching black nail polish. She had long, jet-black hair with hot pink highlights, which caused Georgie to stare for a brief moment.

They both gathered the papers, and as the woman handed them to Georgie, she introduced herself. "*Dios mío, perdóname.* I'm Lilliana Perez. We'll be teaching together since I'm the special education inclusion teacher for the eighth grade!"

Georgie put the papers back in her folder. "I'm so glad to meet you. Do you know where to go from here?" Noticing little heart tattoos with black writing on Lilliana's two wrists, she couldn't help squinting to read them. On her left wrist was, *Viejo*. On her right, *Vieja*.

Lilliana rubbed the back of her neck. "*Sí*, I went to middle school in this building years ago. Can we sit together? I'm a nervous wreck. This is my first job out of college as if you can't tell. *Estoy asustado.*"

Georgie smiled. "I am so relieved to hear someone else is, too. So excited we'll be working together. Did you look at your folder yet? I haven't had a minute free to myself. You might be carrying more things than me, too!" She could see Lilliana had three bags of materials along with her laptop.

Lilliana clutched her items tightly. "No, I am so overwhelmed, I have barely slept since I was hired, and am so worried these kids will know more than I do." Lilliana was biting her lip. "Have a lot riding on this job."

Georgie declared with a clear and confident tone, "I student taught last semester in a sixth grade in south Jersey, and I have to tell you, I'm worried about the same thing. I dreamed about being an elementary teacher, but there were no jobs for that age group. How I managed to get hired for middle school where the kids are bigger than me is a shock. I read on-line we need to fake it; fake a lot for the first few weeks. Fake, we know their games. Fake, we know everything. Fake we are mean. Fake. Sounds like a plan?" And Georgie cringed, glancing her way. "Hopefully I didn't scare you too much!"

Lilliana shook her head. "I read the same article and will follow your lead. Seems logical. Tough, firm, mean. The problem is I am easygoing, a mush, so it will be hard!" Lilliana led the way along the quiet hallway behind the rest of the group.

Georgie kept pace with Lilliana as she walked. "Me too, but we can relax in January and be ourselves by then." It was as if Lilliana was deliberately strolling to stay away from the others.

Lilliana whispered, "*Sí*, but we have to keep talking to each other to make sure we are on the same page, and if it doesn't work, we have to help each other out!"

Georgie's pulse increased as they started to walk up the stairway. "To be honest, I don't have a lot of knowledge about students with special needs. You will have to help me out a lot."

Lilliana's voice was firm. "My professors said general education teachers might need help, but we'll work things out. I'm happy to help you as long as you help me too. It's all about the kids." She smiled at Georgie and paused at the top of the staircase before opening the stairwell door.

Georgie pressed the palms of her hand to her heart. "Good, me too. They paired us well."

Lilliana opened the door, holding it for Georgie to walk through. "Also, as I am Cuban, I can translate for the kids and parents too." She led Georgie along the second-floor hallway where the smell of ammonia was steady, making her cough a little. "We have a large Spanish speaking population. Are you bilingual?"

Georgie coughed a little, rubbing her watery eyes. "I guess they just painted this floor." She refocused, "Spanish? Afraid not. Few years of Spanish in high school, but that's about it." Georgie glanced at the baby blue lockers lining the wall. While the paint was fresh, the corners of the lockers were rusty, old, and sharp-edged.

"*Bueno*. Just ask me, and I'll help you out. Maybe we should buddy up to our mentor teacher?" Lilliana bit her fingernail.

Georgie confided, "Ugh, I met a mentor teacher earlier today, and his tips involve alcohol and vacations. We need to find the right mentor teacher!" Georgie and Lilliana smiled at each other as they saw the digital sign with white neon lettering which read Eden Hills Computer Lab.

CHAPTER 3

Georgie's arms had goosebumps from the air-conditioning cranking in the vast, sterile room filled with dozens of white computers for as far as the eye could see. Blank whiteboards filled the front and right wall, while large white cabinets lined the left-side wall. The strong smell of disinfectant made several teachers sneeze. Leaning across to Lilliana, Georgie rubbed her arms up and down, "You were smart to pack a sweatshirt. It's freezing in here."

"I went to school here years ago. Some rooms have air-conditioning like this one, but most of the other parts of the building don't - the evils of an old building. Anyway, always be ready for any temperature during the year. This applies to the winter too!" Lilliana started to open her mouth again when the lights were turned on and off abruptly.

It was hard to see at first, but Georgie slowly recognized him. It was the man who had been trying to "mentor" her earlier in the cafeteria. He seemed to have taken a shower, found a razor, and put on a sharp suit.

He scanned the group. "Welcome everyone to the technology training session. My name is Alex Williams, and I'm not only the technology teacher but also a mentor teacher. For that reason, I'm here to help you out all year, especially when it comes to report cards, progress reports, and exam grades. We're implementing an online portal that will enable you to hone your skills further with remote learning experiences for the kids. Maybe even engage the parents virtually too! The first thing I did, putting the lights on and off, may save your voice and patience when starting the class.

It gets the students' attention and commands respect in a quick, easy way. Feel free to try it with your students. Trust me, it works!" He walked over to the teacher in the front seat, "Can you hand these out for me, please?" Glancing around the room, he rubbed his chest and clapped his hands. "Be sure to get the handout to take notes. Let's begin as we have many things to learn in a short time!"

For the next two hours, Alex Williams instructed the group with vital details about all district technology programs. Between his verbal instruction and PowerPoint presentation, the reference tools he provided were crucial skills for the staff to have, in order for them to complete their tasks independently.

The bell rang as Alex completed the last slide of the PowerPoint. "Thank you all for your attention, and again, if you need support from me, don't hesitate to ask. Have a great school year!" The group applauded loudly. He, in turn, coughed, gathered his things carefully, and left the room without making eye contact with anyone.

Turning to Lilliana, Georgie raised her eyebrows, "I am shocked he was so impressive. When I first met him, he seemed nuts!" Georgie rubbed her hands together, "Anyway, I think I could do all those things with some practice."

Lilliana grabbed Georgie's arm. "*Sí, asere!* And he didn't have a ring on, and he was good looking. Might be promising eye candy! Doesn't he look like John Legend but a little older? You do know who he is, right? The amazing musician?"

Georgie rolled her eyes, "I know I'm older than you by a good decade, but yes, I know who John Legend is, and I agree with you."

In reality, Georgie felt a little shocked with herself. She was so focused on trying to learn way too much information in a short amount of time, but Lilliana was right about Alex on all counts. On top of him being deadly attractive, he oozed intelligence and competence, which was even more of a highlight for the day. With Alex Williams cleaned up, it was no wonder that district was top in the state. He was more impressive than some of the administrators she had met at the interview, so it was a relief to know he was one of her mentor teachers. She could only imagine what the other mentors were like.

"He is amazing, but I have to tell you a story about him." As Lilliana was about to share a little bit more insight on Alex, a lanky, freckled guy approached them.

Carrying his laptop, a folder and wearing a Boston Red Sox golf shirt, he blurted out, "Hey, I'm Carl. I overheard you. Lilliana, is it? You know your way around here. Can I follow you to lunch? I think we're all teaching the eighth graders together. Maybe figure out some stuff while we eat?"

Lilliana nodded while Georgie took all her items. "Carl, nice to meet you. Yes, let's find the room with pizza and eat straight away. According to the schedule, we don't have much time!"

"Wow, you are right. *Vamos!*"

Lilliana led the way to lunch. "We have a big meeting right after we eat. Dr. Salva is speaking!"

CHAPTER 4

Georgie's heart raced as she sat, looking around the packed cafeteria. She was exhausted already, and still had another half day to go. Lilliana had become a terrific person to connect with earlier in the day. She knew the lay of the land and introduced Georgie to many staff members, although most of the names were a bit of a blur. Her gaze fixated on Alex, who was seated at the back with a woman in blue scrubs, a white ribbon holding her ponytail back. The woman was laughing at something hilarious. Julia and Jose walked into the cafeteria together, circling the room to chat with the staff briefly.

Abruptly, the lights flicked on and off. When Georgie looked over at the light switch, she saw the man she had met a few days ago, Superintendent Dr. Jonathan Salva. He was impeccably dressed in a tailored navy-blue suit with greased-back, black-dyed hair which would not move in a gale-force wind. She saw Julia grind her teeth as Dr. Salva sauntered over to the microphone. Shaking his hand, the teaching staff waited like dutiful children listening to their parents. Dr. Salva stood behind her as they waited for Jose to join them at the front. Jose finished a text message before walking with a fast-paced stride toward the other administrators. Taking the opposite side of the podium, he stood with a wide stance a considerable distance from Julia, and even further away from Dr. Salva.

Julia's chin was high, and there was a gleam in her eye. "Welcome back, everyone! I am pleased to stand along with Mr. Jose Gonzalez. We also have the great pleasure of having Dr. Jonathan Salva with us today!"

The staff applauded loudly as Dr. Salva, rubbing his hands together, stepped slowly toward the microphone, waiting for the applause to subside. Standing with his shoulders straight, back rigid, Dr. Salva began speaking. "Boy, I'm not sure if the applause was because you are happy I'm still here, or because you have heard the rumors that I'm going to be retiring soon." He laughed, as did others in the room. He rubbed his dimpled chin. "Seriously, I am thrilled about this new school year. It's year number fifty for me in education, and I have *loved* every minute. Ms. Bradley assures me we will have a marvelous year fulfilling our building and district goals. We've hired a boatload of amazing new teachers, so I welcome you all. I also want to reassure everyone that this year will be the smoothest in a long time. Let's get the show on the road. I have a busy day all over the district. I'm sure you're all ready to make a difference in the students' lives! Good luck. Then, waving goodbye to the staff, he exited out the nearest door as if he was on fire.

Julia stood at the podium, "Looking around the room, I believe we have the most talented group of teachers yet. We are focused, as you know, on increasing proficiency in student test scores, especially in English. I ask the veteran staff members to help the new group of teachers in any way possible since we have the largest number of students in over five years. Our demographics also include students who speak over thirty different languages, so we are one of the most diverse communities in the state. It is exciting but also challenging. Some of our new staff members also speak different languages, so get to know each other, and help one another." Julia looked directly at some staff members, nodding as if she was speaking directly to them. "Let's get down to business. Lesson plans are to be submitted electronically every Monday morning without exception. They are to be sent to us as well as your content area supervisors in the central office, so everyone is on the same page as to what you are doing. This year, to help with more collaboration time, we will not have faculty meetings every Wednesday. We have scheduled prep time to meet."

Cheers came from many of the veteran teachers, causing Julia to pause. "Jose and I heard you last year. Since you need more time, you will have it. Your mailboxes in the office have your updated class schedules for the first day. We will continue to put hard copies in your mailboxes, but after the first week, it will all be online. The sooner you get used to the new program, the better." She nodded and stepped aside. "Jose, you're up next."

Jose sauntered to the podium, hands in his pockets. Any clapping came from the new staff members only. "Welcome back, everyone! Please keep to the bell schedules as it impacts the movement of students for a timely change in the class period. I'll continue to update the class rosters and email you of any changes. We anticipate new students, as always, until the second and even the third week of school. Realize the enrollment numbers are fluid all year long. Discipline is the central role I have in the building, so if you have any issues with a student, do not hesitate to contact me. I'll figure things out. We will be starting classroom observations soon. The schedule is more demanding than in prior years. I look forward to seeing you working with the students. Have a good year." Then with a slight wave, Jose moved toward the wall, leaning on it.

Julia returned to the microphone. "Last but not least, for the new staff, we're in the business of keeping everyone safe in this building. We will have monthly fire drills, lockdown drills, and shelter-in-place exercises as per state code. You are the role models for our students. Make sure you know the procedures for your room location. We work hand-in-hand with the police, as well as with the fire services in town to ensure our safety is the top priority. This year we also have security guards in front, along with metal detectors. Know that Dr. Salva, along with the board of education, has our best interests in mind. I am confident, working together, we will have a safe, productive learning environment for our kids. Any issues, as always, don't sit on the information - share it! We need to keep ahead of things not only in the building but online as well. In the past, online posts enabled us to figure things out early. It's best to be proactive. This has to continue. If you see or hear anything, say something." And nodding Julia concluded, "Now, I leave the remainder of this meeting to your union president, Mr.

Alex Williams." Applause erupted as Julia shook Alex's hand before she exited, followed by Jose, moving slowly behind her.

Georgie, continuing to write notes so she would remember all the information, sighed. Alex moved at a snail's pace to the podium, cleared his throat a little and spoke. "Now, now, thank you so much, everyone! We had a terrific orientation this morning for the twenty-two new staff members. This afternoon, after this meeting, I will be working with the rest of the staff. We will top off the day with happy hour at Rosie's. I expect one hundred percent participation of the new staff members. After meeting everyone, I firmly believe we have hired an amazing group of staff members. Due to the high levels of understanding, I was able to teach the new group in two hours, so the rest of you better watch out today! Seriously, our new hires are highly competent. Now, one thing Julia mentioned was room sharing. No one has only one room this year. Everyone will share at least one room." There was a grumble of chatter, so he paused. "That is a huge change for many of us who have been here for a long time. I have already met with the administration. There are no grievances, as this is within the parameters of our contract. We will need to be the consummate professionals I know we are." Alex pointed to the back of the room, "Last but not least, I need to introduce our school nurse, Renata Washington."

Georgie looked at the woman whom Alex had been sitting with earlier. Renata smiled and waved as all the staff turned to look at her. She had a pile of files on her lap along with a marble-covered notebook.

Alex continued, "Renata handles all things medical. If there are any issues at all with you, your students, anything, please do not hesitate to contact her. Confidentiality is practically her middle name. Seriously, I work collaboratively with the administration to make sure the custodians keep the building clean. If you have a concern, let me know via email or stop by my classroom. This year, I have an open schedule in the computer lab, so whole groups can work on lessons. You know, in meeting with building goals, English classes have priority as we have new software programs to help raise test scores. I will work with you any day, any time! Have a fabulous year! Veteran teachers, I will see you all in a few minutes in my room." The staff applauded as Alex beamed with a relaxed smile across his face. Several teachers met him with hugs.

Before leaving the meeting, Georgie squeezed her eyes tight and gasped as she gathered her items. When she opened her eyes, she noticed Lilliana and Bob Arthur speaking in low, hushed voices in Spanish. Bob was another newbie. He was over six-foot-tall, in his mid-twenties with reddish hair and freckles. All of a sudden, they were fleeing out of the room. Lilliana turned, "Georgie, we gotta go! *Rapida.*"

Georgie called out to them as they scurried ahead. "Hey, guys, wait for me."

CHAPTER 5

Lilliana held the door open to Room 212 for Georgie and Bob. "We don't have a lot of time to get things done. I talked to some other special education teachers, and we are going to be having a ton of meetings with all the transfer students."

Georgie flipped the room lights on and looked around. The sunny, bright room had four sets of windows facing west. She was disappointed, as the natural light would only illuminate the room for half the day. The baby blue marble tiles on the floor complimented the stark white paint on the walls. The lights lined the dingy white ceiling tiles, which surrounded a projector hanging in the center of the room. Her eyes discovered a massive set of bare brown bulletin boards. The materials she purchased at the teacher store would look perfect on them! She whispered, "My first real classroom." Georgie hid a slight smile as her heart raced. She was all ready to place her items down when she noticed a thin layer of dust on top of the desk. Her mouth opened and closed without speaking, before blowing the dust off the counter.

Lilliana smiled warmly, "Our new home away from home, *Srta. Nelson*."

Bob exclaimed, "Yo, do you guys mind if we work together? Maybe we can help each other with stuff, like share tips or something? Anything to make this easier." He started dragging a few student chairs to form a circle in front of the room.

Lilliana placed her things next to one of the desks in the circle. She nervously played with her necklace. "*Sí*, Bob."

Bob threw his Eden Hills bag on the ground. "My class lists are huge compared to what they were when I was hired two months ago. It sucks."

Georgie stuttered, "Why the big increase?"

Lilliana tilted her head, "I forgot, you're not from around here. Eden Hills is one of the oldest towns in the state with tons of land. We've had a construction boom over the last few years with condos popping up everywhere, so the population has skyrocketed." Lilliana rolled her eyes. "They have expanded this building a few times since I graduated." She took out a tissue and giggling dusted off a few desks with a napkin from her bag. "This is a heck of a lot cleaner than when I was here, that's for sure! Take a good look around. This will be our home away from home until June."

Bob, chewing gum, flopped into a chair, opened his laptop. "Let's get going. I saw an email. We have to submit our lesson plans electronically using the online district template."

Lilliana exclaimed, "*Dios de bendiga*. I had no idea they had an electronic format for these until Alex's workshop. I wish they'd told us earlier. I could have done this last week."

Bob shook his head. "How are we going to get two weeks' worth of lessons typed into this format so fast? I will be working on this all weekend." They continued working in silence for some time.

Georgie had nearly finished the first week of lessons and was now typing in the second week. "This should get easier the more we do it, yes? The template is better than old school pen and paper. When do you think these are due? First thing after the weekend?"

Alex suddenly appeared at the door. "They are not due until next Monday. Guys, you have a week, relax."

Georgie squinted. "Are you sure? We can't get behind before we've even started."

Alex slowly glanced at her laptop. "Julia sent an email. Yikes, you guys are my prize pupils, so if you are stressed, I can only imagine what the others are like."

"Why are we your prized pupils?" Georgie asked, teeth clenched.

He chuckled, which led to a coughing fit, making his eyes glassy, and his cheeks turn purple. "You are the closest to my classroom. I'm next door to you. If you guys are frazzled, I'm sure there are nineteen others in the same boat. On top of that, the veteran teachers I trained are freaking out over the new program I taught them. Take a deep breath, guys."

Lilliana barked, "Georgie, we have an IEP meeting early next week. I thought it was happening soon since the student is medically fragile. I saw the email."

Georgie's head emerged from staring at her laptop. "IEP meeting? I have no idea what you are talking about."

Lilliana's mouth fell open. "We have IEP meetings for all special education students at least once a year. Please tell me you know that."

Georgie shrugged, glancing at Bob, who also shrugged.

Lilliana rubbed her eyes. "Guys, a student with a disability is called a classified student. Don't worry; I'll forward meeting notices to you so you can put them on your schedule. Just so you know, if you are invited, you must attend. It's the law."

Georgie nodded her head, vigorously, "I knew but never expected a meeting so early in the year."

Lilliana's voice was monotone, "Get ready because they are coming fast and furious. This student, Jason Rollins, needs a heart transplant so we will meet with him, his parents, and pertinent staff tomorrow after school." Lilliana's hand was over her heart.

Georgie's mouth dropped. "Oh my God, what do I have to do? How do I even prepare? Lilliana, I only had one class about children with disabilities."

Lilliana's eyes dazzled. "Don't worry," she told them. "That's why I'm here. I met with Renata two weeks ago. It seems the student, Jason, is on grade level academically but will be out a lot."

"What do I do at the meeting?" Georgie pulled out a notebook, grabbed a pen, and jotted down the student's name. Alex leaned against the front wall watching the new teachers' interaction.

Lilliana walked over to Georgie and touched her arm. "You listen, take notes, ask questions if you want. Jason has an oxygen tank, and a one-to-one paraprofessional to help him around the building. If he does not get a heart soon, well, it's not good. You focus on finishing the plans. I'll finish his paperwork. One thing at a time. Bob, he's in your class, too, so I will fill you in."

Bob closed his laptop and shoved it into his backpack. Grabbing his sweatshirt, he spoke in a trembling voice, "I've got to go. I'm spent. I still have to do some emails at home. Thanks to both of you, at least I won't sink for the next two weeks. My wife told me it would be a struggle, but this is beyond anything I could have ever imagined."

Alex chimed in as Bob flew out the door. "It's a lot harder than you think, I'll tell you that. If you want to book some computer time, no worries, I'll put you on top of the list. Let me check on the others now since it seems like you are all in good shape for the kids next week." Alex strolled over to Georgie's desk. Her eyebrows raised as she asked, "Do you think so?"

Alex knocked on her desk and, with a deep, gratifying sigh, he smiled. "You've got this, Georgie. I know it!" Then off he went.

Georgie and Lilliana were alone working in the classroom for another two hours when Jose walked in.

His eyes narrowed. "Ladies, how are you doing? Everything coming along?"

Lilliana closed her laptop. "Yes, Mr. Gonzalez. We are all set! The IEP meeting after school will be high intensity. Excited to get going."

Jose glanced at Georgie's laptop. "Glad to hear, Lilliana. Any issues with the kids, let me know. I have a son classified with autism at the high school. I'll help you advocate for the kids any time. Just let me know."

Lilliana started to pack her bag. "I can't thank you enough, especially when it comes to social skills. Some pupils may have issues with making friends. Three students need behavioral plans implemented; which reminds me, Georgie, I'll get some resources printed out for you." And grabbing a book out of her bag Lilliana darted out of the room, saying, "Be back in a second."

Georgie's mouth went dry as Jose remained in the room, arms folded as if trying to avoid conversation. Her skin flushed along her neck as she tried to focus on typing her lesson plans.

Jose cleared his throat as he strolled around the classroom perimeter. He approached Georgie's desk, leaning over her shoulder. "Um, glancing at your plans, they seem fine, but you need a lot more work compared to what the other teachers have done so far. Night," and he sauntered out of the room whistling.

Lilliana bounced back into the room with a pile of papers in her hand. "I am so excited to get started with the kids. Wasn't that nice of Jose to stop in to check on us?" Lilliana placed the pages on top of Georgie's desk.

Georgie's stomach was cramping as if a welterweight punched her. "What have other teachers done? I'm already behind?"

Lilliana reviewed Georgie's plans. "Look, you have to type in the homework, then you are done! Not a problem. That will take only five more minutes. I have a hard time believing all the others are where you are. Don't compare, but you do, don't you! I can wait for you." Lilliana leaned against the wall, checking her emails and texts on her phone.

After a few minutes, Georgie, having re-read her plans, rubbed her strained eyes. "Yes! Done! At least for today." As she packed up, she told Lilliana, "Thanks for making copies of the student documents. I need more explanation on some of their needs. It helps so much with the planning. I only know two weeks of the curriculum, never mind the needs of students with special needs. They are all so different." She pushed her hair out of her face, stretching her arms high over her head.

Lilliana bit her lip. "They are, but I can help. That's my job. I have a photographic memory, so it is a big plus. Otherwise, it's a lot to memorize to know a twenty- or thirty-page document on each kid!"

Georgie stood and shook out her legs. "Yes, thanks for staying with me. You are sweet." After she re-read her schedule, Georgie hoped she could learn all the students' names quickly. She whispered, "Nerves, Georgie, nerves. It's a sign to go home."

Georgie placed her materials on the teacher's desk at the front of the room. The last item she put in the drawer was her beloved silver Cross pen, a cherished gift she had received when she finished college. She rubbed it for good luck, put it in the top of the drawer, and locked the desk with the tiny key on her set of room keys. Locking it would be fine. She placed her laptop in her backpack and pausing to look at her classroom said, "This will be a great year." Glancing at her filthy hands she took out some hand disinfectant and rubbed the grime away.

At that moment, Carl walked into the room. "Hey guys, finally found you. Alex wants me to remind everyone about happy hour after school today at Rosie's. He told me to tell you, especially Georgie. You need to attend. Maybe we could all meet and talk about how to attack the numbers of kids we have. It's a ton of work! Lilliana, I hope you go too!" Message delivered Carl quickly left. Lilliana had noticed his cell phone had a Red Sox emblem cover on it, much like her ex-boyfriend's.

Georgie began flipping through her folder, looking for the lists, thinking Carl must be mistaken. She was shaking her head until she opened the file and looked closely at the pages. "I have five sections of classes." Georgie found the totals on each page. "I have thirty-five kids in each class! That's not what they told me at the interview at all."

Lilliana counted the names on her papers. "I have eleven classified students in each section. Lots of responsibility; trust me. Student teaching, I only had four." She bit her fingernail.

Georgie called out, "I'll meet you there. I need to re-organize my class lists."

Lilliana turned to Georgie, "Are you *loca*? Do that at home, please! We need to socialize to make sure we know who to get help from, and also to de-stress a bit. Let's go before we get to the place too late. I feel like it's the right thing to do."

Georgie exhaled. "You're right. I have a few days to get it all together. I'm overloaded with information as it is." Georgie smiled. "This better be good, Lilliana," and she followed Lilliana out into the hallway. As ringtones echoed around the corridors with different sounds, Georgie looked at her phone, seeing it showed the name and address of Rosie's.

CHAPTER 6

The watering hole was located a few blocks from Eden Hills in a neighboring town. It was at a dead end on the corner of a desolate block. The parking lot in the back was barely visible unless approached directly. Rosie's red blinking sign was small, almost secretive. Georgie pulled into a spot, seeing Lilliana sitting in her car. Knocking on Lilliana's window, Georgie startled her. "Is everything OK, Lilliana? You didn't have to wait for me."

Lilliana popped out of her car, sweating excessively. She wiped her brow, fluffed the black dress clinging to her body, and slammed the car door shut. Her fresh red lipstick was as bright as an apple. "I didn't want to go in on my own. All of this is new to me, and my heart is racing. Truthfully, I thought you might bail on me. I'm used to that."

They strolled toward the entrance. Georgie nodded, squeezing Lilliana's hand. "I agree, but it's exciting too. Let's do this. You talked me into it, after all."

Inside, there was a small U-shaped bar with a dozen or so brown leather barstools filled with teachers. Maroon plastic tablecloths covered the rickety wooden tables, providing some color in the room since the dark wood panels on the walls were dated. Decorations were minimal, but the large copper ceiling made the space bright and warm. The noise level of the crowd drowned out the '80s pop music blaring out. A popcorn machine in the corner emitted delicious buttery smells as the two girls entered the room.

At the bar Georgie ordered drinks for both of them, treating Lilliana to a Mojito. Toasting each other, they glanced around and recognized a few of the new teachers sitting at a table. Walking over, they both said, "Hi guys, can we sit with you?"

Bob moved his sweatshirt and bag off a few empty seats. "Sure, sit. I was saving you some seats. I was going to go home when I got the text. Can't miss out on some fun! Did you guys see our lists of students? Man, tons of rugrats." Georgie and Lilliana sat, leaning in to hear the conversation better.

"Yes," Georgie's eyebrows were raised. "Can the lists be right? I was told about twenty-five kids to a class."

Bob sipped a large gulp of Budweiser from a can. "Yup. The school is way overcrowded this year. My wife has worked in one of the grammar schools for a few years. She says they're bursting at the seams there too. I bet they put out another referendum soon for another addition to the building. Last year she had close to thirty-five kids. No freakin surprise. Look at all the new condos everywhere! What do you expect? Anyways, when were you guys hired?"

Georgie knew little about the town. "I was interviewed last week and hired by the central office staff. It's been a bit of a whirlwind." Her face was turning as bright as a stop sign.

Lilliana beamed with confidence. "Don't worry. I told you I was hired weeks ago so I can help you out. Plus, I'm a local."

Georgie's stomach churned. "I only found one teacher resource guide in my mailbox. I'll need to get more information." Slowly, she sipped her vodka tonic.

Bob bragged, "I was hired early in the summer because of the football coaching job. You're all in for a treat. I've tried to get into Eden Hills for years. It took a while because of the good reputation and insane salary guide. It is a top-notch district, you know."

Georgie's leg jumped. "I read something about the district getting a lot of funding but did not realize it was so prestigious."

Lilliana's eyebrows furrowed as she tried to understand. "Didn't you do your due diligence before you were interviewed? I researched and had about ten other districts looking at me. Eden Hills was the place I wanted

32

to work. Giving back to my hometown is special. Now I have to work hard to keep the job."

Georgie fiddled with her glass. "This is a second career for me. Working as an editor was not as glamorous as I expected, but it helped me pay for graduate school these last few years."

"That's cool. Why teaching?" Bob tilted his body toward Georgie.

"Love kids, always have, but I have a lot of responsibilities with my family, so I couldn't leave the job until I had all my ducks lined up. Now they are as lined up as they are ever going to be." Georgie felt a fluttering in her stomach.

Lilliana slouched in her chair. "We can go over things this weekend if you want, Georgie. Heading to the shore to Mommy and Papi's beach house rental for one last *fiesta* but we can meet up Monday."

Georgie's eyes looked heavenward. "Sounds ideal. The district laptop is a godsend! Been without a computer for a few days, so I'll call you if that works for you."

They were interrupted by Alex who joined them drinking, what seemed to be, ginger ale. For a slightly less formal look than his staff workshops, he had removed his tie and jacket. The top button on his white dress shirt was open. "You all look serious. What's the deal? Good orientation? Got any questions for me? I was the one who texted about happy hour, so I have your numbers, and you have mine."

Her pulse raced as Georgie exclaimed, "Your presentation was fabulous. I learned a lot."

Alex clapped his hands. "Glad you thought so. A lot of information early on, so it might take a while to sink in. Swim or run, do something to decompress. What are the plans for the weekend?"

"Walking on the beach is about it for me. Living at the beach always helps." Georgie flipped her hair back.

Lilliana laughed playfully, "*La playa?* Which one?"

Georgie spoke in a quieter voice than usual, "Shellview."

Alex coughed while making intense eye contact with Georgie. "I'm in the neighboring town, Dove Cove. I moved there two years ago. Love the area." He chewed on a piece of ice from his glass.

Georgie blushed. "It's what I've always called home."

Alex took a deep breath and smiled ear to ear. "Any questions - I'm around. Enjoy the weekend. Oh, and welcome to Eden Hills." And he shuffled away towards the door.

Georgie watched Alex leave. There was something about him she couldn't fathom. She rubbed her chin, "He seems as if he might have our backs."

Lilliana rubbed her hands. "Well, he seems to be definitely on our team so far."

Georgie confided, nodding slowly, "Seems so, but let's make a pact to focus on our job and our kids. It takes time to figure out which side people are on." Leaning over, Georgie whispered, "Listen, be careful with Alex. Seriously. Talk to me if you want to vent, and I'll do the same. I feel like this is a game. Who will make it until the end and get tenure? It's a long four years until that happens. I don't mean to act like a big sister or anything."

Lilliana nursed her Mojito, hardly taking any sips. "So, no dating him, I suppose? Not for me, he's way too old, but you? There are more than enough people my age here for me to focus my attention on."

Georgie jerked her head back. "Don't mix business with pleasure. I would not even consider a date with him. Please! I think schools are gossipy places. Well, that's what I read anyway."

"You're right. We have enough on our plates. I saw an updated email that administrative observations would start the first few weeks of school. For now, it's time to loosen up." Lilliana swung her glass, clinking Georgie's glass.

Lifting her glass Georgie sipped the last bit of liquid. "My mind is racing. So much to learn so quickly. Don't you think? I found the class syllabus online; it's substantial."

Bob walked back to the table with a tray of shot glasses. Carl followed him, carrying some meatballs and chicken wings for the group to share. "Enough of the serious chit chat, guys. Let's toast to a great year." He winked at Lilliana, then smirked at Georgie before pulling a chair next to Lilliana and placing the food on the table. The four of them each took a shot glass, clicking them together. As Georgie choked it back, she noticed Lilliana throwing the clear liquid over her shoulder to avoid drinking it. Carl and Bob high-fived each other, then they each grabbed a chicken wing as the waitress brought napkins and plates. Roars of laughter erupted at different sections of the bar. Happy hour was raging. Georgie smiled as she looked around the bustling room. Leaning towards Lilliana, Georgie sipped her drink. "I'm glad you talked me into this. Just what I needed."

Maybe it was the booze, but Georgie wondered what it would be like to go on a date with Alex. She hadn't been out on a date for some time. Well, not since… Oh well, she wasn't going to dwell on that.

CHAPTER 7

Georgie spent more time than expected over the weekend on her lesson planning. Several times she went for a walk on the beach to clear her head, which helped tremendously, along with a few calls to Lilliana. She fell asleep at her kitchen table twice, trying to rework the lessons based on Lilliana's feedback and suggestions based on each student's needs. They decided to meet after school during the week and review the lessons to make sure things were going to flow well. Georgie decided to allot more time for her students to complete her tasks as her expectations were high. Considering she had never taught at this grade level; she was not sure what they could or could not do.

Labor Day evening, she received an email invitation to meet with Julia for an hour before school started the next day. Georgie tossed and turned that night, driving extra early to school in preparation. She had chosen to wear a green linen dress with matching jewelry along with a ring, which was a gift from her beloved mother. Georgie always wore it for good luck, wanting to keep her parents' spirit close for such important events. She hoped she would beat Julia to the school so she would look prompt. However, Julia was already in the main office, filling the staff mailboxes with handwritten notes.

Julia was wearing a mint green wrap dress, pearl necklace, and matching wedges. As Georgie walked into the room, Julia noted, "Brilliant thinking," and pointed to their similarly colored dress choices. Then she got down to business. "Thank you, Georgie, for getting here early! I thought we could meet now for a little while. Please come back to my office. How was your weekend?"

Georgie followed her, trying to keep up the pace. "It flew by. But I was able to get a lot of work done. Excited about this position." She sat in one of the smooth black leather chairs as Julia closed the door to her office.

Julia sat next to her in a chair where it was closer and more intimate. "I wanted to meet with you individually since I was not part of the hiring process, although I am thrilled they found you. Once I saw you went to Teachers University, I knew you were of a high caliber. I am currently a student there for my doctorate with Dr. Montross as my mentor."

Georgie's eyes danced. "Dr. Montross is amazing. She was my mentor, as well."

Julia nodded her head rapidly, "I know. I spoke to Dr. Montross at length about you after you were interviewed. Magna cum laude, prior career experience as an editor at the *New York Tribune*, volunteering in a local church - Georgie, you are the real deal. I only connected you with your mother after speaking with your boss at the newspaper. It seems as if you want to make a name for yourself, so I understand all too well."

"Wow. I only hope I can fulfill your high expectations." Georgie's hands trembled, and she felt dizzy.

Julia's face turned upward. "I have no doubts. That is why I insisted on hiring you above all other candidates and why I recommended they hire you on a pay level higher than the salary guide. Dr. Salva was also impressed and fully backs you as a candidate. Now, the reason why you are hired is simple but challenging. We have one sector of the population not meeting high levels of proficiency on state tests: grade eight English. I believe with your skills, along with your in-class support teacher, we can raise those scores. So, if you need further professional development or support, I will make it happen."

"I understand." Georgie gulped hard - more pressure on top of her own self-inflicted stress.

"I scheduled you and Lilliana Perez to be together for much of the day so you can work as closely as possible to help our students achieve. To try to set you up to succeed, we can continue to meet and brainstorm as much as possible. I hope that works for you." Julia leaned back with a crisp nod.

"I understand." *Deep breaths, Georgie!* Thoughts whirled through her mind.

Julia pursed her lips. "I can see you are getting red in the face and neck. Please, this is not intended to add to the pressure of a new job. I wanted you to be clear about my expectations. Come to me for anything, concerns, problems, etc. I am always here. When I am not, well..." Julia chuckled and leaned against her desk. "I am always here. Any questions so far?"

Georgie proclaimed, "No, I think I have things under control. Is there someone else I should seek out for help? I don't want to bother you all the time. Teachers who may be able to mentor me or suggest things?"

Julia leaned in to talk. "Great question. There are curriculum supervisors you can email about the English content. They are responsive but not located in the building. My first suggestion would be to get to know Alex Williams; he ran the technology segment last week."

Georgie closed her eyes and compulsively nodded. "Yes, I met him."

Julia, speaking in a steady voice, walked around her desk to sit. "He's been here as long as I have. You can imagine Alex knows a lot about what goes on, in and out of the classroom, if you get my drift. Talk to him. He is an invaluable resource. I have to be honest. We've had a high turnover in the last few years. We both try to help teachers stay, but sometimes it can be a difficult climate. I will leave it there." Julia shuffled the papers on her desk, then turned her computer on.

Georgie frowned. "So, many teachers in the building are not tenured?"

"There are only a handful of teachers who have stayed. Others have left for many reasons." Julia sat back, breathing deeply. "The kids are terrific, parents are involved, the salary guide is good, but burnout is high. There's a lot of pressure on everyone. All I can tell you is, please know I am on your side. So is Alex. To be clear, we want you to soar. When that happens, the kids do the same. That is the goal!" Julia pumped her fists.

Georgie offered Julia a firm handshake while saying, "Thanks for taking the time to speak to me, Ms. Bradley."

Julia slowly walked Georgie to the door. "Call me, Julia. Also, I am working on my dissertation this year, using the district data in English, so your class grades will be part of my study. All I ask is you make sure the data goes into the district database system Alex taught you. The sooner you can input the grades the better. Understand, it doesn't reflect on you or your job at all, but I need to keep looking at it. Have to compare it to other school grades in the district, even from last year." Her eyebrows were raised. "It's a lot of work, but a doctorate is on my bucket list."

Georgie reassured Julia with confidence. "We'll go over the program this week again, so we both know what to do."

Julia's hand pressed her stomach as she beamed. "Fantastic! Keep me in the loop."

"I won't let you down." Georgie gave a quick shake of her head. As she turned, she vaguely recognized the woman approaching.

Julia tilted her head to the side. "Georgie, have you met Renata, our vital school nurse? She's a lifesaver."

Renata rolled her eyes as she shook Georgie's hand. "Oh boy, corny jokes, here we go. Really, Julia? Ha. Nice to meet you, Georgie. My office is down the hall if you're looking for me."

Then raising her eyes, Renata asked, "Sorry to interrupt, but can I speak with you Julia, for a second?"

After Georgie had left, Julia motioned Renata into her office. "Come in. From the look in your eyes, I'm thinking we're already having issues." Renata closed the door as Julia leaned against her desk. "Spill it."

Renata pushed her hair behind her ear. "Last week, when I came in to organize my office, Tiffany gave me the wrong set of keys. I thought they were my set of keys, but there were two extra keys I have never seen before." She took the set of keys out of her pocketbook. "In the corner of my office, there's a locked room I could never open, so I put a filing cabinet against it. You know, forgot about it since I've never had the keys." She took a rusty gold key off the keyring. "*Finally*, this key opened the door."

Julia shook her head. "I have no idea about the room or this key. It's all news to me. What did you find?"

Renata shrugged her shoulders. "Filing cabinets. Old as dirt." She took a second smaller key off the keyring. "This opens all the cabinets, but you have to see the place. It looks like it hasn't been cleaned in years. I mean, you could smell the mold and mildew. We need the custodians down there big time."

Julia placed both keys on her desk. "Consider it done." She crossed her arms and pursed her lips.

Renata's phone buzzed, so she glanced at the message. "Sorry, I have to get this. A mom is dropping off some meds." Renata walked to the door and turned to Julia. "From the looks of the place, it doesn't seem as if anyone has been in that closet in a *long time*." Renata then darted out the door.

Julia stared at the keys while her blood boiled.

CHAPTER 8

Alex walked into Room 212 to find Georgie and Lilliana hovering over a book in the front of the classroom.

"Happy first day with the angels! I saw the kids, and they are all fired up and ready to go. There sure are a lot of them this year." Glancing at his watch, "Student entrance is in about ten minutes."

Georgie closed the book. "Excited to hear, right, Lilliana?"

She nodded. "Brings back a lot of memories from when I was in middle school. I'm a little nervous. I have to admit."

Alex held on to the door. "We all are, don't worry. I just wanted to wish you luck. Remember my schedule, so if I am open, reserve the space early." Suddenly he started coughing loudly, uncontrollably.

Georgie moved closer to him. "Can I get you some water? I have a cough drop in my bag." She exchanged an alarming glance with Lilliana.

He shook his head, wiped his mouth with a tissue, and took a deep, clear breath. "I'm good. I'm used to it by now. Don't worry. I'm positive I am not contagious." He faked a smile as he took several deep, slow breaths, which caused a little bit of a stutter. "Anyway, don't forget teacher observations start fast in the building," Alex spoke at a slow rate. "You will each be observed three times minimum. It can be announced or not announced, so don't be shocked." He was about to leave but turned back. "Also, always have your lesson plans and class lists on the desk in the event it happens." He was impressed Georgie and Lilliana were writing every word of what he was sharing. "Sooner you get into the routine, the better. If I can help you integrate technology into the lesson, it impresses the administration."

Georgie was starting to warm to Alex more than at their first meetings. "I may take you up on that. Next week might be perfect for my plans for the first project."

Alex gave her a thumbs up, "Sure, email me. Better get back, I have to be in my room. Do me a favor, always be where you are supposed to be at all times." He quickly left the room as he started coughing loudly again.

Lilliana's mouth tightened. "*Dios bendiga.* I hope Alex is OK. Sounds like a brutal cold."

Georgie tilted her head, making firm eye contact with her. "It did. I hope he feels better. He has been very helpful so far."

The bell rang for the first period of the school year. Georgie's first class would be packed, meaning she would barely have enough desks for each of them. She unlocked her drawer to grab a marker to write both hers, and Lilliana's, first and last names on the whiteboard. Turning around, she needed to lean against the wall for support, surprised to see Jose in her classroom. Unable to speak, she watched him walk around in silence, clenching his jaw. She was relieved that Lilliana arrived while he was still in the classroom.

Lilliana's voice rose with excitement as she welcomed him, cheerfully. As he left as quickly as he had walked in, Lilliana exclaimed, "Was that weird or nice?"

Georgie's face was flush with warmth. "Not sure, Lilliana. Let's focus on the kids. I hear them coming."

Lilliana chimed in, "Remember, we have an IEP meeting tomorrow."

"How could I forget, partner? How about we welcome the kids together? We are a team, after all." They stood at the doorway, asking students if they needed any help finding their classroom.

As the students filed into the room one by one, both teachers asked them to find a seat where they were most comfortable. From there, both Lilliana and Georgie would set firm limits. They also needed to articulate rules without hesitation to ensure the students knew who the boss was. Georgie was determined to know most of the names of her students. She used pencil and paper to map out a seating chart that could be adjusted with a few sweeps of the eraser since administration shared that the enrollment would change daily. As the day continued and she met more students, she felt confident with Lilliana's expertise in special education. Georgie was sure to learn a lot from her even though Lilliana, at times, had shaky hands and lost focus. One on one with the students, Lilliana had a friendly yet firm rapport with the students, consistent in each class period.

By the last period, Georgie waved her over as the students copied their homework assignments. "We've made it through the entire first day without any major issues. What do you think?"

Lilliana blew out a series of short breaths to gain control. "So far, so good is right. I am a little anxious but thought I would calm down a bit more."

In a soft tone, Georgie chose her words carefully, "Just relax. Do you want to take a seat in the back for a few minutes?"

Lilliana covered her mouth with her hand. "*Un minuto.* I didn't think teaching would be so hard, so many balls in the air."

Georgie strolled around the room, checking on her students, stopping at each desk while they worked. This was the first time she had disagreed with her teaching partner. She was on an adrenaline high. *Fulfilling a dream is more like it!*

The bell rang, signaling the last period of the day. Julia and Jose were meeting in a small conference room in the main office. Julia smiled. "Well, that was some first day of school! Went pretty well, considering we compressed a few days of professional development and orientation into one day last week."

Jose nodded, "We're doing the best we can with the time we have. Between the budget cuts last year and the construction projects, we are lucky we have even opened on time!"

Julia stopped writing. "Agreed. How do you think things went today?" She nodded - for once, Jose was right. "I was impressed with the new staff members so far. Thanks for floating around today. Did you see any issues or red flags? Considering the last-minute hires, I think being fully staffed from day one is fantastic."

After a loud yawn, Jose gave a blasé shrug. "Staff wise, they seem pretty decent. Hey, the workshop went smoothly." Jose had only stuck his head in the room for a minute, instead of staying for the duration of the presentation. Julia grabbed a pen to take notes. "Alex did a great overview of the programs. Boy, he was outstanding! He may not realize it yet, but he is a solid future administrator. Would you like me to approach him about enrolling in some graduate classes? You never know."

Julia crossed her hands in front of her chest, saying, "I have already discussed it with him, and I believe he is almost done. What about the new staff? Do you anticipate anyone being difficult or mediocre? I want to know sooner than later, so we are not in the same situation as last year with so many vacancies throughout the year. It was a disaster continually hiring substitutes."

Julia rubbed her chin. "As you know, classroom instruction suffered. Dr. Salva expects us to meet the 10 percent increase in achievement. It's frustrating this is the only school in the district that's not award winning." She looked away. "But with everything last year, I'm not surprised. We looked like we hired a bunch of incompetent staff members." She drilled her nails into the table. "It was bad luck…"

Jose cut Julia off. "That was not on us. They are brighter and more enthusiastic than any of last year's hires, with a few concerns, but I'll watch them. I give you my word. Maybe the colleges are preparing them better. Who knows? Bottom line, we have a fresh new year, and we worked hard to make sure the issues from last year are in the past."

He always thought Julia worried too much about the small things. If he were in charge, he would be keeping his eye on the global issues of the building. He had control of the situation, and it would all work out in the end, at least in his perspective.

Julia moved closer to the table, leaning in. "Can you make me a promise? We need to focus on our school building goals and *only those goals*. High test scores have to be the focus. We need to keep that goal at the forefront of all faculty meetings this year and cut off any negativity or innuendos, especially about last year and even previous years."

Jose knew his job was safe no matter what happened, so he only half-listened. Julia was up for tenure in her principal position. With such commotion and controversy in the building last year, one more minor issue this year might see her winging her way back to the classroom. Her dreams of running an award-winning middle school would be over. With her out of the way, his dreams would be fulfilled!

Finally, Julia broke the long moment of silence. "You're right. We are fully staffed, and that's all that matters right now. The student body is packed in, and the board of education has major decisions to make regarding the leadership positions of the future. It is no secret my job is on the line." Her eyes were fixated on Jose. "It should also be understood you report to me directly, not the superintendent and not to any other administrators at the high school or elementary schools. I… need… to know what goes on in this building. Please give me the professional courtesy to let me figure things out in my building first… That includes staff issues."

Jose grabbed the blank notepad and pencil. "Is that it?"

Julia stood. "Facilities need to be up to code at all times too. Do you understand? I already dealt with an issue with the custodians this morning. It will be resolved by the end of the day."

Jose stared at her as she spoke, but he was busier counting the minutes until he and his kids could get out of town next weekend. He needed to escape Eden Hills as it was choking him already. "Sounds like we started on the right foot."

Julia rubbed her hands together. "Glad to hear we're on the same page. Let's hope for a fantastic year!" As they departed, her big, bright, fake grin hurt her face. She knew she was on shaky ground, and that she couldn't trust Jose one hundred percent. Still, she would sort it in the end, one way or another.

As Jose walked back to his office to grab his keys, he looked out the window to see the new teachers walking to their cars. It was already nearly four o'clock. He put a piece of gum in his mouth, chewing it slowly. Out of the corner of his eye, he saw one teacher walking to her car far behind the others. Moving closer to the window, he chewed so hard he bit his tongue, causing it to bleed. "Ouch! Damnit."

As the car left the lot, Jose snapped a photo of Georgie's license plate, saying, "Enjoy your free time while it lasts. Game on."

CHAPTER 9

Georgie arrived earlier than the previous day to prepare for the IEP meeting for her student in the afternoon. She placed her laptop on her desk and drank some coffee to try to wake up. She had slept or eaten little, since her stomach was doing flips. Turning on her computer, she was looking for the student's documents to review when Jose knocked on her door.

He avoided direct eye contact as he said, "Georgie, I hope you are ready for the school day."

Georgie felt like her insides were vibrating as she stood up. "Beyond excited. Brushing up for the IEP meeting I have with my student Jason Rollins today."

"Tell me about him." Jose walked around the classroom, looking closely at the newly decorated bulletin boards with their colorful charts. Georgie and Lilliana had taken extra care to make the room look aesthetically pleasing for the students.

Georgie felt as if his questions were a type of pop quiz. "He is a classified child, medically fragile, who works on grade level. He is a transfer student who will most likely be out more than he is in school due to his health."

Jose glanced out the window. "What else?"

"Not sure what else you want to know. I provided some input to Lilliana, who has worked on his goals and objectives for the document. We've been working well together right from day one." Her stomach was cramping, as it had been almost every day since she had started this job. "I am looking forward to meeting his family to help them in any way I can." Georgie rubbed the back of her neck.

Jose moved a straight desk crooked. "Make sure you know as much as you can in case the family asks. They want to make sure he is not just a number, that he is an individual. Not sure you are there yet. Keep that in mind for every meeting. It seems like you will need a lot of luck today." He sauntered out, passing Lilliana on the way.

Lilliana threw her things down, *"Buenos dias.* Is everything OK? I'm not late or anything." She threw her things on the large teacher desk she and Georgie were sharing.

Georgie collapsed in her chair. "He was quizzing me on Jason's background. I feel like I failed."

"Are you kidding?" Lilliana moved closer to Georgie. "We know all we can, based on the documents. Don't take it personally. Plus, I have the paperwork all set, thanks to you!"

Georgie shrugged her shoulders. "I guess you're right. I'm probably paranoid."

Lilliana leaned against the wall, "Listen, I spoke to one of his son's teachers at the high school; they love Jose. She told me he is an involved dad, always there for anything. I guess that is how he acts with all the kids; as if they are his own. I'm sure we are well prepared for the meeting." Lilliana's hands shook a little. "I've been in a dozen or so IEP meetings. One thing to keep in mind is it is about the student's needs. I expect the family will do most of the talking. Maybe the medical staff will discuss ways to ensure he is safely educated in the building. I am going to offer to work with him when he is out, so they will be pleased that he is getting a consistent education. We've worked it out!"

"Wow, fabulous. You're making me feel much better." Georgie rubbed her cherry red cheeks. "I guess it is a carry-over from my other job. People were out to get you at all times. I"ll ease up, I promise."

In the last period of the day, Georgie and Lilliana pulled some student desks together to prepare for their first IEP meeting. As Lilliana typed, Georgie looked closer at Lilliana's wrists. "Hey, would you mind telling me about your tattoos."

"*Sí*. My parents left Cuba with me when I was only three years old." She turned her wrists over and held up her left hand, explaining, "This heart is for my grandma." Then pointing to her right wrist, "This is for my grandpa. I look at them every day. It reminds me to thank them for their sacrifices for me. They helped us get out of Cuba safely. Now, I want to make them proud. Give back, you know."

Georgie was in awe. "Do you ever get to see them?"

She shook her head. "No, but since I was in high school, I send them money so they can buy food, necessities. The more I make, the more I send them."

"They must be so proud of you!" Georgie patted Lilliana's folded hands.

"Oh, yes, they are. Everything I do is to make them proud!" Lilliana blushed. "Are you ready for your crash course in special education?"

Georgie took out a piece of paper and a pen. "Go for it! I'm ready."

Lilliana was wringing her hands. "The special education supervisor walked me through their IEP program last week when I came in to get some materials. You do know what IEP stands for?"

"Individualized education program. Yes, I learned that, at least. It is the legal document for the special needs students. I saw a few in my practicum, but I don't know all the details. I just know I have to follow it." Georgie sipped a little ginger ale. She had continued to be nauseous for nearly a week.

"Don't worry. I almost finished making copies of their paperwork for you. So many kids with complex needs. So far, each is different." Lilliana opened her folder to show her some papers.

"Different? What do you mean?" Georgie glanced at the files on the computer.

Lilliana sat crossed leg. "Seems like the group falls into three classification categories: learning disabilities, attention deficit, autism. I will continue to forward you their modifications and accommodations for you to learn how to work with them. Thanks for being so open to all this."

Georgie's eyes grew wide. "Open to it? I'll do my best, but how do I do that exactly? I am going to need you."

Lilliana took a bite of her apple. "My professor mentioned sometimes you guys, you know, general education teachers, refuse to follow the needs of the kids. I was afraid you would be against what I was asking you to do for the kids. The last thing I needed to get was a hard time for my first job." She exhaled. "Confrontation is something I struggle with."

Georgie rubbed her sweaty hands together. "I know so little about what you are talking about. I'll work with you, not against you. It will be a learning curve for me, but I'm here for the kids."

Lilliana agreed. "I will help you any way I can, but I don't have much information either. Not even sure where we go to get the rest of the curriculum guides or textbooks. I emailed the supervisors, and they wrote back to tell me the material would be in our boxes or emailed to us directly. As of now, nothing. I'll keep checking our mailboxes in the main office. I am not good at last minute things. Otherwise, my anxiety kicks in!"

"I found a few things yesterday. Once I am done, I'll give them to you." Georgie glanced at the clock in the room. "Hate to say it, but we have ten minutes until the meeting. We should go. You returning after the meeting?" Georgie threw out her can of ginger ale.

Lilliana took her bag and a large pile of papers in the folder. "*Sí*, I don't want to carry all this home."

Lilliana and Georgie hurried to the IEP meeting near the main office. The small conference room was practically full. There were several teachers, Julia, Renata, the occupational therapist, the physical therapist, the child-study team members, and Jason's physician who had dialed in on the phone. Leading the meeting was Jason himself, who set a tone, more of optimism than negativity or fear. Jason could pass for any other student wearing jeans and a New York Giant T-shirt. One visible exception was the tubing wrapped around his ears to his nose. While the backpack on the floor looked like it was merely for school books, upon closer examination, it contained an oxygen tank.

Jason began, "Thanks for coming here today to meet about me. I want to thank you ahead of time for your help this year. I'm excited to be in middle school. Gonna sound weird, but I can't wait to work hard." Although he laughed, Jason had to gasp for air from the oxygen machine keeping him alive.

Georgie watched as this student she had feared the previous day put an entire room of adults at ease. His medical history was intense and complicated.

Julia leaned in. "We are thrilled to have you at Eden Hills, Jason. I hope you find the building easily accessible to get from class to class. We have a brand-new elevator in the wing of the building where all of your classes are located."

Renata asked a series of questions about his health status as they continued to discuss technical and medical issues with the physician on the phone. Both Renata and the physician reassured the group Jason was ready, willing, and able to attend the new school.

Lilliana told Jason, "I will be in charge of your academics while in school. If, for whatever reason, you are not here, I can work with you at home as needed, so there is continuity. Sounds like a plan, Jason?"

His breathing was slow and labored. "You're gonna come to my house? Cool, Ms. Perez."

At the end of the meeting, Mrs. Rollins chewed the inside of her cheek. "I can rest my head on my pillow tonight, knowing Jason is safe in your hands during the day. I have huge faith. Jason will have an amazing year." Looking at the table, she took her hand and placed it on top of Jason's hand. "Hopefully, he will get his new heart soon!"

"Mom, I already have a heart. I now need a *good* one," Jason chimed in, which made everyone laugh.

Linda requested, "Let's show you around, so you are all set for tomorrow." The room emptied, leaving Mrs. Rollins alone with Julia.

Mrs. Rollins blocked the doorway, hyperventilating. "Ms. Bradley, to be clear, my son better be safe here." Her tone was sharp, biting. "Bullying problems. Too much work. No caring teachers. You have no idea what happened over the years. We moved here for peace, and he better get it here. I can't move him again. It's not fair. Eden Hills is his *fifth school* in as many years." A tear rolled down her cheek.

Julia offered her a tissue from the box on the table. "You are in a different place here in Eden Hills, Mrs. Rollins. I will make it my business to make sure Jason has a fantastic experience." She scanned the room for a piece of paper and pen, finding the items in a cabinet. She started writing. "This is my cell phone number. I can be reached at any time." She handed it to Mrs. Rollins. "Call me or text me at any time. No issue is too small."

Mrs. Rollins sniffed as she clutched the paper. Almost as if it was a million-dollar lottery ticket. "I'm shocked you would give me your cell phone number. That's a first." And her eyebrows lifted.

Julia nodded. "This is how it works here. Come on. I'll walk you out so you can complete any last-minute paperwork. We can take it one day at a time."

"That's been my motto since the day he was born." Mrs. Rollins let out a heavy sigh.

As Lilliana, Georgie and Jason approached the stairs, Lilliana pointed up, "Jason, do you want to walk up the stairs or take the elevator?"

Jason licked his lips. "Where do we have to go?"

Georgie explained, "All your classes are on the second floor for the full day, except lunch and some specials. Some days you may need to go up and down a few times."

Jason paid close attention. "How about we take the elevator today for practice? Tomorrow, if I feel good, I will try the stairs."

Lilliana agreed as they walked to the elevator. "Go ahead and press the button." She winked at Georgie. "Perfect plan. We can also allow you to have one friend keep you company when you use it if you want."

Jason watched the doors of the shiny, silver elevator open. "That's awesome. Never had that before in my other schools." He pressed the second-floor button. "I don't want to be different because I'm sick."

As the three of them watched the doors close, Lilliana and Georgie exchanged glances, grinning.

"Who knows? Maybe tomorrow might even be the day I get my heart. Never can tell."

CHAPTER 10

Georgie decided to read her emails before going home since Jason's meeting had lasted almost an hour. It seemed information was shared primarily in emails at Eden Hills, so she had to stay on the ball. That is when Georgie's heart sank. She fell back into her chair.

TO: Georgie Nelson
FM: Jose Gonzalez
RE: IEP meeting

As per our conversation this morning, I did not feel you were prepared enough for the student's IEP meeting that took place. You must take an active interest in all students. Next time work closely with the special educator to be more proficient with the student's needs. I expect you to be more prepared for the next meeting.

Alex called out from the hall, "Have a great night."

Georgie was nearly crying. She mumbled, "You too."

Alex slowly walked into the room. "You are not as chipper as I would have thought. I know you're a newbie, but hey, how bad can it be?" She pointed to her message. He looked at her laptop and read the email. "Georgie, he is like this with everyone. This is nothing new."

"I knew some information on the child, but not all of it. He is not wrong." She closed the laptop carefully.

"Hey, it was your first IEP meeting, and you are brand new. He knows it. Look, he has a history of putting things in writing that do not need to be said. I always suggest sleeping on it, writing a rebuttal, blind copy me for my file as the union representative. If you want to go over it with me, I'm a good sounding board. Text me so we can go over it."

"Can I let it go? I don't want any problems," Georgie sighed dejectedly.

Alex shrugged his shoulders. "Your decision."

She squeezed her eyes shut. "Is Jose starting a file on me? It's what - day two?"

Alex sat on the desk for a short time in silence, hesitating before speaking. Then he confided, "If you must know, Georgie. You have his daughter Angelina's job. He is not going to play nice with you. Now at least, you know it ahead of time." He rubbed his hands together.

"His daughter's job?" Georgie felt nauseous.

Alex chose his words deliberately. "She applied, but you got the job. I'm sorry to say, but this type of nonsense may continue with you."

"What do you think I should do?" she muttered. Georgie's cheeks were flushed.

As he slowly stood, Alex coughed. "Let's walk out together. Follow my lead." Alex took out his phone, texted something to someone, then put it back in his pocket.

Georgie noticed Alex take a puff of an inhaler as they walked to the elevator. She was not sure if shuffling was on purpose, or if this was his average speed. They walked into the main office, where Julia greeted them both. Georgie's body was trembling.

"Hey, Alex. Georgie, great child study team meeting today. You provided valuable input. You and Lilliana did your homework, that's for sure. Nice job escorting Jason around, so he is prepared for tomorrow when his classmates are here. I know his mother was extremely relieved to see how caring the staff is." Julia stood right outside Jose's office door.

Georgie gulped hard, unable to speak.

Alex puffed out his chest. "Georgie and I are heading out for the day. Two days down, one hundred seventy-eight days to go! Night, Julia. Night, Jose!"

As they walked out, Georgie looked into Jose's office. She was confident Jose had heard every word of Julia's praise. He called out, "See you tomorrow."

Georgie followed Alex out in silence. As she walked to the bottom step in front of the school with Alex, she knew the two teams in the game. She also knew she would lose more sleep tonight, figuring out her next play.

Julia walked into Jose's office and closed the door.

"Leave Georgie alone, Jose. She is way too valuable for your bullying. We need her more than ever, do you understand?"

Jose crossed his arms. Julia was livid. "I received a call from Dr. Salva today. He has decided not to retire this year. He has extended his contract for another three years." She glared at him. "A little heads up on your father in-law's plans would have been appreciated."

Jose slammed his fists on his desk and jumped to his feet. "I had no idea! He doesn't exactly confide in me these days."

Julia stormed out, slamming the door. He was unable to concentrate on the documents he had been working on. Shaking, he shook his head, muttering, "Another three years. Now what?"

After wrestling with what to do for most of the night, Georgie decided not to write a rebuttal to Jose. Feeling slightly guilty, she intended instead to be over-prepared for the next meeting. She was more embarrassed Alex had gotten involved in something so minor.

Georgie's lesson focused on obtaining a writing sample from each student about their summer experience. The fifty-five-minute class flew along with ease. The only sound in the room were students, either typing on their laptops or writing with a pen on paper.

As the students moved out smoothly for lunch, Georgie and Lilliana stood at the door monitoring the hallways between the change of classes. "Georgie, that group was a nice bunch, but their writing skills are all over the place. We may need to rework our lesson plans again for this group. I think we might have scared them into being good; so now we have to work on their basic skills. I guess that means it's working." Lilliana dared not smile as she watched the students moving along the hall.

Georgie noticed the issues too. "You're right. I assumed they were much higher than they are. I will rework the lessons and email them to you for your input. Any suggestions?"

"There are some fantastic basic skills programs online we can infuse into the lesson, maybe. I'll forward you some links at lunch." Lilliana bit her lip. "I hope you don't mind my suggestion."

Georgie shook her head. "No, I love your resources, but I don't think we have time with so much to cover."

Lilliana raised her eyebrows, "You will be making a mistake to fly through the lessons. A few of the students are lost." The bell rang.

Georgie fidgeted as her stomach was bloated so much she needed to sit. "Um, let me take a closer look at things. We have a lot riding on their test scores with Julia. I can't cut back the lessons."

Lilliana ran her hands through her hair as she counted to ten to herself. "That's not what I'm saying. Simply tweak the lessons. Maybe do some skill-building as a warm-up activity once or twice a week?" Her fists were tight, fingernails biting into the palms of her hands.

Georgie's stomach pains subsided. She refocused on what Lilliana mentioned and gave her a thumbs up. "That sounds better. I thought you meant doing the whole lesson reviewing skills since the curriculum is rigorous."

Lilliana's eyes looked heavenward. "That doesn't even make sense. Give me a little more credit." She joked, "I didn't recently graduate from college. Ha ha! Looking at your lessons, they are comprehensive. Much better than what my student-teacher showed me."

Georgie was able to stand again as the students entered. She confided in Lilliana. "I have to thank Alex for the tip. Fingers crossed it works with the rest of the classes. Have to say, it's either beginner's luck or the kids are scared early in the year. Weren't you surprised how easily they have adjusted to the rules so far? I found myself chatting with them more than anything. They crack me up." Georgie didn't smile either, only giving an evil eye to a boy who was teasing another boy. She jotted some notes about the class with her Cross pen, gripping it tightly. Georgie was confident the superstition was helping her already with her new career.

Being so impressed with Lilliana's knowledge, Georgie only hoped she could remember which student sat at which desk in each period. Hard when you have six boys named Ricky, six Pablos, plus four Emmas among the students. Still, she was determined to memorize their names as quickly as possible. It was essential to build a positive rapport with them as she managed the overloaded class. Glancing across at Lilliana standing near the window, she received a wink.

At teacher prep time, Georgie and Lilliana returned to their first-period classroom. Georgie lowered her voice, "I am not crazy about the teachers' room. There's so much to do. Meeting a ton of people is not high on my list of priorities."

Lilliana nodded. "*Sí*. Do you get many emails from parents? Many of them send me emails all day long."

Georgie looked closely at her emails. "Me too. It's only September! I wonder what it will be like after a marking period. Oh, I almost forgot. I emailed Alex to make an appointment in the computer lab. Thought they could do some research for the next story. What do you think?"

Lilliana's eyes gleamed. "Love it! Some of the kids are getting too chatty, too fast. Also, at lunch duty, I saw some boys in the fourth-period class giving each other dirty looks."

Georgie continued typing an email and nodded. "Yes, I guess the honeymoon might be coming to an end. The teasing was relentless yesterday at lunch. I've been making a little cheat sheet so we can tell the other teachers. Tell the guys, you know, Bob and Carl. Good to tag-team all of the troublemakers early. Say, when is there another IEP meeting? I need to be better prepared than the last one." Jose's letter of reprimand still haunted her.

"Yikes, Jason is out already. I'm calling later to see what's going on. Being on the transplant list means it could be any time." Lilliana wrote something on a sticky note. "Oh, the next IEP meeting. It's sometime soon." She looked at her emails. "Found it. I am forwarding you the notice."

"I appreciate it! I want to be on top of my game at all times," stated Georgie firmly.

"I feel the same pressure as you do," Lilliana acknowledged.

Georgie rubbed her bloated tummy. If Lilliana only knew!

CHAPTER 11

About a week later, Georgie parked her car at her regular hour, in her usual spot, on what should have been a typical day at Eden Hills. Georgie did not feel normal whatsoever. She had had a hard time eating anything for a few days. Even the raisin cinnamon bagel in her bag from her favorite bakery was too much for her. She could barely move as her stomach cramped. While wanting to get upstairs to her room, Georgie was not feeling at all well, so she went to Renata's office, seeing as it was closer than her classroom. Nausea suddenly overcame her for a moment. She found she needed to use the bathroom. Plus, the stomach pains were the worst she had ever felt in her life.

Renata, also an early bird, was already at work, washing her hands at the sink. Turning towards Georgie as she walked in, she looked at her closely, "You look pale. Want to lie on the cot?"

Without a word, Georgie did so until she was startled. "Oh, no! I am worried I'll be late for my first-period class so let me text Lilliana." She took out her phone, slowly pressed Lilliana's number, feeling dizzy.

Renata saw Georgie suddenly grasp the right side of her stomach. She looked gray. "Are you in pain? Tell me how you are feeling."

Her face grimaced in pain. "I've been feeling nauseous for a few days now, but it comes and goes. Little pain on the right side. Threw up a bit outside near my car this morning. Thought it would go away. It's weird since I don't eat much. Don't feel well at all! I feel like I need to go to the bathroom, but I'm in too much pain."

Renata pressed on Georgie's right side of her stomach, causing Georgie to scream. "Oh, my God! The pain. I can't."

Renata raised her eyebrows. "That is your appendix. We need to get you to the hospital." Renata dialed 911 from her cell phone, telling them to come to the side entrance of the school. Next, she texted Julia to get to her office ASAP.

Georgie was in agony. "I can drive myself! Please, don't make a big deal about this!"

Renata held her hand. "No way, Georgie. We follow procedures. Relax, I won't leave you. We're getting an ambulance. You're going to the hospital."

Julia stormed into the office. "What's going on, Renata?"

Renata pointed toward Georgie, who was lying on a cot in the fetal position, sobbing. Julia walked over and grabbed her hand. "Everything is alright. You're in great hands."

After three years at the middle school, Renata knew all the paramedics, along with most of the police officers working in town. Dialing another number, she spoke firmly, "Get me Chief Odin. Yes, this is an emergency. We need to get Georgie Nelson to the hospital. Now. It's her appendix. Blood pressure is getting lower. Move it!"

Julia sat still, looking in amazement at the nurse. "Wow, you have guts talking to Chief Odin that way. Good for you. I am texting Jose to let him know I am going to follow Georgie to the hospital in my car. Can you go in the ambulance with her? I'm calling for another nurse to cover you."

Renata winked at Julia while Georgie groaned in pain and started to perspire.

Putting her coat on, Julia told Georgie, "Don't worry. We have an excellent hospital nearby. Who can we call for you, Georgie?"

"I… I… I don't have anyone. But I can take an Uber or a cab. I don't need an ambulance." She winced once again with pain.

Julia whispered closer to her ear, "They are already on their way, so don't worry. Are you positive there's no-one I can call for you?"

Georgie shook her head.

A few minutes later, Jose entered the room, a genuine look of horror on his face. "What can I do?" As Julia's stomach was flipping, Jose lowered his voice, "Get out of here. I'll cover the building."

Julia smiled. "I'm going as well as Renata. Another nurse is coming in now to cover. If you need me, text me, but for now, it's your building. Tell the secretaries what is going on."

Georgie, wincing in pain, whispered to Renata, "Oh, I have a cousin, Clare, but she's a few hours away."

Julia stepped away from them into the corner of the office to call Dr. Salva. She noticed the filing cabinet covering the door Renata mentioned on the first day of school. Shaking her head, she made a mental note to make sure the custodians followed through with her request. Dr. Salva's voice snapped her back to the issue at hand. "We have a teacher going to the hospital. Jose is in charge until I get back. I wanted you to know."

Dr. Salva barked, "Keep me updated. Who is it?"

She winced, whispering, "Georgie Nelson. I will. The paramedics are here. We are heading out now."

Renata consulted with the paramedics while they carefully placed Georgie on a gurney. She then followed them out of her office and into the ambulance waiting outside the side door. "Georgie, I'll keep you company and call your cousin." Having forgotten her pocketbook and coat, Renata turned back to her office. She needed to lock her desk and filing cabinets too.

Jose said, "Consider her classes covered."

"I'll keep you updated and will be back as soon as I can," Julia yelled from a distance as she raced towards her car.

Renata finished double-checking the locks in her office and turning back to Jose, said in a rushed voice, "I think her appendix might burst if we don't get there fast. She might be out a while, so be prepared for a short-term coverage plan. Just saying." She darted off, jumping in the back of the ambulance

Jose raised his eyebrows, calling out to her. "Hopefully, it is nothing too serious." Watching the ambulance speed out of sight, he grinned as warmth spread throughout his chest.

Once in the main office, Jose walked over to Tiffany and scribbled a phone number down. "Tell her she needs to be here as soon as possible." Rubbing his hands together and licking his lips, he decided to stroll around the building. There was a certain air of confidence, almost pride in himself. At last, he was where he wanted to be. Now he was in charge.

Georgie was quickly admitted into the hospital while Renata looked after her things. Georgie's heart pounded while they moved her onto a bed in the emergency room where the doctors assessed her needs. She could barely keep her eyes open as she answered questions. Renata receded into the background, giving her the privacy to share whatever was needed.

A petite nurse in baggy blue scrubs approached Renata. "Hi, I am Amal. Do you know if Ms. Nelson has family or someone to call?"

Renata answered, "Truthfully, she says there is a cousin several hours away, but I did not want to do that until I knew what was going on."

Amal blinked rapidly, "Well, we need someone who can authorize information for the next steps."

"I'm the school nurse. Poor thing is a brand-new teacher." Renata looked at the last few numbers texted on Georgie's phone and saw the name Clare along with a Maryland area code. "I may have it here. Calling Clare now."

"Sounds good. Let me go see what is going on," and Amal gave Renata the forms to fill out since Georgie had given Renata her wallet. After completing the paperwork, Renata spoke with Clare over the phone.

Julia arrived shortly afterwards and sat with Renata, who looked like a wreck. Julia shook her head and cleared her throat. "We're off to a busy school year already. Well, this is hospital visit number one. Care to make a bet how many more we'll have this year? What did we have last year, twenty visits?"

Renata smirked, "Let's see. There was the mean girl fight in the bathroom where one girl threw the toilet paper holder. They hit one another in the nose; that was fun too. Hey, how about the basketball player dislocating his knee? An ugly one." She glanced at her emails. "Oh, of course, Alex's collapse was the scariest. Must have sat here for hours with him with the MRIs, CTs, pulmonary function tests. He never shared anything with me at all, but I still worry about him."

"I worry about Alex every day but don't like to say it out loud. Now Georgie. So much for having a calm year." Julia started pacing.

Renata's phone rang with the ringtone, "Somewhere Over the Rainbow," blaring at a high volume. "It's Clare, Georgie's cousin." Julia nodded, biting her lip. Renata answered, explaining what had happened, asking, "Is there anything we need to know about her health history?" Putting her thumbs up as Julia looked on, she continued, "Does she have any immediate family nearby?" Julia started to pace again. Renata chuckled, "I know, it's a shame it's so early in the year, but we will help out, no worries. Clare, you've been most helpful. I'll call you later when we know something."

Julia sat, leaning in. "What's the deal?"

Renata rubbed her cheek. "Well, the good news is she has no significant health history."

Julia exhaled. "Well, that is a huge relief. What else did you find out?"

"Clare disclosed that Georgie's mother passed away a few years ago of a massive heart attack. Her father is in a home in South Jersey with dementia. She had a brother who died, but she didn't go into detail. That's about it. It sounds like no one is local at all."

Rubbing her hands together, Julia raised her eyebrows. "Georgie is going to need some help."

Renata stretched her arms. "I can stay tonight if you want?"

Julia's muscles tightened. "Don't be silly. I am here. Jose can cover the building. I'm sure he's in his element."

Renata laughed before becoming serious. "I am so worried that maybe it's her appendix. Did they say anything?"

Julia shook her head. "Maybe, but they are doing other tests as we speak."

"Poor girl. I meant what I told Clare. I will help her out in any way I can."

Julia glanced at her phone. "You are so good. Let's see what happens. Well, Jose has her classes covered; he's put Angelina in." Despite sounding confident, Julia was a little concerned. She hoped Angelina was the right choice.

Renata hesitated only slightly before saying, "Jose introduced me to her over the summer. She seemed nice enough. You know they had a rough time at the Gonzalez house." She leaned in closer to Julia. "His wife left him a few weeks ago. Dinner one night, gone the next. She met someone online, ran off to Florida."

Julia's mouth fell open, and guardedly whispered, "No! I can't believe it. Mind you, Maritza never was nice, so maybe he is better off. Sad to say, I don't know how they stayed together so long. The one good thing about Jose is, he's a wonderful father, but now he has his hands full. How about the son? He must be in tenth grade now. I presume both kids are not with her?"

Renata rubbed her neck. "No, the kids are with Jose. With his son's special needs, I guess it's the best thing for all of them."

Thinking about what she had heard, Julia wondered if this might explain Jose's behavior. But then again, he had always been a bit off.

Amal came out with the doctor. Both looked concerned.

The tall, buxom, blond doctor was no more than thirty years old. "I am Dr. Stein. We need to get Georgie into surgery quickly before her appendix bursts. Give us a few hours; you may want to go home, get some rest. It looks routine. She is healthy, so it shouldn't be complicated, but you never know. We'll let you know how it goes. Any questions?"

Julia sighed. "No, please keep us updated. However, I would prefer to wait. Is there somewhere I could stay?"

Amal pointed to the end of the hallway. "There is a waiting room which is more private. I can take you to it, but first, we need to get things organized for Georgie."

⇥+⇤

Sometime later, Amal came back to escort them to the private waiting room where they were to wait until they heard back from Dr. Stein. Renata gasped when her phone alarm buzzed. "Jeez, I need to get back to school to give some meds to a child. Do you want me to come back?"

Julia insisted, "Not necessary. I'm here. Go home once you've finished. I'll text you with any news."

The wait was a long one, made more frustrating by having no one to speak to about things. Julia was reading her emails on her phone when she felt as if someone was staring at her. Her heart nearly jumped out of her chest as it was none other than her old friend Marko Medrano, heading directly toward her.

His grin was broad. "Julia Bradley, as I live and breathe!"

Marko was a former athlete who had not slacked off with the years. He had light brown skin, and his slender, muscular frame moved straight toward her. His icy-blue eyes dazzled; his dark brown suit and red tie were hard to miss.

As she looked at him, Julia saw his hair had turned a 'salt and pepper' color since the last time they had seen each other, but he was still deadly attractive. She frowned, "What are you doing here?"

He kissed her on both cheeks, saying, "Saw you fly through the door while I was with a client. A lawyer's job is always needed, you know."

At first, she stuttered a little. "I… I have a new teacher in surgery. What's going on with you? How is the new district? The… new wife?"

Marko pulled her gently by the arm. They were now sitting very close to each other on the waiting room couch. "New district stinks, the new wife is not great. I'm looking to make a change in both areas. I miss Eden Hills and running into you more often, but the bigger districts are the way to go. More work means more business to pay the bills." There was a pregnant pause before he went on. "I was sorry to hear about Brendan. He was a special guy. How are you doing?"

Julia's voice was cold and emotionless. "As fine as someone can be after her fiancé has been killed." She sighed. "You know, good days, bad ones. I'm focusing on getting the school on the blue-ribbon list. The newbies are a promising group, including the one in surgery." She took out a mint. "Sorry about the wife; number… what? Four?"

He started to sweat a little. "Yes, but don't say it too loudly. I'd better go. If you need me for anything, call. Good seeing you." He hugged her a little too long, but she didn't seem to be bothered by the embrace.

"You too. Don't be a stranger." As she watched him leave, she remembered how, before Brendan, he had been the best thing she had ever let go.

❧ ❧

Several hours later, Julia, still waiting for word on Georgie, was speaking with Tiffany who was filling her in on all the things Jose had done or changed during the brief time Julia was out of the building. Without Tiffany's ears and eyes, things could go awry fast with Jose at the helm. Julia laughed, "Well, sounds like everything is still standing without me. See you tomorrow. As usual, you saved the day." Finishing the call, she waved to Renata, who had decided to come back, after all, to check up on her.

When Dr. Stein appeared, she looked exhausted as she spoke in a flat voice. "Georgie's going to be out of it for a while, but we'll move her to a room in a few hours. There were no issues at all. Standard appendectomy - recovering for a few days then as good as new. It's late, so you might want to come back in the morning. Good thing you got her here when you did. It seems like she has been symptomatic for a few days."

Julia rubbed her temple. "I'll wait for her to wake up. I don't want her to be alone."

After Dr. Stein left, Julia took Renata by the shoulders. "Renata, go home to Daisy."

Renata bowed her head, "I will after I share the good news with Clare. She sounded worried. Good thing Georgie's healthy." She started to walk while dialing. "If I can do anything, I am a text away. I'll come by over the weekend. I'm sure she'll be here a day or so."

Julia called out to Renata. "Go, I insist. Regards to Daisy." Julia then wrote the same text to Jose and Dr. Salva since she did not have the energy to compose different updates. As a nurse walked by, Julia interrupted her midstride, "Excuse me, is there a chapel here?" The nurse directed her to the small, dark room with six benches, a crucifix, and a table of half-lit plastic candles running low on power. Sitting in the last pew in the row, she composed some mental prayers of thanks for the safe, comfortable procedure for her ace in the hole.

CHAPTER 12

Georgie's blurry vision only saw a bright white room as bells were ringing in her ears. Confused, she tried to wipe her face with her hands but noticed a tight cream cloth around her arm with wires connected to machines. An attempt to lick her lips was fruitless as her mouth was as dry as a desert. *What the hell happened to me?*

Julia poured some water into a plastic cup and held it to Georgie's mouth. "Here, drink some." You took a bit longer than we expected to wake up, but I am happy to see you looking back at me."

Georgie was discombobulated. She swished the water around her mouth, then swallowed some more. Blushing, she shrugged her shoulders. "The last thing I remember, I was telling some nurse about my bowel movements. Something about my breakfast? What happened? Surgery? Appendix? It's a kind of blur." Julia placed the cup on the tray next to the bed.

Julia, nodding, leaned in closer towards her. "Exactly. The doctors had to take your appendix out before it ruptured. Dr. Stein, your doctor - who, by the way, looks like she is seventeen years old - said you did great! You have to stay here for a few days. And you'll need to take a few days' rest afterwards, but otherwise, you are good to go. Are you in pain?"

"Not when I press this!" Georgie pressed a red button the nurse had shown her for drugs. "God, I love this button. I may need these drugs more often! Julia, you didn't stay the night, I hope."

Julia patted her hand. "Sure did. I can't have one of my most valuable teachers waking up to… well, this place is not exactly a five-star hotel. Anyway, many graduates work here, so in a way, I have been reuniting with friends. Feeling old too. Students I taught early in my career are running the place!"

Georgie smelled Clorox and coughed. "Well, now I'm awake, please go home. I'll be back to work as soon as possible. I promise."

Julia knew Georgie had no family coming to see her. "I don't mind keeping you company for a little while."

"I insist. I'm fine. I better call my cousin and my dad's nursing home. Must let them know where I am." She looked around for her phone.

Julia texted Renata to let her know Georgie was awake. "Relax, consider it done. Just get better. That's all we can ask for."

"Thank you. I don't know what to say other than I am touched."

Julia held Georgie's phone. "Look, I've put my cell number on your phone, so don't hesitate to let me know how you are doing. Come back when you are ready. We need you!" Satisfied Georgie would be resting, Julia left her, going straight to her office to find a few dozen voicemail messages.

Not long afterwards, a thin, tall Asian man in white scrubs walked into Georgie's room. "Hi, Georgie, I'm Al, your nurse. I'm not sure if you can remember me speaking to you a few times already, but remember to press the red button when you need some relief from the pain. In a few minutes, we are going to do some more blood work on you as requested by Dr. Stein."

Georgie's head tilted to the side, "What tests?"

Al's tone was flat, "Some blood tests."

"Blood tests for what?"

"Dr. Stein will discuss it with you. Are you able to understand what I am saying, or are you still a bit groggy?"

Georgie giggled. "I love these drugs, Al. Not groggy, just relaxed."

Al checked the machines, took her temperature, and then her blood pressure. "Great. I'm glad you are feeling better. Dr. Stein is coming in shortly."

Georgie watched Al do further assessments in silence. Then she closed her eyes for a few minutes. Hearing someone enter the room, she opened her eyes to find Renata at her bedside.

Renata smiled. "Yay, Georgie, you are looking much better than the last time I saw you! How are you feeling?"

Georgie had some pink in her cheeks. "Much better. Thank you for all you did for me!"

"Any time. Boy, I spoke with Clare, and she is as sweet as you are. Do you want to chat or watch some TV?"

Yawning, Georgie shrugged her shoulders.

Renata took the TV clicker from the table and laughed, "Trashy TV it is!" The pair watched a reality show for some mindless entertainment. After an hour, Renata left to find Al as Georgie had fallen asleep.

Not far from the nurse's station, Renata found Al typing information into a computer. She fumbled for words, "I thought you said Dr. Stein was coming to check on her. An emergency, I imagine?"

Al glanced around, "I'm not sure, sorry. Normally they are in right away, but they are looking into some things."

"What things?"

"I am not at liberty to say. But I have been taking more blood."

"This is not normal?" Renata was alarmed.

Al tried to reassure her, but as a part-time ER nurse, Renata was an expert.

"It's usually normal to take more blood when needed; please don't worry. Georgie is in excellent hands." After a short pause, he informed her, "Err… I know they are consulting with another hospital for some information."

Renata's voice rose a pitch, "Another hospital? Why?"

"I don't know. The doctor will come when she gets all the information. Please be patient. I'm sure there is nothing to panic about."

Renata's mind was racing as she meandered back to Georgie's room. She rubbed her hands together as she walked into Georgie's room, quietly sitting down so as not to wake her. Renata's leg was jumping as she waited for some news.

Georgie opened her eyes. "Renata, you saved my life. I will be forever grateful."

"Hey, I see the drugs are working. And anyway, that is my job. How are you feeling without your appendix?"

"Not in pain. You know what? I haven't seen the doctor yet."

Renata changed the channel on the TV. "Surgery is surgery; it's always serious. They can never be too careful."

Georgie's breathing was shallow. She shuddered, "How was school? I'd better text Lilliana, otherwise, she might be upset with me. We had plans for the kids to go to the computer lab. Oh well, I guess another day."

Renata patted Georgie's hand. "Everything has been taken care of. Lilliana has things under control. Everything is under control." Under the bed, Renata's toe was tapping like a woodpecker on a hollow branch. It was the way she channeled her energy, especially when she lied through her teeth.

⚊⫟ ⫟⚊

After some considerable time, Dr. Stein arrived. "Hey Georgie, we met a few times quickly. Glad to see you looking much better now. How are you feeling?"

Georgie rocked back and forth, "A little sore, but from the surgery, not like I have felt the last few days."

"Good, I am glad." Dr. Stein's voice softened. "Georgie, we have done some additional blood tests, but are still awaiting some of the results. It may take a few days for a few of them. I want to be honest with you. We are consulting with experts from another hospital. There was an unusual circumstance very few of us had ever witnessed at this hospital."

Renata turned to Georgie. "Would you like me to step out?"

"No, please stay." Georgie gripped Renata's hand tight. "What do you mean?"

Dr. Stein started slowly, "When we sent your appendix for pathology analysis, we... err... found a mass of rare cells."

Georgie's head flinched back slightly as did Renata's.

"What?" said Georgie.

Dr. Stein lowered her voice. "It appears you had some rare types of cells in your appendix. They are small, uncommon. I have only read about these in textbooks, quite frankly. When I discussed the pathology results with several other physicians, no-one has had any experience with them. They suggested I speak to an expert, but there are only a very few in the country. When we scanned you before surgery, the cells did not light up since they were too small. I have conferred with other experts who suggested we take some more blood to see what your levels were after the surgery. At this point, this is where we are. Do you have any questions?"

Georgie lay in bed, blinking quickly and biting her lip. As strong as Renata was, she too sat in silence, her face frozen, eyes wide open. It was as if all the air had been sucked out of the room. Both women were too blindsided to ask any questions.

Finally, Dr. Stein broke the silence. "I know this comes as a shock to both of you, but luckily we found it by accident. When the blood work comes back, you can make some decisions as to what the next steps are that you are going to take. Do either of you have any questions?"

Georgie did a double-take. "Mass? Abnormal cells? I didn't know there could be a good mass."

Dr. Stein patted her on the legs. "Let's talk further when you return to my office. I should have more information by then. When all the test results come back, you should see an expert. I know enough to know I am not that person."

Georgie blurted out, "When can I go back to work? I'm brand new and have a lot riding on this job."

"I understand. We'll have a follow-up appointment. Let's go from there. I have to make sure you heal from the surgery first. When will that be? I'm not sure. Let's give it about a week to see what happens. First things first, let's get you home. I am thinking in a day or two. Sound good?" And the doctor patted Georgie's bed.

Georgie sighed. "Sounds like a fabulous idea. Get me out of here!"

CHAPTER 13

A few days later, Renata pulled up in front of Georgie's house in the quiet, serene beach town of Shellview, New Jersey. Number 17 Birdbath Drive was a stately, four-floor white Victorian home decorated with wilting purple wisteria hanging from faded white wicker baskets. The open porches on each floor held old white wooden lounge chairs which had toppled over. As Renata looked closer, she saw that the house was desperate for a paint job. While each house on the block had minor variations, Georgie's was the most in need of repair. The houses were tightly packed next to one another, being separated by only a small garden or path. The bushes in front were overgrown, needing a trim. Despite it being dated, it was still a sight to behold.

Renata gasped. "Georgie, your home is exquisite. Wow! When can I move in?" Georgie smiled back in silence. Renata got out of the car and inhaled the fresh salt air, hearing the roar of the waves a block away and the sound of windchimes in the distance. Renata suddenly felt under-dressed in ripped jeans, rainbow sneakers, and an old Bruce Springsteen concert T-shirt. This town was hoity-toity, even empty. She darted around to help Georgie walk from the curb to the porch. "This is not like Eden Hills *at all*. You truly live in… freaking… paradise."

As Georgie fumbled for her keys to open the black front door, Renata noticed how tired and pale she looked from the hour drive. Quickly Renata went back to her car, opened the trunk, and gathered up some more packages. Returning, her hands were full of plastic bags filled with food.

"It looks as if there must have been many parties here! When you invite me, I might never freaking leave!"

Ambling into the house, Georgie sighed, "Thanks. It was my parents' home. Guess you can tell I haven't made many changes since they lived here."

Renata was already on her way back to the car, to grab more stuff. Which was good, as Georgie wasn't in the mood to discuss her family. All she yearned for now was to go to bed.

Slamming the trunk closed, Renata carried the last of the bags into the house, closing the heavy front door with her foot. As she returned, Georgie said, "Being home calms me; it brings me peace. Let me give you some money for the groceries. It looks like I'm going to be eating like a queen for the week." Taking her wallet out, she worried she did not have enough cash. Lately, she seemed to be short of money a lot.

"Not on your life! I know where you live, so I always know where to come for a good home-cooked meal. That's all you owe me."

Placing the remainder of the bags on the cream marble kitchen island, Renata glanced around the open plan area of the first floor. The living room and kitchen, all faded white, were splashed with patriotic decorations. Red, white, and blue candles on the tables, American flag pillows, and stained-glass eagle lamps enhanced the rooms. Until Renata spotted the large painting over the center of the room, everything looked as if it could have been from the Civil War.

"Huh, spectacular. Where is this?" She asked. After a closer inspection, she read the inscription: *An Irish Landscape.*

The painting showed gigantic cliffs with various hues of green mountainous hills. As she looked closer, Renata could see small rock formations which must have signified parcels of land. "My, oh my." Turning around, she found Georgie sitting on the silver metal bar stool at the kitchen counter, head in her hands, yawning. Renata cringed and took out her car keys. Glancing at the cobwebs in the corner of the room, she decided to take a broom and give the place "a lick and a promise" another time.

In truth, Georgie was relieved to have some help. At this time of the year along the shore, neighbors were sporadic. It was nearly a ghost town. Most stores only opened on the weekends. "Thank you for everything again. You have done so much already. You don't have to take me to the doctor this week. I can Uber it," she told Renata gently but tiredly.

Renata moved closer to Georgie. "Please, let me help you. You don't know me very well, but I don't take no for an answer. Anyway, I can see you need to get some rest. I'll text Lilliana to call you later, after you adjust a bit. She can't wait to talk to you. Oh, and Alex wants to drop by since he lives nearby; here is the schedule," and Renata pulled out a piece of paper, handing it to Georgie.

It was clear her new colleagues had planned this out carefully. Refocusing her eyes, Georgie read the paper as she sauntered into the living room where she flopped onto the sofa, mouth agape. "A schedule? You did all this for me? I don't know what to say." Shaking her head, Georgie put her hand over her mouth, as her eyes filled with tears.

Seeing her yawn, Renata thought it time to leave. "I'm heading out otherwise I might stay here forever. That sheet has all our numbers on, so feel free to text anytime you need something. Will Clare visit?"

Laying her head on the pillow, Georgie shook her head. "I told her not to bother since she has a new job. Hopefully, I can get some work from Lilliana to keep me busy."

Renata rattled her car keys. "I understand. I'll see you for your appointment with Dr. Stein in a few days. Make sure you keep walking too. It's big-time important for your recovery." But Georgie was already closing her eyes, so Renata slipped out the door.

⚔︎ ⚔︎

The next day, Georgie had no choice but to take it easy. She checked the schedule, realizing Alex was coming by to check in on her, so she took a well-needed shower. She hoped the hot water worked since it was unreliable these days. She was excited to be seeing another human being. The bonus was, he promised to bring her work laptop, along with a pile of essays she needed to grade. She couldn't wait to see how the students had done with her assignments. She also wanted to input the grades into the database for Julia. The last thing Georgie wanted was to let anyone down. Since she had left her school laptop in school, and her own computer had died of old age right before school started, she only had her cell phone.

The doorbell rang. Georgie called out, "Come in." She was making iced tea in the kitchen.

"Am I interrupting something?" Alex wore a crisp red golf shirt, navy-blue pants and loafers. His arms were full of what she had texted him she needed.

For some reason unknown to her, Georgie choked up. "No, not at all. Happy to see you. It's so lovely of you to visit and help me out. I appreciate you being part of the schedule to check up on me." And she smiled ear to ear as their eyes met.

"It's my pleasure, neighbor! Dove Cove is nice, and far enough away from Eden Hills so I can hide from school business." He laughed and jokingly said, "No pressure, but please hurry up and get back soon. Everyone misses you. Poor Lilliana needs you for sure!"

He placed her school laptop on the dining room table along with a thick pile of papers in a folder. "Here are your things. Lilliana gave the kids with laptops your email, so be prepared for many more assignments being emailed to you directly."

Georgie slapped her hands against her cheeks. "Wow, this is great! I'm not that sure they miss me. They barely know my name, before bam, I'm out. Not a good look." She started to slip on her sneakers.

"You can't help it if your appendix wanted to get the hell out of your body! Calm down." He looked around the room, stretching his arms. "Seriously though, how are you doing?" And he coughed deeply as he leant against the nearest chair.

She tied her shoelaces. "I have to exercise a little every day. Do you want to walk with me a little? I've got to get out of here; otherwise, I'm gonna lose my mind. Ignore my crazy hair, ugly old sweats, won't you?"

Alex didn't notice anything of the sort. To him, she looked gorgeous, a sight for sore eyes, so he told her, "You look amazing, considering. Sure, let's walk. This is the best time of the day before the sunsets. It's what I love the most about Shellview."

She looked at him a little closer, realizing as handsome as he was, he was also as thin as a rail; in fact, too thin. "I agree. I heard a rumor you had a rough time last year, health-wise. Are you feeling better?"

Alex was struggling to hold the heavy door open for them to leave, letting the light in from the sun. He lied straight to her face, "Feeling outstanding! Do you have *anything* with caffeine in it, to take on our journey?"

"Good idea!" Georgie went to the refrigerator in the kitchen to get some water and a bottle of her homemade iced tea. On the way to join Alex outside, she stopped a moment to check her image in the mirror only to see, what she considered, to be an imposter. She looked the same on the outside but now had something sinister growing inside her. Much like a backpack filled with dynamite; waiting, ready to explode at any given moment. What a roller coaster ride the last few days had been. *When would it end? One day healthy, the next minute, surgery... mass... cells?* Shaking off her scary thoughts, she decided to do what she did best - file it away and plug along.

Opening the door to the front porch, Georgie found Alex with his eyes closed as the late afternoon sun beat on his relaxed black skin. He looked as if he was in a deep trance. She hated to interrupt his thoughts. Standing next to him, Georgie handed him the iced tea bottle. By accident, their hands brushed against each other.

Alex was startled by the coldness of the bottle. He was also tired, worn out from the day. Opening the lid, he quickly guzzled down the entire bottle, as if it would miraculously give him the energy to walk anywhere with Georgie. "I needed that." He said before catching her staring at him. "I know what you're thinking."

"I'm not thinking about you." Georgie pushed her curly hair off her face, tying it up with an elastic band which had been wrapped around her wrist.

"You think I look like an older, but I believe wiser and definitely hotter, John Legend," and he laughed. "The kids tell me all the time. If I had a penny for every time someone told me that, I'd retire in a minute." He gazed at her house. "I'm admiring this home of yours. I bet there are some *juicy* stories." Alex joined Georgie, and they went down the stairs.

With a giggle, Georgie shrugged. "Nah, simple story. I was raised here with my family my entire life. Wonderful parents, fantastic brother - my twin, in fact."

Following her lead, they headed west toward the ocean. She walked nice and slow, which was the perfect pace for him. "Cool. Having a twin brother must have been fascinating. I have a brother, too. Do you have Wonder Twin powers?"

Georgie reminisced. "I wish we did; he would still be here. Derek played college football." With a slight smile, she added, "Immensely talented. He was such an amazing quarterback, recruited by four division one universities. It was tough on his body, though. He was injured too many times, had countless surgeries." Georgie spoke in a quiet voice. "They gave him tons of medication. He overdosed on opioids three years ago. It sucked. His death broke all our hearts." She felt a thickness in her throat and took a moment to control herself and swallow the feeling before concluding. "Two days after his funeral, my mom had a massive heart attack. It was devastating."

Alex stopped walking. His mouth opened, but for a few seconds, nothing came out. He was speechless. Then he said, "I don't even know what to say."

Her stomach cramped, so Georgie drank a sip of water and strolled on, saying, "Nothing to say. I kept my father together, took care of him until I couldn't do it anymore. Last year Dad's dementia became too difficult for me to handle; especially on my own. I couldn't carry-on caring for him myself, so he's in a safe place, ten minutes from here."

A gust of wind blew, causing the tall sea-grass from the dunes to sway fast from left to right. Georgie took a deep breath. "After ten *long* years, I left my editorial position. I was done! My parents wanted it for me, but I didn't want it for me. It was such a cut-throat, backstabbing environment, especially when all I have ever wanted to do is teach kids."

They crossed the empty two-lane street toward the wood-planked boardwalk. "I was looking towards having a more rewarding career, a better life. I was thrilled with my decisions until my damn appendix the other day!" Georgie laughed nervously. She had never shared this with anyone. They both kicked off their shoes before heading for the sandy, narrow beach path.

"Wow," said Alex. "That's quite a story. How are you doing? Do you have anyone special to help you out?" He placed his shoes next to Georgie's sneakers neatly on the planks; side by side like two eggs in a carton.

Georgie led Alex through the narrow path and twelve-foot dunes until they emerged onto the flat, cool, soft sand. Turning she saw Alex struggling a little behind her, so she waited.

Taking in a long, deep breath of air, she realized she too was pretty winded, so she sat down. "Well, this looks like a perfect place to plop, I'd say."

Alex sat next to her, covering a yawn with his hand. Georgie looked out toward the high tide. "I was dating a lawyer for a while when all this happened, but he appeared to have the sensitivity chip missing. He was nowhere to be seen when I needed him most. Before I even noticed it, our relationship had tanked. According to his text, he didn't want the drama."

Georgie sipped her water. She looked at Alex staring at her with his mouth open again, speechless. "You asked, Mr. Williams."

"Ms. Nelson, that is one of the *worst* stories I've heard in a long time! Awful." Then he pointed to the ocean. "At least you have this. Hell, even I find the ocean healing. That's why I moved here." He rubbed his hands together, then coughed so hard he had to take out a tissue and blot his lips. "I appreciate you telling me. Trust me; I keep things close to the chest. What you tell me goes nowhere. No worries, I'm here for you. After all, we're neighbors. Well... practically."

Georgie's eyes welled up behind the eyelids. "The generosity I have experienced in the short time at Eden Hills - you, Renata, Julia, Lilliana... it's been amazing. I can't say enough about how much I needed to find some good faith in people. It's been a long while." And she buried her feet in the sand with her hands. Alex mirrored her behavior.

"As a whole, we're a good group of people." And he paused before continuing, "Listen, I've had my share of loss too. We all have. It's a big burden; especially when you need people. If they disappear, it is disheartening. Please, your ex-boyfriend lawyer needs to meet my ex-fiancé nurse. They sound *perfect* for each other. As for me? I am too much work to marry. Can't make it up." He shook his head.

Georgie shrugged her shoulders. "Her loss." She high-fived him. "Well, neighbor, if you need anything, I am only a few minutes away. Ready to go back?" And Georgie pointed in the direction of her house. She yawned loudly, "I apologize. I can't believe how this walk has tired me out." Standing, she brushed off the sand.

Alex led the way. "I'm tired too. Listen, we have a schedule to help you out, but I'll let the others know I'm your main point person. After all, I'm only eight minutes from here, according to Google maps. Everyone else is way too far. Oh, and you didn't hear it from me, but Lilliana has her hands full with your sub." His legs were wobbly as he walked along the narrow path.

"My sub?" Georgie exclaimed from behind him.

Alex yelled over his shoulder so Georgie could hear him over the crashing waves, "Yes, but I have it handled." He found their shoes precisely where they left them.

Georgie slipped on her sneakers. "I don't know how to thank you. It's a relief. It's a dream job."

Alex coughed a little bit as they continued back to the house. "I know. I have your back. I *will always* have your back. This conversation goes nowhere. To be honest, I did a bit of recon on you. Tell me about your famous mother!"

They had arrived at her front step. "No way, that's for next time..." said Georgie as she started climbing the steps to her house, leaving Alex watching her from the sidewalk.

Alex suddenly realized that he did not feel sick for the first time in many, many months. He rubbed his eyes. "Maybe a dose of Georgie Nelson a day would keep all his doctors away," he thought as he left humming a lively jazz tune.

CHAPTER 14

Despite the offers of help, Georgie took an Uber to the office for her appointment with Dr. Stein. She couldn't take Renata away from her job, no matter how supportive she was. After what seemed like hours waiting, the nurse called her name out. "Georgie Nelson, Dr. Stein is ready for you."

Biting her tongue nervously, Georgie followed her into the examination room without a word, sitting on the paper-covered reclining table. Dr. Stein walked in right away with a folder and shook her hand. "Well, you are looking much better than the last time I saw you. How are you feeling?"

Georgie rubbed her hands on her legs. "Great. When can I go back to work?"

As she lay down on the examination room table, the doctor moved Georgie's blouse then her pants to check the scar. "Healing nicely. How about eating, drinking, exercising?"

Georgie had all the right answers. "I eat three meals a day, thanks to some wonderful colleagues, I mean friends, cooking for me. Drinking lots of liquids, sleeping is fine. Have no energy sometimes after my walks, though."

"How long are you walking?"

"About thirty minutes a day."

"Very good, exercise is always important to do. I'm glad to see you have recovered so nicely. Excellent. We received some of the test results we ran in the hospital."

Georgie was hesitant to ask, "I thought you got everything out. I'm OK, right?"

Dr. Stein paused before saying, "Well, the tests have led me to refer you to an oncologist for more support. Some of the elevated markers are concerning."

"What does that mean? Is an oncologist to do with cancer? Are those cells? Masses? *Cancer?* What are the markers?" Her face had started to flush, heart thumping a million miles a minute.

Dr. Stein pursed her lips. "Those cells are a rare form of cancer, called neuroendocrine cancer. That means you need further discussion with another specialist, an oncologist. Do you have any gastrointestinal symptoms? Eating? Diarrhea? What is this?" Dr. Stein looked closely at Georgie's red face and neck. "How long have you been having this redness, this flushing?"

Georgie bit her lip. "Over a few months, but only sometimes. When I am stressed, which is often, I guess."

Dr. Stein spoke sternly. "This is not the time to be coy or underestimate anything with me. Anything else?"

"Eating has been hard. Whatever I eat, I am off to the bathroom. I'm embarrassed to say it out loud." Georgie's voice weakened.

"How about your energy levels?" queried Dr. Stein.

Georgie mumbled, "I noticed over the spring of last year that I needed to nap more. I've had a full-time schedule. Working during the day, graduate school at night. Issues with my father which have been going on for years. It's been a lot."

Dr. Stein smiled. "I am sorry if I am coming across firm, but I need you to focus on things differently." Taking hold of Georgie's hand, the doctor sat next to her on the table. "You are young and strong. You can get through this. That much, I know. If you have any questions, you call me. You can go back to work from the surgery. But, please make sure you see the oncologist as soon as possible. Good luck." And she patted Georgie on the shoulder.

After the doctor had left, Georgie sat in the office in silence, not moving for several minutes. The appointment had not gone at all as she had expected. She was supposed to be excellent, healthy. Damn it. She could no longer be in denial with this cancer thing. She got dressed then texted Renata. *Can we talk, please?*

Renata responded right back. *Call me, no kids around.*

Georgie paced the office. She had heard what she had heard, but to say it aloud would make it real. Calling Renata, a lump in her throat, Georgie's eyes bulged, "I have a rare type of cancer called neuroendocrine cancer. I don't know where to begin."

"I'm here for you, don't worry. I am going to research as much as I can for you. Just go home and take it easy. Can I drop by your house tomorrow?"

Georgie's voice was shaky. "Yes, if it's not too much trouble." She touched her face with her hand; it was stinging a bit with the redness.

Walking outside, Georgie sighed before calling an Uber. She leaned against the wall of the building, hoping her stomach would stop cramping before the ride home. She hated to admit it, but her stomach issues were a constant problem lately. When the Uber arrived, he honked several times for attention before she realized it was for her. Apologizing to the driver, she asked him to put the music off as she kept her window wide open. There was not enough air or silence for her to think straight. As shitty as she felt, Georgie knew she was going to have a sleepless night.

The following day Renata stopped by with a large file filled with neuroendocrine cancer information. Renata had a lightness in her chest. "My wife and I tried to find out as much as possible about neuroendocrine cancer, but there is not enough information on the Internet. Some of the information is contradictory, too. This type of cancer has few experts available in the country. Luckily, we live close to a couple of world-class doctors."

Georgie looked at the information garnered from the few websites, along with Renata's resources, before making a list of questions for the doctor. "The problem is, I have no idea where to begin. I've had symptoms, but it seemed like normal stuff, but I guess it wasn't."

Renata recommended, "Try to make a log. Think back to when you first started feeling symptomatic. Think hard. It helps the doctor understand how you are feeling now."

Sitting back in the chair, Georgie shared, "I thought about how I could have possibly gotten this. I know my extended family members don't have any of these issues, whatsoever. I even double-checked with Clare. Everyone is in good health."

Renata felt she needed to change the subject to concentrate Georgie's mind on the future instead of the past. Pointing to the list of doctors, she raised her eyebrows. "You don't have a lot to choose from. I would suggest calling the one in New York. It's the closest, as the others are in Denver, Philadelphia, Iowa, California, even Europe." Eyebrows were raised, her voice monotone.

Georgie grabbed her cell phone. "I suppose there's no better time like the present." Calling the number, she made an appointment for the following week. Ending the brief exchange, she shrugged her shoulders. "Well, that was easy. I appreciate you being here Renata and listening to me."

Renata moved closer to Georgie, pleading, "I want to go with you. You might need a second set of ears. The information is a lot to absorb."

Georgie nodded her head slowly. "I think that might be best, please. In the meantime, I will create a diary of my symptoms, just as you suggested to prepare for the appointment. Renata, this conversation stays with us, this cancer crap. Please! I don't want to risk my job. Oh my god, I forgot to call Julia." Her hands trembled.

Renata waved her hands as if saying relax. "Remember, we have some holidays next week, so it's not a full week. You still need to chill."

"Duh, I forgot about the holiday - what a relief, since I have the oncologist on Tuesday. We're off until Thursday. Works out perfectly." Georgie smiled, dropped her shoulders, rubbing her hands on her pants. They were sweating every time she started to think about what she was facing.

Georgie dialed Julia's number and danced a little in place. "Yes, I can return Thursday! Can't wait!"

Renata's phone buzzed. "Yes, Daisy, I'm on my way home now." Rolling her eyes, "I promise I can get the groceries you ordered online." She turned to Georgie. "My wife is not happy with me these days. Long nights at school, then ER shifts don't necessarily lead to a happy marriage. Who would have thought?" Renata rummaged through her pocketbook for her keys.

Georgie bit her lip then grimaced. "I can't take you away from your family with my appointment."

Renata shook her keys high in the air. "Found them, yay." Looking straight at Georgie's eyes. "Nonsense! You are a priority for me. Besides we don't celebrate any freaking holidays. I'm driving, so text me the time. Take the weekend to process all of this. It is a lot to take in. Know you have many people in your corner. Think of all the kids in your classroom who need you to come back and rip them a new one if they misbehave! Seriously, call me if you want to talk." And Renata moved to the doorway, waving goodbye.

Georgie waved, "Bye. I'm good. Get home safe." She walked to the door, watching Renata speed off, honking her horn. Shaking her head, she wondered what she had done to deserve such kind people in her life.

⚔️

Georgie wanted to go for a walk, but instead, looked at the piles of papers she needed to grade. However, the minute she started to read the first essay, she fell asleep on her couch. When Georgie awoke a few hours later, she called Lilliana for a chat to see how things were going. She had missed a few texts from her over the past few days.

"Lilliana, my partner in crime, how are you? How are the kids?" Georgie curled up in a ball on the couch.

Lilliana cleared her throat, "*Dios te bendiga*! I am fine! How are you feeling?"

Georgie smiled, hearing Lilliana's voice. "Much better. On the mend. What have I missed?"

Lilliana was jumpy. "Well, other than we miss you, of course, things are going well. The substitute is following your lesson plans for the most part. The kids seem to like her but not as much as you, so don't worry, *mi amiga*. I've been out to Rosie's with her a few times with a bunch of the teachers. She appears to know everyone!"

"How come she knows everyone?" Georgie's pursed her lips.

"She is Jose's daughter, Angelina. Not sure if you knew. She's also the superintendent's granddaughter. Not sure if you knew that either." Lilliana giggled.

Georgie's mouth dropped. "Wow. I had no clue at all that these people were related."

Lilliana spoke in hushed tones as if someone could hear her share a secret. "She tried for a job in the district, but it didn't work out. Not sure what job, but she seems to try hard. The only issue so far is she took some photos of the kids and wanted to post them on her social media. I told her to check with someone first since it did not seem like a good idea to me."

Georgie covered her mouth. "Good thing you said something to her! What happened? Did she listen to you?"

"Luckily, Alex walked in, and she discussed it with him. He instructed her not to post *anything* and not to take a photo of any student with her cell phone. Strangely, she did not seem bothered. Anyway, glad you are coming back. You will be here in time for back to school night; that's all that matters. I'm so happy I don't have to do it without you! Do you need anything?" Lilliana talked so quickly Georgie could hardly follow.

Georgie was getting nervous, hearing all the information. She paced around the room before answering, "No, nothing at all. I have the essays. Alex has been dropping things off too. I figured I would bring everything with me when I come back. Alex is coming here over the weekend. I'm hoping he can show me how to put the grades into the program again. It seems there are a lot of steps." She opened her laptop and turned it on.

Lilliana reassured her. "*Por favor,* don't worry about it. When you get back, you'll need to be tough, as the kids keep you on your toes. Also, our schedules have changed a bit. We both now have double lunch duty instead of hall duty. It's a killer. I can barely go out on Thursday night, but I'm managing."

Georgie rubbed her eyes. "Ha, I have not seen a Thursday night out in ages. Well, I better get going. You have a terrific weekend. I'll be posting the grades in a jiffy in case Julia is looking for them." She typed in her passcodes and clicked on the program.

"Georgie, relax. She has not asked, so I would not rush. I did talk to some other teachers. We are doing well, considering you are not here. We can review things once you get back."

"Thank you for being so understanding," said Georgie as she sat at her counter, biting her nails.

Lilliana's voice was soft. "Hey, it's not your fault you got sick. If you had not done the plans, that would have been the bigger issue. The kids did a pretty good job. Trust me, even Angelina can follow them. With my help - a lot of it at times - we get through. See you next week. Happy to hear your voice. If you want to Facetime or chat, let me know. *Buenos Noches*," and Lilliana ended the call.

"Knock, knock. How are you feeling, Georgie?" It was Alex at the door with a bag of groceries and a container of soup.

She glanced at her watch, then hopped off the chair and fixed her sweats so they looked less wrinkled. "Come in. Great news, I am ready to return to Eden Hills. Yay!"

Alex placed the items on the kitchen table as he had the previous few afternoons. "Great news is right! Everything is going pretty well." He coughed so harshly, there was some blood in his hand, which he quickly wiped with tissue from his pocket. "I have another pile of student work in my car. How much writing are they doing? If you don't raise the test scores, I don't know who will."

"Speaking of test scores, would you mind showing me again how to input the grades? I've started but decided I'd better ask. With so much on my mind, I don't want to input things incorrectly," and she pointed to her computer.

He pushed it aside. "Sure thing. But how about we eat first? One thing at a time."

She moved back to the chair at the empty counter space. "I would like that. Did you make soup?" Georgie rubbed her hands together before taking out a pot and placing it on the stove.

His gaunt cheekbones were prominent from smiling. "I did. I have been eating it a lot lately. It's bone broth. Very healthy for you with all the vegetables. I have had some health issues myself, but I try to take good care of myself." Alex took some fruit and vegetables from out of the bag and placed them in the refrigerator. This was his routine now.

"How long have you not been feeling well?" asked Georgie, grabbing two bowls along with spoons.

He opened the container and dumped the soup into the pot. "Quite a while. It goes back to when I first started working at Eden Hills. I reacted to something in the building; a few of us did. Needed an inhaler. Got worse, then better, then bad again."

"So, you have asthma?" Georgie filled two glasses of water without asking. By now, she knew what Alex liked.

He turned on the stove, stirring the pot with the ladle she placed by him. "That's it. I don't know what I have. I don't feel great. No one seems to know what the hell is wrong with me. Seen doctors over and over again, but no-one can make any sense of things," explained Alex as he stirred the pot of soup as it gently boiled.

"You mentioned an ex-fiancé the other day?" Georgie didn't look up as she folded two napkins, placing them alongside the place settings.

Alex hesitated before answering. "I was engaged after being with her for too many years. She was a nurse who smoked like a chimney. I suppose I should have seen that as a red flag but the things you do for love. What can I say? I used to joke, telling her she was trying to kill me since I couldn't breathe at times. One day, she decided she didn't want to date a patient. In a way, I get it. I have been frustrated for years with not feeling well. My quality of life, at times, sucks. Have to tell you, being sick makes you realize what is important. Friends, family, love," and he quickly turned to look at Georgie.

Her arms had goosebumps as she quietly replied, "True. It does make you think about life differently. After my brother and mother's deaths, I certainly reassessed things."

After pouring the soup into both bowls Alex, sitting at the counter across from Georgie, laughed. "Do you know, you must be the only person I know not on social media. I only found information about your mother, but you are like a ghost. Well, at least on social media."

She blew on the soup to cool it off. "Yes, I've made sure there is as little as possible out there. As far as I know, only you and Julia are aware of her fame. I want to be successful with my accomplishments, not on the back of her coattails. That's why editing was so hard. Big shoes to fill when you have a mother who earned a Pulitzer Prize in journalism at such a young age. It was a double-edged sword for a kid."

"I read her work; her writing was extraordinary." He leaned forward on his elbows.

Her eyebrows raised. "I am *amazed* at how much you have found out about me in such a short time."

Coughing a little, Alex removed his glasses. Folding them he placed them down next to his plate as he did before every meal. "Took no time at all. I am constantly researching important issues in my position as union rep."

"Was I 'an important issue'?" She asked, surprised, while twirling her hair.

Alex sipped the soup on his spoon. "Not every day a second career teacher is hired, especially in Eden Hills. Don't be too flattered." He teased. "I look into everyone. It's like my job to keep an eye on things." He sipped another spoonful of broth. "Well, luckily, you are on the mend! That's the main thing." And he winked at her.

Georgie ate another spoonful of soup. "Mm. This is awesome. How about after we eat, you show me the electronic grading system, then we can go walk on the beach?" Georgie stirred her soup, eyes down, trying to keep her composure. She was flattered, regardless of what he said. "I could use a walk to calm me before the chaos of next week." Suddenly her stomach cramped, so she crossed her arms. "Oh, and you can tell me more about how my substitute teacher happens to be related to two of the most powerful men in Eden Hills."

Alex bit his lip. "Whoops. You found out. It is no big deal. It's not like she is vying for your job or anything. Think of it as some sub covering your class, Georgie. Leave it alone. Trust me, and you have nothing to worry about. Let's eat. This amazing dinner I brought you is much more interesting than all that crap."

CHAPTER 15

Since she was heading into New York City fifty miles away, Georgie had asked Renata to pick her up two hours before the appointment so they would make it on time. Georgie wanted to make a good impression on the doctor for some reason, so she dressed in a sophisticated gray pantsuit with matching heels; almost as if she were interviewing for a job. She noticed her clothing was much looser than when she last wore it a few weeks before her job interview at Eden Hills.

Now, here she was sitting in Dr. Grace Hendi's office waiting for her first, and hopefully last, oncology visit. Her briefcase contained health logs, copies of scans, blood work, along with discharge papers from her appendectomy. She could not think of anything else to bring except her notepad, which listed nearly thirty questions.

Renata sat next to Georgie, also having decided to get dolled up in her most elegant dress, with pearls around her neck and diamond earrings in her ears. After a weekend of researching information with Daisy, they had discovered that, while it was considered a rare disease, neuroendocrine cancer incident rates were increasing. Interestingly, there were several global online support groups, along with many local state groups. When Renata posed questions in any of the groups, many patients and caregivers responded with thoughtful and practical insights. Eventually, she would share all the information with Georgie, but one step at a time.

Upon entering the office, the receptionist provided Georgie with a clipboard containing ten pages of paperwork attached. Current medication lists, physician contacts, family history, present symptoms, plus insurance releases were all included in the packet. After Georgie had completed the paperwork, she and Renata chatted about little things, such as the weather. Minutes seemed like hours until a tall brunette male nurse in his twenties called out, "Georgie Nelson, Dr. Hendi can see you now."

The two women stood and having gathered their belongings, they followed him into the doctor's small office. "My name is Francisco. Good morning. Before you see the doctor Georgie, can you come with me for a few minutes?"

She quietly followed him into the phlebotomist station. The empty, sterile space reeked of a combination of Lysol and coffee which nearly choked her.

Francisco rubbed her arm, saying, "I'm going to take your vitals first, then some blood." He typed some information into the computer.

To fill the time, Georgie blabbered on, "The office is empty. I'm kinda surprised." She rolled up her sleeves since she anticipated his next steps. Her eyes blinked rapidly as she sighed deeply.

Francisco rolled the blood pressure cup on Georgie's upper arm. "This is a time when we see new patients. Also, some patients are in the back receiving treatments." He saw the numbers and typed the results into the computer. "Your blood pressure is normal."

"I'm shocked it's normal. I'm pretty nervous," Georgie told him, clearing her throat.

Francisco waved her on to the scale. "Understood. That's natural. Let's see your weight."

"Truthfully, I haven't been able to eat much. I've lost some weight since the surgery, over five pounds." She felt like her heart would pound through her dress.

"Eight pounds, exactly. I'll note that in the file." Francisco walked her back to the office and placed a paper on the doctor's desk. "All set. Dr. Hendi will be with you in a moment."

With a quick knock at the door, Dr. Hendi walked into the office. She was wearing a white coat with her name in script on the right side. The slightly overweight brunette with brown skin, brown eyes, and black-rimmed glasses sat behind her desk and opened a large file filled with papers presumably to do with Georgie.

Dr. Hendi smiled warmly, "Georgie Nelson. Wow, I can see the piles of research you have done on your lap! There is a lot of fantastic information online, but I caution you some of the sites are incorrect, *be careful*. Georgie, what brings you here today?"

Georgie cleared her throat while Renata laid a hand on Georgie's shoulder. "I had emergency surgery about a week ago for my appendix. To my surprise, and I guess the doctor's, they found some weird cells. Later the doctor said it was a mass. At my last appointment, she called it a neuroendocrine tumor, and that I needed to see an expert. I'm thankful to find you. Very happy you could see me so quickly too." She cleared her throat. "Also, hoping you can help me. Please."

Dr. Hendi looked Georgie directly in the eyes, head tilted to the side. "How are you feeling?"

Georgie took a couple of clear breaths. "Tired, nauseous, sweating a lot - bathroom issues too, but I thought it was nerves." She shrugged her shoulders and rubbed her sweaty palms on her lap.

Dr. Hendi lowered her voice, "I looked over your blood work. Some of the markers are normal, but there is a high one, which is serotonin. There are other tests we can do, which I am ordering. You are one of the lucky ones." She leaned forward toward Georgie. "Many patients never have any symptoms, so by the time we find something, it can be too late."

Georgie and Renata were fixated on the doctor's every word. She moved from behind her desk, pulling a chair closer to Georgie. "I'll order a Gallium scan. It can find tiny tumors, and it's also great at detecting this type of cancer. Fortunately, many hospitals now have this type of scan available, which was not the case several years ago."

Georgie felt a tingling in her chest. Her mind flitted between trust and worry.

"After that, we can go from there. I also want you to do a urine test. Once we get those results, we meet again to see what course of treatment you require, if any."

Georgie wet her lips. "If any?"

"Some patients just need to be monitored without medication. Some need monthly shots of medication long term, maybe targeted therapy even. It all depends. I can only tell you which you may need once we have current blood work. We want to redo it now that your appendix has been removed. I also like to do my own blood work since it's sent to my typical labs. If the scan comes back clear, *which it may*, we might be able to monitor you every few months with no action unless needed."

"What do you mean?" Georgie responded in a quiet voice, her eyes widening. She did not expect to hear Dr. Hendi raise this as a possibility.

Dr. Hendi's voice was flat. "Once you have this slow-growing cancer, it may come back to some other place, at any time. The markers help us, but frankly, they can be nonspecific, meaning they may or may not tell us about any activity. Neuroendocrine cancer is a rare, sneaky type of cancer."

Georgie's voice was weak and unsteady, "Are you saying I can be fine for a long time, but that it can come back?"

"It may. We will watch you closely."

Georgie felt numb all over. "I can work, can't I? I want to live my life."

"It all depends on how you feel. As the disease progresses, rest, nutritional support, modifications with your lifestyle have to take place. Let us not put the cart before the horse. You need the scan and blood work first."

Picking up the phone, her voice was monotone, "Francisco, we need a Gallium scan for Georgie." As she placed the phone receiver down, she elaborated, "All the tests are done as an outpatient. We work with a hospital close by; they are hands-on, so we get the results back quickly. We'll meet again once we have all the results. It does take some time as these are special tests. Questions?"

Georgie looked at her pad. "I think all these questions can wait until we know what it shows."

"You can ask me anything, but I don't know what more I can say until we know more. Every case is different; every one with neuroendocrine cancer is different. There are different locations, rates of growth of the tumors, symptoms, blood work. Listen, we're in this together."

"Well, as long as I can keep working. That is the best news." And Georgie leaned back feeling slightly relieved.

Renata cleared her throat. "Doctor, what is the cause? What do you think?"

"You know there are so many factors we are unsure of such as genetics, environmental - nothing to pinpoint. Sorry, I don't have an answer. It's best to focus on what we have at hand now. Georgie is getting the right care. You know, many people go to many different types of doctors until they find the correct diagnosis. One step at a time."

Renata grabbed her friend's hand tightly and nodded, "Thank you, Dr. Hendi. You have been most helpful."

Dr. Hendi tilted her head to the side. "Francisco is going to take more blood from you before you go. The scan order is in the works, along with the insurance approvals. What else do you have for me? Your blood pressure is fine; weight fine…" The doctor shook Georgie's hand with both her hands like a warm hug. "Georgie, until the next time. It's been a pleasure meeting you."

After Francisco took her blood, Georgie approached the receptionist for the next appointment at the front desk. The receptionist tapped her pen on the table as she looked at the calendar. "Let's give the blood work a little more time. Dr. Hendi also wrote you a prescription for a urine test, which takes about a week to get the results. That takes us three weeks out."

Georgie put the date on her phone for the appointment. "In another three weeks, I should know where I'm at. Very good."

The receptionist waved, "See you then."

As they walked out of the office, Georgie turned to Renata. "I am wiped. Can we go home?"

Putting her arm around her new friend, Renata rubbed her shoulder. "Home it is. You did great, you know."

Georgie's mind raced. Turning to Renata, she hugged her, crying a little and saying, "I'm relieved. I think I'm going to be all right with this. Well, at least I'm cautiously optimistic." Then pulling away, she put her shoulders back. "I'm *so happy* to go back to work. Can't wait to see the kids. Renata, before we head to the car, do you mind if we stop at the church over there? It's been a while for me, but I have to thank God for you, my doctor, hell… for everyone. Need a minute." Her ears were ringing as she felt a wave of heat over her chest and face.

Georgie, with Renata following behind, walked up the steps of the sizable Gothic-style church she had never been to before. Entering the dark, dimly lit block-long building with high ceilings, Georgie noted it was empty. She heard her heels echo as she chose a warped wooden pew to sit in and pray. She stared in awe at the stained-glass windows depicting saints and biblical stories. They reminded her of the church her family used to attend when she was young. The candles flickering along the walls illuminated the chapel, like a hug welcoming her home. Georgie recalled a Catholic superstition that when entering a new church, you were to make three prayer intentions. At times like this, she could use all the luck she could get. Faith? She was not sure what she believed anymore. She closed her eyes tight to pray for her three wishes. As a little girl, she had always prayed for others, but today, the prayers were all for herself. She pleaded for grace. *Haven't I been through enough?*

⊰⊱

Sometime later at Eden Hills, Julia was sitting at her desk when her cell phone rang. It was Georgie, which was a pleasant surprise. She crossed her fingers as she asked, "Georgie, how are you feeling?"

Georgie smiled. "I'm feeling great. I wanted to confirm my return on Thursday!"

Julia cheered. "Happy to hear! Everyone is going to be happy to see you, especially your students. When you come in, let's meet in my office. We'll get things going in the right direction for you."

"I look forward to it. I'm working on some essays right now."

"I don't have to tell you, but don't overdo it. Once you are back, you are back."

Georgie's stomach felt like it was full of butterflies. "Alex says the same thing every time he stops by."

"He has stopped by, huh?" Julia's head tilted to the side. "Funny, he has been out of school for a few days. Well, I'm glad he has been a good support system for you. See you soon!"

Julia immediately texted Jose the excellent news. As she tossed the cell phone, she had not felt this relieved in a long time. She called Tiffany. "Georgie is back, so no more of Angelina, but feel free to use her in other places. I heard the kids like her!"

⚔+⟊

Jose's phone buzzed as he walked to his car. He was on his way to get his son from the high school. Reading the text, he cursed under his breath. Unlocking the driver's door, he saw something glistening in the passenger seat along with a red backpack he knew belonged to Angelina. Turning on the ignition, he dialed her number, but it went to voicemail.

Grasping the St. Joseph's medal from around his neck, he screamed into the phone. "How many times am I going to tell you when you borrow the car, clean up after yourself. Your backpack is here, along with other stuff. You are too old for this!"

Pressing the end button, he grabbed a silver pen sparkling in the light. It looked expensive. Upon closer examination, he saw it had the initials 'GN' engraved on it. Furious, he redialed Angelina's number.

"Glad you answered the phone this time! Meet me at school *right now.* You have two feet - you can walk. You have to return something to the building before you get yourself into trouble. No excuses this time."

CHAPTER 16

On Thursday morning, Alex was in front of Georgie's house earlier than promised, in order to be her very own chauffeur for the drive to Eden Hills on her first day back. Georgie and Alex took several trips to the house, carrying all the materials she had graded during her absence. Between the laptop and three backpacks filled with essays, she was thankful for the extra pair of hands. She hated to admit it, but she was feeling tired already, and the day had barely begun.

Wearing an old but favorite good luck dress, Georgie settled into the car. "This almost feels like the first day of school again. I appreciate all you have done for me; I couldn't have done it without you. Your cooking has been amazing. If I have not said it before, I do value our friendship." As the car began to move, she glanced over at Alex, who looked exhausted. "Alex, Julia says you've been out. I hope it's not my fault. You have been doing so much for me."

Alex merged onto the highway, driving a little below the speed limit. "Nah, had to get some tests done, new doctors. No biggie. Jeez, I didn't realize she was keeping tabs on me. I need to have a chat with her." He chuckled, almost to himself.

"No, please. Julia sounded surprised, that's all." Georgie bit her nails, worried about having spoken.

Alex rubbed his chest. "Well, in my career, I have rarely been out. Do you know how many sick days, along with tons of personal days I have?

That's what happens when you are strong and tough, like me. Hell, I've been teaching for close to thirty years."

"Wow! I did not realize you had taught so long. Hope you don't mind me saying you look good for your age," and she giggled.

He looked at her fast, sticking his tongue out at her. "Julia, Jose, and I all started together. They went the administration route, but I stayed in the classroom and got involved with the union in order to have a say. I learned fast it's important to know what the hell is going on as much as possible." Alex put his signal on to move into the slow lane of the three-lane highway.

"How so? Care to share?" Georgie was relaxed as Alex drove at the speed limit even though other cars were whizzing past them.

Noticing Georgie's arms had goosebumps, he lowered the air-conditioning. "Not yet. Let's say I watch everything and everyone closely. I need to know what goes on in the building from behind the scenes. Julia and I have an agreement, a good understanding of what is working. If something needs to change, I'm often the first one to tell her. We work well together to make sure we do as much as we can, so everyone in the building is safe. Some days are easier than others."

Georgie crossed her arms. "Quite frankly, it sounds as if you are speaking cryptically."

Alex turned the radio station to jazz music. "Rambling. Just ignore me. Julia takes good care of you, so don't worry."

"What about Jose? I hadn't realized he was related to the superintendent." Her heart raced.

He changed the radio station channel again. "Worry about your job and working with the kids. Julia and I watch out for you and the other newbies, as long as you work hard." He started to hum the song.

Georgie decided to change the subject. "I'll drive myself home today. So happy to see my car again. I hope it's alright since it's been in the parking lot for so long."

The exit sign for Eden Hills was in sight as Alex beamed. "It's fine. I'm friendly with the chief of police, so I asked Chief Odin to patrol the lot every once in a while. He's kept an eye on it. No worries."

"Thanks so much. What a great town Eden Hills is." Georgie's cheeks flushed.

With a few minutes left in the drive, Georgie was getting nervous until she heard her favorite song on the radio. "Funny, I heard this same song the first day I pulled into the parking lot at Eden Hills."

Alex turned the Bon Jovi song abruptly to a jazz station. "Sorry, but *this* is music, Ms. Nelson. Let's wait until it's over! Put off work a bit longer." Georgie and Alex closed their eyes as the melody sank into their skin, bones, blood, soul for the next precious moments. When the last horn faded silent, they both opened their eyes, calm and relaxed. Even if only for a brief time, they escaped to a field of blissful sunflowers blowing kisses to the sun. Alex's heart radiated through his chest. "Mm… now let's go inspire some kids."

Georgie met with Julia for only a few minutes. Then carrying Georgie's bags, she walked with her to her classroom. Georgie gulped, "I put the grades into the system on an ongoing basis, so you had your data for your research."

"I looked! It's impressive how many assignments you were able to grade. You've learnt the grading program so quickly and are well ahead of some of the veteran teachers in doing the grades already. I am sending you an email to commend you for all the work you've done while you were out. Beyond my expectations!"

Georgie's mouth dropped; she was almost crying with relief. Walking into her classroom was exhilarating! She found Lilliana waiting with a cup of tea and bagel for her to eat for breakfast. "Lilliana, you are a sight for sore eyes!"

Lilliana was clad all in black as usual. Looking, Georgie saw her silver Cross pen lying on the floor next to her desk. Picking it up, she held it tight. "Great to see this again, too."

Lilliana clapped loudly. "*Felicidades.* Happy to have you back. Julia, her plans saved us. With such specific details, we were on autopilot most of the time. The students wrote a lot!"

"I know, I saw the results in the grade book. Lilliana, you are getting an email from me commending you on your hard work. I received a few phone calls from parents concerned about Georgie being out, but they were pleased to get responses from you when they had questions." She placed Georgie's things down. "Oh, not to put pressure on either of you, but back to school night is next week, so check your emails regarding the schedule," whereupon, Julia quickly left.

Georgie sat, took the lid off the tea. Her face was flushed, and her stomach felt cramped. The bagel would have to wait. Wiping the desk with her hand, white dust scattered in the air. "Wow, dirty here today."

Lilliana dusted off some desks in the back. "I've been speaking to the custodians. Some days are cleaner than others. Let me look at you. Fabulous to have you back!" Lilliana clapped her hands, cheering. "How did the surgery go? Are you feeling better? I've never had surgery before."

Georgie cleared her throat, "Much better. Just a little tired. I don't know how to thank you. How about I treat you to dinner?"

"Dinner sounds great. It worked out fine. Angelina, as I told you on the phone, was fine, considering." She shrugged her shoulders.

Georgie unpacked her things. "Considering what? I know nothing about her."

Lilliana darted to close the door, before moving closer to Georgie and lowering her voice, "Considering I was working with her and her family connections. *Can we say nepotism?* Did you think I would complain about her? She was a body in the room. I had to cover practically everything. Some of the tenured teachers were not happy with me doing everything in here. No idea how they knew, but they did. I didn't want to say anything, since Jose was *always* around checking on the class."

Georgie took some deep breaths. "Was she not helpful or good with the kids?"

Lilliana opened her laptop. "Angelina was like a kid herself! She was out every night with some of the new teachers. Some days, she smelled like cigarettes and booze. Yet the kids loved her! Many of them knew her from town. A few kids are her brother's friends, mother's friends, grandmother's friends. It goes on and on! We were in school at the same time but had different groups of friends. Get my drift? If anything, it added to my anxiety, but that's what therapists and medications are for, right?"

Georgie covered her mouth in shock. "You could have told me on the phone."

"No way. Let's move on. Look, because I was nice about everything, I am getting a good email from Julia! I can't wait to print that email out. Yay, I can add it to my file! Oh, and Jose *loves* me now since I put up with his daughter. I know I made her look good. Angelina told me she is top of the list now to sub here in the building, even with you back. It's a win, win!"

Georgie laughed. "Well done! I am so sorry I was not here."

Lilliana shook her head. "I'm not mad at you, more frustrated with Angelina. Let's get back to me supporting the kids I need to support. There are three IEP meetings next week for some new kids, and I have to prepare. Maybe we can go over the goals and objectives a bit next week. I think we need to work late, up until back to school night and forget dinner for now."

"Sounds like a plan." Georgie noticed the bell was going to ring in a few minutes as she tried to process things. "I need to use the restroom quickly. Also, to book the computer lab for tomorrow."

Lilliana raised her eyebrows. "I booked the lab already. Go to the bathroom. We don't have much time!"

❈

That afternoon, Georgie was getting her third wind for the day thanks to her guzzling caffeine any free moment she had. Secretly, she loved lunch duty, hanging out with the kids, interacting with them in a less structured environment. She felt alive! It made her forget her health issues too. She high-fived a student as she walked around the room, monitoring the hundreds of students. The high-pitched sound of the kids' screams did not even bother her.

Georgie did not notice Jose standing in the corner, chatting with some students. She sat next to one of the students who needed her help with a math problem. As she clarified a step, Jose strutted over, saying, "Ms. Nelson, it is unacceptable to sit on duty."

Georgie covered her mouth with her hand, embarrassed by how he spoke to her in front of the group. "Mr. Gonzalez, I am helping my student with a math problem."

"You are assigned lunch duty, which means you stand," he retorted before storming off.

Bob walked over to console Georgie. "What the hell was that?"

Georgie rapidly blinked back tears, quickly looking out the window so the students couldn't see she was upset.

"Do you want to go for a walk? Better pull yourself together." He looked around to see if Jose had left.

Her voice cracked, "Yes, I need a few minutes. See you in a little while."

Georgie walked quickly to her classroom, which she knew would be empty. She slammed the door, nearly crying. Walking over to her desk, Georgie opened the drawer that held her special pen. She gripped it tightly and found a blank piece of paper so she could write everything that happened.

Alex had heard the door bang from his room. Knocking gently, he called out, "Can I come in?" Slowly opening the door, he saw her sitting upright, eyes filled with tears, scribbling furiously. Leaning against the wall, he gazed at her. "What happened? It couldn't have been that bad."

"I think Jose is writing me up for sitting while I helped a student. I don't know what I've done to him!"

"I can go talk to him if you would like."

"No, but I am thankful my observation is by Julia, not Jose. I don't know what more to do. I've only just gotten back."

"If Julia does your observations, then that's all that matters. These write-ups, trust me, he does this to many staff members, it won't be a big deal." Alex found he wanted to push back the hair from her pretty face.

Georgie's laptop buzzed, alerting her to a new email which had arrived, as expected.

Alex moving closer, read the email with her by leaning close over her shoulder. Clearing his throat, he was able to prevent a cough as he bent over. He could not help but smell her perfume, and he liked it.

TO: *Ms. Nelson*
FM: *Mr. Gonzalez*
RE: *Lunch Duty Assignment*

As per my conversation, you are to remain standing during your lunch duty assignment. Sitting on duty is not expected. You are to monitor the students to ensure their safety. It should never happen again.

Alex could do nothing but chuckle. Jose was being petty, which was nothing new, but Georgie was devastated. Her hands were shaking, her eyes blinking wildly.

"Jose has been doing this for years. Write a response and bcc me so I can keep a file. If it makes you feel better, sleep on it, then write a response. Tomorrow you won't be writing with emotion. Pass the word on to your crew, so they know how to handle this when it happens to them."

Georgie shut her laptop, suddenly feeling better. "You have a calming way, but I think I am the only one Jose has singled out like this."

"You are not, believe me. It happens to *everyone*. Want to go to Rosie's after school?"

"I wish I had the time. I'm exhausted. Rain-check, please!"

Alex shook his head, teasing, "I cooked enough gluten-free food for you to eat in a lifetime! You owe me. Now is the time for some crap in your gut instead of all that healthy stuff. Tomorrow after school. I'm not taking no for an answer." He waited for her to look up, but she didn't, so he turned to leave, his heart feeling as if it was shrinking. When Georgie called his name, he stopped, swallowing hard.

"Alex, you are right. Tomorrow is going to be a better day. Rosie's on me!"

Georgie decided she needed to rest during the weekend while doing her twenty-four-hour urine test for Dr. Hendi.

On the way out of school for the day, Georgie stopped by Renata's office. Renata was on the phone, but she waved Georgie in. "Daisy, I hope to be home on time today! I freaking promise. Don't threaten me with the kids. I am in the ER on Saturday all day." She threw her phone in her bag and turned to Georgie. "How was your first day?"

"Fine. Glad to be back. Is everything OK with Daisy? I feel bad. I hope all the time you have spent helping me is not causing any issues."

"Not you. It's between this job and my weekend ER shifts. We hardly see each other. She doesn't understand how important this year is for me. It is my tenure year for Christ's sake! While I love it here, she is not crazy about the hours or the salary. With the twins, and her not working, there's a lot on my plate."

Renata looked at a family photo of happier times. Showing Georgie the picture, she beamed, "This was when we adopted the girls four years ago. It was my idea we would share parenting and work duties. Daisy's recent health issues have stopped her from taking any shifts at the hospital yet. It's been tense between us for some time. It can't be easy for Daisy. I mean, she's with the kids all day. Anyway, enough about me, sorry. I could do with more help in this office too. I'll have to speak to Julia."

Julia walked in, saying, "I heard my name. I hope it is in a good way! How's it going, ladies?"

Georgie grabbed her things. "Had to thank Renata for her help. She was invaluable. See you both tomorrow."

Julia raised her eyebrows, "What is going on, Renata? You looked frazzled."

"It's the same old issue, Julia. I need more help in this office, even answering phones would help. Can't get it all done." She snapped a rubber band around her wrist harder and harder.

Julia leaned in. "I see you running around all the time. Let me talk to Jose. We can make a schedule and get you some extra help. Phones, messages we can handle."

Renata hugged Julia. "Have I ever told you you're my favorite principal ever?"

"I'm your *only* principal, my *favorite* nurse in Eden Hills. Consider it done," and Julia scurried out.

Renata felt like she hit the lottery. She whispered, "Hate to say it, but Julia might have saved my marriage!" Rubbing her face, Renata called Daisy. "Honey, what can I get from the market for us? I'm making dinner tonight."

CHAPTER 17

Georgie walked into school the following day with more energy than the previous one. Sleeping nearly ten hours had helped, but she had forgotten to write her rebuttal to Jose. Not enough time to do that or eat, for that matter. She started work on responding to some emails from parents. There were a few who were concerned about the workload she was expecting. Just as she was formulating a response, her phone rang.

"Georgie, this is Francisco from Dr. Hendi's office. I am calling about your Gallium scan appointment. Everything is approved with your insurance. We have you scheduled for next week, but we received a call that there is a cancellation. If you can make it this evening, we can squeeze you in."

Georgie answered without thinking, "Yes, of course! Do I need to take anything? Any preparation?"

"Did you eat anything today?"

"No." Georgie pushed her hair back.

"Perfect. No food or water for the rest of the day. We will see you at five at the hospital. Start to finish, it takes about two hours, so it's not bad."

Georgie gulped some air. "So glad you called. Nice to get this over with."

"Absolutely. Once we get the results, we can move your appointment closer then go from there." Francisco ended the call.

Georgie looked out the window for a moment to gather her thoughts when Jose walked into the room. She got to her feet. "Good morning, Jose. Getting ready for the day."

"Were you on a personal call on your cell phone? You should know better. I will let it go this time, but next time, no cell phones." He left as quietly as he had entered.

Georgie pushed her hair back when Renata knocked on her door, holding a folder. "Hey, Georgie, thanks to you, I have help in my office. Stop by anytime - you're my good luck charm!"

"So are you! They rescheduled my scan for this evening. I am so relieved to get it done. Being busy helps to not think about it."

"Do you need me to go with you? Keep you company?"

"No way! Go home. Be with your family. I insist."

"I made an amazing dinner last night for Daisy and the girls, so I'm out of the doghouse. She Googled some further information for you." Renata handed Georgie the folder. "May sound weird, but I asked her to do some research for you. It has given her a purpose, making her feel needed while she is out of work. Don't hesitate to contact her, as well. She can't wait to meet you. Some night when you are on your feet, you have to come over to meet the family! Better run."

As Renata left, Lilliana walked in. "Georgie! Did you hear the news! Jason Rollins got a heart last night! Best news ever!"

Both cheered. Georgie wiggled her hips, "Hope that's a good sign for a great day!"

When the bell rang, Georgie and Lilliana escorted their students into the computer lab for their first period of the day. Julia and Alex welcomed the group as they quietly filed into the classroom in an organized manner. Julia stood to the side, impressed by how much control Georgie and Lilliana had attained in such a short time. Even with an overcrowded classroom, it was operating as smooth as silk. Julia moved on to another room for one of her eighty classroom teacher observations for the school year.

Lilliana and Georgie bounced around the classroom, instructing students individually and monitoring their progress. Alex sat back at his computer to watch. He realized how quickly the time had passed with this group since they were so busy and on task.

When the bell rang, Georgie's eyes danced. "I take the groaning sounds to mean you want to stay another period! Oh well, we will be back in Mr. Williams's lab next week to finish. Terrific job, guys! Have a nice weekend."

The students packed to leave while Lilliana helped organize a student's disheveled papers into his backpack.

"I will have the notes from the week posted on the website in case someone missed something," Georgie announced. The students left the room slowly in silence. Once the last student had left, Alex was finally alone with the two women.

He pumped his fists. "You guys have this down pat! I know some tenured teachers who couldn't manage that group of kids - nicely *done*! Would you mind taking a suggestion from me? Julia should observe you next week while you are here for the next lesson. You both have nothing to worry about. Get it over with, come on!" Alex told them.

Georgie and Lilliana looked at each other in a panic. Lilliana took the lead. "So soon in the school year?"

"It's good to get it over. Let the administration see how good you are. They start making decisions real fast about re-hires for the non-tenured staff. Knock it out of the park early, get your name out there. It's a good thing, I swear. I would never steer you wrong." Turning, he stifled a yawn.

Georgie was hesitant. "Isn't it too early?"

"Trust me, have Julia see you. I know she saw a little bit today. She had to be impressed. Get ahead of the rest of the non tenured teachers. You have to be observed at least three times this year. Have her observe you the next time you are in here - shall we say Wednesday?"

"Yes, with this group," Georgie's eyebrows drew together.

Alex nodded, "Do it. Email an invite to her. You are helping her out. Trust me. She wants to catch you doing a good job so she can document it."

"Well, if that's the best way to go, I will. Thanks."

"Are you guys going to Rosie's today after work?" Alex's eyes narrowed. "Heard a few are going for some drinks. It might be good to unwind a bit."

Lilliana waved her arms. "I'm going for sure."

Alex looked at Georgie, waiting for her response. "Work hard; play hard. What about it, Georgie?"

"Err… I'm sorry, but I can't make it." She was going to have to rush to make the scan appointment at five o'clock.

Alex tilted his head down and frowned, "You owe me, remember! Another rain check is fine. You have two minutes until the next class. If I don't see you, have a nice weekend." Georgie and Lilliana went off to their next class.

Turning away, Alex coughed so hard he had to sit in order to get some air. It was becoming more and more of a problem. He looked at the calendar on the wall while shaking his head, the results from his recent tests were taking a long time. He took out a medicine container and popped the new pill of the month into his mouth, hoping this latest and greatest remedy would help.

⚒

Georgie and Lilliana arrived in their classroom across the hallway, where most of the students were already working. While Lilliana took attendance, Georgie took Alex's advice to invite Julia into her first-period class next week for observation. Alex was right - get it over and done. Lilliana moved to Georgie with a slow smile, "It's nice to be praised for our work and end the week on a positive note. Alex didn't have to say all that to us."

Georgie's knees buckled, "You're right. I think he's on our side after all. You, by the way, look so pretty, Lilliana. New dress?" Her co-worker wore a colorful knee-length lace dress. "Have fun at Rosie's. We'll have to go another time."

Lilliana walked away towards a student as Georgie gave herself a pep talk. 'Five hours until the scan. Keep it together!'

On her way out of school, Georgie checked her emails for any last-minute memos. She was surprised to receive a message from Julia, who wanted to see her ASAP. Georgie needed to make the scan appointment and had only a few minutes to spare to get there. Georgie stumbled back a step when she found Jose sitting in Julia's office.

Julia waved Georgie into her office. With a serious, even tone, she sat up straight at her desk. "I know you are running out, but we were just talking about you."

Georgie stood with her mouth open, unable to speak.

"We were going over the observation schedule. I told Jose how you and Lilliana took the initiative to invite me in to see both of you next week. I appreciate the invitation! I saw you with the kids. Considering you have been out, I would never have guessed it." She winked at Georgie. "Jose would like to do your second observation. Can you be sure to do the same thing with him if you have a special lesson planned? I'm certain he will see you shine. Jose, anything to add?"

He shook his head. "Nope. Looking forward to seeing you in action, Georgie."

"Sounds great." Georgie was a terrible liar.

Leaving the office, Georgie's stomach was churning, nauseous to the point where she almost vomited. The fresh air helped; almost like a refreshing dip in the pool on a hot summer day. Not sure how long it would take to get to the hospital, she found herself running out of the school. At this moment, Jose was the least of her problems.

⚔ ⚔

Georgie's hands trembled as she arrived at the hospital in plenty of time for her scan. As she sat in the registration area, her palms were sweaty, her stomach cramping. Her leg jumped as she waited for her name to be called. The waiting room was quiet, as if no one else needed a scan or was sick. The silence was unnerving.

Tempted to check her emails from school, she looked at her phone one last time then turned it off. She wanted to be present in the moment. Closing her eyes, she was trying to recall her prayers when she heard her name called. Jumping in her seat, she saw a tall middle-aged African American woman with blue scrubs, holding some papers and smiling at her. "Georgie Nelson? Hi, my dear! I am Veronica. Please come with me. I'll be conducting your scan today."

Georgie pasted a fake smile on her face as she followed Veronica into a room the size of a closet, just a few steps away.

Veronica was all business. "Take a seat, so we can get the show on the road."

Georgie was freezing as she sat on the cold, hard, dirt brown recliner. Veronica returned with a silver metal case along with a warm blanket, which she handed to Georgie. It was as if she'd read her mind. She put the blanket over her, tucking it tightly around her body. "Actually feels wonderful."

Veronica patted her on the back. "That's the best part, I think. Like a spa, but not." Finding Georgie's vein in her right arm, she squeezed a silver metal substance from a syringe into it. "Okie Dokie. You have to sit for about forty-five minutes. Then I'll be back to put you into the scan. Any questions? Do you need anything?"

Georgie shook her head.

"Rest. I'll be back in a jiffy." Veronica took the metal container out of the room, closed the door slowly and shut off the lights.

Georgie realized this was the most she had sat still in days, deciding to use the time to make a mental list of things to prepare for work the next week. She found it better to focus on actions she could control than the unknown. It seemed like days and days before Veronica called her name again.

"Let's get you scanned, my dear!" and Veronica flicked on the lights, giving Georgie the thumbs up. "Follow me."

Veronica escorted Georgie into a large room. In the center was a machine which looked like a giant white doughnut with a metal table in the middle. Veronica tapped it. "Georgie, please lie here for me." Georgie put her head on a pillow that Veronica provided. Next, a pillow was placed under Georgie's knees, with Veronica strapping her legs and chest in place using black Velcro straps.

"Now put your hands over your head and get as comfy as you can. You will need to stay very still for the entire test." Georgie followed the instructions while Veronica double-checked that the body straps were correctly placed. Then she patted Georgie's hand, "This will take about twenty minutes, my dear. Stay as still as possible, and I'll see you in a few minutes. I'm only in the room right next door, so I can hear you if you need me." Humming she exited to the separate smaller adjacent room with a glass partition which had a large table of computers. To Georgie, it looked like NASA ground control.

Veronica spoke on a microphone, "Georgie, can you hear me, my dear?"

Georgie looked at the plain, white ceiling tiles. "Yes, I can."

"You will hear some noises while the table moves. Don't worry. It's the machine working. You just stay still." Georgie closed her eyes.

"OK, here we go."

The minute she heard the first noise from the machine, Georgie remembered the words to the many prayers she had learnt as a little girl in Catholic school. As they came back to her, they gave her the peace of mind she so desperately needed.

CHAPTER 18

During the weekend, Georgie kept busy planning mini-lessons for those students who needed extra reinforcement with their grammar. It was a pleasant diversion from checking her phone every few minutes to see if the doctor had called with the scan results.

Renata's text provided Georgie with exceptional comfort. *No news is good news.* Georgie told herself, over and over, to stay calm. Not being able to sleep again, she arrived at school at the crack of dawn Monday morning. She was surprised to find Lilliana already in the classroom, typing on her laptop. "Hey, is everything all right?"

"We have big things going on this week, so I figured I'd get an early start." Suddenly Lillian's voice broke, and she started to cry.

"What is wrong? Everything will be alright. We have everything organized."

"Had a rough weekend, got blown off by *mi novio.* My anxiety is through the roof."

Georgie joined her. "I'm so sorry. I didn't know you were even seeing anyone. Do you want to talk about it?"

Lilliana nodded as she blotted her tears with a tissue. She stood sniffing, walked to the door, looked around the hallway, then slammed it. "It's kinda complicated. You must not say a word to anyone. *No one knows!*"

Georgie shrugged her shoulders, "I won't say anything, but why would anyone here care? No one knows your personal stuff. Come on, people break up all the time. No worries, everything will be fine, I'm sure."

Lilliana sat back down, ripping the tissue in her hands and looking at the floor. She mumbled something in a low voice.

Georgie's head darted forward. "I can't understand what you are saying. You will feel better when you talk it through. I promise I won't say a word."

Lilliana covered her face with her hands, "I made a big mistake! He works in the district."

"Is he a teacher in the building?" Georgie gripped the sides of the desk.

"*Si*, I didn't want to say anything. It happened when you were out."

"Well, avoid him. It's a huge building, and it's not as if we work with many teachers directly." Georgie tilted her head.

Lilliana stared at Georgie as she bit her lip.

Georgie's eyes grew bigger. "It's someone we work with directly?"

Lilliana paused, looking away, "It's Bob, the dopey new football coach."

"Bob? Married Bob?" She rubbed her forehead. "What the hell, Lilliana?"

"He told me they had a bad marriage, and I believed him. Now I have to see him every day."

Georgie tapped the desktop with her fingers. "I don't know what to say."

"There is more." Lilliana sobbed, "I saw him with Angelina."

"No way!" Georgie rubbed her hot cheeks, hoping to cool them.

"Yes! They left Rosie's together on Friday. I am sure something is going on." She took another tissue out of her bag and blew her nose.

Georgie leaned in with a low voice, saying, "Well, you're lucky it's over. Don't date *anyone* here. If this stuff gets out, who the hell knows what will happen."

Lilliana dabbed her eyes. "What are you saying? You're involved with Alex. I know it! I can tell."

"What! No! We are friends, good friends. But that's all!" Georgie crossed her arms over her chest.

"Well, keep it that way. I want to keep my job. Now Angelina knows about us, and if it gets back to my Papi, I'm dead. It's a small world in this town, you know. My mommy will be so disappointed too. It goes on and on! My family has worked so hard to give me so much. I can't disappoint them."

Georgie rushed her speech. "I'm glad you talked to me, but let's focus on what we have to do here. Forget Angelina, along with the lying Bob. To think he seemed so happily married at Rosie's. What an ass! His wife works in the grammar school for God's sake. He has to know it will get back to her."

Lilliana sighed several times, as her leg jumped. "Well, he doesn't seem to care. He told me she was dating someone in the district too. Who knows! I'm glad you didn't suspect anything when he was around. It makes me feel better."

"I had no clue," and Georgie covered her mouth with her hand. Her head was spinning, and the day hardly started.

"Let's keep it that way. Anyway, I met someone new last night online. Really excited to meet him later this week. *Screw Bob!* This guy has been texting me, so we will see how it goes." Lilliana opened her laptop.

Georgie could not help but chuckle. "Lilliana, as long as you stay clear of all the guys at work." She used to have the energy to date at Lilliana's age but always avoided co-workers. It sounded like Lilliana could use a friend, so she reached out and patted her arm, "Hey, let's go to Rosie's after school, you and me. Sound like a plan? My treat. I owe you so much! We can talk about work tomorrow."

Lilliana cheered up. "*Eso es maravilloso!* I'm in. That would be nice. What happened to you? Something other than work?"

Georgie clapped. "Forget Bob and Angelina. Life is too short. I got you!"

❧✦❧

Georgie had a fun, light-hearted dinner with Lilliana. They returned from Rosie's with plenty of time to spare to find Alex in their classroom. Georgie was thrilled to see him. "Any last-minute tips for back to school night?"

He sat yawning, looking at his lesson plan book. "We have a short schedule with the parents, like ten minutes, so introduce yourself, give them a copy of the syllabus, expectations, blah, blah, say good night. The best advice I learned as a first-year teacher was: if you don't know the answer, say, 'I don't know, but I'll get back to you.' There is nothing wrong with not knowing all the answers. Honesty is the best policy. However, be sure to get back to them within a short window – an immediate response works wonders. It's their child's life, and middle school kids don't tell their parents much, if anything at all, so they rely on you for the low down." He stretched his arms. "Whatever, don't fear them, and you'll do fine. Woops, better go! Time is money." Alex headed to his room, where he had a coughing fit. Shaking, he took an inhaler from his pocket.

"Ready for tonight, Alex?" Julia had startled him from behind as he choked on the medicine.

Alex coughed again as he opened his room, "Ready as always!" He rubbed his chest, trying to hide his inhaler. "The new technology we ordered this summer is amazing, Julia. The teachers are pretty proficient with the basics." Taking a few breaths, he continued, "I've made appointments with much of the staff already for the next month. We'll be packed in!"

Julia let out a huge massive sigh of relief. "How about the new group of teachers? They receptive?"

"They were my first customers. Very impressed with that crew." Alex started to turn on computers. "They're the last people to worry about."

"You know I trust your judgment," Julia bumped shoulders with him, unexpectedly feeling a hard bone. "Say, how is graduate school going? How many credits left?"

He did not answer directly. "Administration is not easy. You make it look easy, but it's not at all. Really hard to be on top of everyone and everything *all the time*." He was shaking his head, raising his eyebrows.

She stepped back to stare at him, biting her lower lip. "If I can do it, you can do it. To think we both started here together, on this floor, in these rooms. Amazing how time flies." For some reason, she had the heebie-jeebies.

Alex sat, turning to Julia. "I'm not finishing my administration degree coursework, I'm afraid. I wanted to tell you myself, in person. I'm putting my paperwork in to retire by the end of this year."

She gripped the back of a chair tight. "I don't know what to say. I'm shocked, yet not shocked. Is it your health...? You have been sick for a long time. You deserve some rest." She bit her lip, trying not to get upset. "You must have hundreds of sick days! You have never been out, until recently, that is."

He looked anywhere but in Julia's eyes. "It's the right time. You have everything under control here. Wait until you see the newbies too. They're good. You will get higher test scores as long as they stay. I'm convinced! And before you know it, we'll be calling you Dr. Bradley," He grinned. "I know how long you've wanted it. You'll have to keep Jose under control without me, boss!"

Julia rubbed her hands together. "Thanks for your vote of confidence. It won't be easy, but I'll try to manage without you. You've been my right-hand man in this place forever. That's the biggest secret to my success, Alex - you. You're my trusted administrator without the title." Her head tilted from side to side. "I am happy for you, but once the cat's out of the bag, beware. Everyone will be upset."

He shrugged his shoulders. "I trust you. Don't tell anyone until I give the OK. Please. I want to do it on my terms."

She put her hand over her heart. "Your secret is safe with me, my friend. It's been a joy! Not even sure I would have stayed here without you. Of course, you were there through my toughest days." And she quickly wiped away a tear. "When Brendan was killed, you kept me going. There are not enough words of thanks for your support."

Alex's voice was monotone. "Well, I definitely would have left without you. That is a fact. As for the other, you needed me. Now go! Time to get the show on the road, my friend."

Julia left in stunned silence. Alex cracked his neck. Completely exhausted, he realized he had five more hours until he could go to bed. It was going to be a considerable challenge. He took a loose pill out of his pocket, swallowing it without water. Barely able to catch his breath, he took one inhale of the three different inhalers from his backpack then immediately coughed so hard, he was sure part of his lung would pop out of his chest. He covered his mouth, but when he took his hand away, he noticed drops of blood on his palm. This was happening all the time now. Taking out his phone, he typed the date and time in the health log app he was required to keep for his latest doctor. He elected to take a nap in Renata's office out of sight for an hour. It was always his last resort when he needed to catch some z's.

Georgie made sure she was early for the main presentation given by Julia in the auditorium. She noticed Julia had changed into a tailored black suit and three-inch heels. Always looking impeccable, tonight Julia was flawless. Georgie thought for a moment perhaps this could be her in a few years: the principal? Would she have the time and health to do what it takes? Turning, Georgie saw Jose leaning against the back wall, as far from Dr. Salva as he could get. Alex sat with Renata in the last row.

Julia welcomed everyone who had crowded inside. "Welcome to Eden Hills Parent Back-to-School Night. Our assistant principal is in the back, Mr. Jose Gonzalez, as well as our superintendent of schools, Dr. Jonathan Salva. Over the next hour, we have a lovely evening planned for all of you, where you will walk in the steps of your children, following their schedules. We have staff situated throughout the building, along with our student council members posted in prime locations in the hallways, if you need some help with directions. Please remember, this is not a conference, but an introduction to your children's new schoolteachers. Enjoy the evening! The bells will ring in approximately five minutes for the first-period class."

Georgie exited the auditorium with her colleagues. Her feet felt like cement, her face already flushed. Lilliana joined her, and together they walked to their classroom presentation. For all the nervousness, the evening went smoothly. Many parents wished Georgie good health for the remainder of the year. As they did, a silent chuckle filled her.

Later Lilliana sighed and wiped her brow. "I have to say that went well, don't you think so, Georgie?"

"I do, but didn't you find it weird how Jose stood in the back of the classroom all night? I'm thankful you were with me. Otherwise, I would feel as if I had a complex or something."

"I guess he does that all the time. Maybe we can talk to the others. See if it has happened to them. Do you think he is worried about us? I thought we did a good job. Sorry, I have to run; some of the teachers are going to Rosie's if you want to go."

Georgie shook her head. "Have fun without me. If you hear anything about Jose, text me."

"I'll try to get some scoop. See you tomorrow." And Lilliana gathered her things and hustled out the door.

Georgie had cramps in her stomach so strong she grabbed the chair. After some time, she finally took her bag and slowly headed home. Rosie's was the last place she wanted to go tonight. Georgie needed to conserve what little energy she had left. She locked her classroom door and decided to take the elevator. Pressing the button, she turned to find Alex ambling towards her. "What's the verdict? Good night or what?"

"Great, thanks so much for checking, but may I ask a question? Is everything all right with Jose? He stood in our room the entire evening. I don't want to worry Lilliana, but I hope we're not in trouble in any way."

Alex tugged on his ear, "Mm… I usually never see him in the classrooms. I guess Julia asked him to do it. Who knows? The main thing is you felt like you had done a good job with the parents who met you."

Georgie shrugged her shoulders. "This is all new for me. I hope it doesn't show."

Alex smiled. "Don't worry, with time many parent questions will come. Around the first marking period grades, you'll be flooded with emails requesting a meeting. They have a hard time letting the strings go, especially when little Johnny Smith forgets, oh, twenty homework assignments. Get ready!" He yawned loudly as they found their cars. Alex needed to take some more days off to recover from tonight for sure.

A few days later, Georgie was working with a small group of students after school when she received the call. Recognizing the number, she requested her students to keep working as she took the call in the hallway. "This is Georgie Nelson." There were too many students in the hall, so no privacy. She walked toward the computer lab, looking in to see if it was empty.

"Georgie, this is Francisco from Dr. Hendi's office. She would like to speak to you."

Georgie grabbed hold of the doorknob, something to keep her from collapsing. Her heart was beating out of her chest until she heard Dr. Hendi's voice say, "Good news. The scan is clear. There is no evidence of disease. We have to wait for the urine test to come back to see the serotonin level present."

Georgie was stunned. "So, I am fine?"

"I want to see you in a week after more of the results come in. Your blood work shows signs of elevated blood serotonin, chromogranin, and another hormone called histamine. I think there is a need to put you on monthly shots. We'll get you started then see how you feel. Since you have had a neuroendocrine tumor once, elevated blood work, and are symptomatic, you need to be treated at this time."

"I understand, Dr. Hendi. I will see you next week. I will do whatever it takes, but I still have a lot of questions."

"Bring them with you. We will talk over any questions you have. Make an appointment for later next week. Hold on."

Georgie could barely speak. "I need an appointment." Her chin trembled. "Yes, I'll be there."

She walked back to her classroom, more confused than before. Her mind racing, she realized she needed to read more about neuroendocrine cancer. On her phone, she put the appointment on her calendar. As she walked into her class, she saw Jose sitting with her group of students.

He waved and met her outside the room. "What were you thinking? Leaving students unattended is unacceptable. What if something happened? Where were you?"

"I had an emergency phone call."

"Back on your cell phone?"

"I have a follow-up doctor's appointment."

"On your own time, Georgie. This can't keep happening. Understand?"

"Yes, sir..." And he stormed off in a blur.

Face flushed, she checked the student's work and tried to compose herself. "Great job, guys. We'll check this tomorrow in class." Watching her students leave, she was disappointed in herself for leaving them alone. Shaking her head, and feeling frustrated with herself, she pounded her fists on the desk. *Damn it, I am going to lose this job! Another reprimand letter any minute, I'm sure.*

On her way out for the day, Georgie stopped by Renata's office, but when she looked in, Georgie saw Renata's hands flailing around as she spoke with Julia. As soon as Renata saw Georgie, she waved her in. "Julia, thanks for listening!"

Julia stood, holding up her hand. "We'll get to the bottom of it, I promise. Georgie! See you tomorrow for your observation. Can't wait!" Julia left them alone.

Renata shook her head. "I cannot believe this is happening!"

"What is wrong?"

Renata showed her the filing cabinet. "Look at the lock. Someone has tampered with it. I have all the students' medications in this cabinet. Notice the scratches on the clasp. Someone is trying to take the medicines. With everything I have to do, trying to catch someone breaking into my office is not high on my list. Julia told me she would take care of it. I am sure she will. How are you feeling?"

Grinning from ear to ear she said, "Good news! My scan is clear!"

Renata gave her the thumbs up. "Well, that has made my day! What a relief!"

"Well, Dr. Hendi wants me on medication, on shots. I don't understand it. I have to read more of the information you gave me. Why do I need it?"

Renata held her arms tight to her body. "Listen, Dr. Hendi took a lot of blood. And she's the expert. Plus, you have not felt well, right? If you need shots, you need shots. The main thing is you feel better."

"Would you show me how? I don't know how to give myself a shot."

Renata patted her hand. "Of course. Text me. I can come to your house or meet you here, whatever you want." Her phone rang, "One minute... Daisy, I am on my way home now. Yes, I'm putting my coat on now. There is good news about Georgie. Can't wait to share when I get home." She pressed the phone off. "Daisy was cheering. Great news about the scan. One step at a time with all this, OK?"

Georgie took her things. "I guess you are right. You have to go, and I have to prepare for my observation! Speaking to Lilliana about it later."

"Let me lock the office, and I'll walk out with you. Hey, have you seen Alex lately?"

"No, come to think of it. I was in Alex's room earlier, but he wasn't there."

"He's been out again, not telling me much. Have to get to the bottom of things with that man next!"

"I had no idea he was out so much either." It seemed as if Georgie was with him all the time out of school.

"He is a sneaky man."

⚊⚌+ +⚌⚊

Alex lay in his bed for the third day after his lung biopsy, recovering alone, in silence, and hoping he would have answers soon about a proper diagnosis. Until he heard something from the doctor, he slept. There had been issues with what should have been a routine procedure, leading to more questions than answers. He was second-guessing having the procedure done in the local hospital rather than the city hospital first recommended.

The phone buzzed again. He glanced at the list of fifteen missed texts from school. Leading the pack checking up on him, was Georgie. He wouldn't dare tell anyone how sick he was, so ignoring all communication, for now, would do. What could he say anyway?

The phone rang. He saw his doctor's name, so he answered. "Yes." He listened to the shocking news. Scratching his head, "I understand. Can your office email me all the results? I'll do what I need to do." He lay still. "I have no interest in suing if that is your concern. I only want to feel better. Yes, immediately."

Hanging up, he threw the cell phone against the wall, nearly breaking it. His eyes were heavy, and his body was weak. Alex would deal with the new doctor's appointment another time. Right now, sleep was all he could manage to do with all the new prescriptions he had received.

CHAPTER 19

Georgie stopped by Alex's classroom the morning of Julia's observation to confirm everything was all set. She was excited to finally get it over with, as it had been a busy few days. "Alex, before I freak out about this observation, thanks for dropping dinner off for me the other night. You're a good friend." She scanned the room for anything that might be out of place. "We are good for the observation today, aren't we? Do you have any questions for me before we come in?"

"No, you have been thorough. *You will do fine.* Don't let the reprimand letter from Jose throw you off. Julia is fair."

"You mean reprimand letters- plural. I got another one this morning. The man waits for me to screw up, I swear. Anyway, I'm so glad you're confident in our abilities. I wish I were. Lilliana has been anxious since I scheduled Julia to come in."

"First observations are always nerve-racking, but as long as you do what you have been doing, you will be fantastic."

Georgie's stomach was cramping as she tapped her finger on the student desk.

"Relax, it will all go well," announced Alex. "I have faith in you. Look around. It's as perfect as you can plan." He saw her flush a little on her neck, so he backed off, stealing glances at her. She was hopping around like a frog leaping from lily pad to lily pad, making sure all the computers were on.

Georgie shook her head. "Lilliana's not here yet. She's always early. I rely on her all the time! Makes no sense."

Alex coughed loudly for several seconds. "Worry about you. You're being observed for your lesson. She will be observed for her role with her students. You need to calm down, please. If she is out, I have your back. Tell me what to do."

Georgie wiped her sweaty hands on her skirt and looked around one more time until she was startled to hear Alex's labored breathing, almost like a rattle. Turning to look at him, he was focused on his computer. When she peered out of the room, she saw Julia coming, so she dashed to her classroom.

Alex was printing emails out when Julia appeared with her laptop in hand. "Morning, you are everywhere these days. Well, we've had some issues with the ceiling tiles in one of our rooms this morning. I had to handle it, as you well know. Georgie emailing me really helped me out with my observation schedule."

"When you're finished, can we have a word about some things?"

"How about now? I'm ready for the observation. Let me close the door. What's going on?"

"Thanks for speaking to the custodians. There are a few concerns again, so I'm glad you know about some of them! It's not easy being in charge, but the cleanliness of the building can't wait, which is why I always appreciate the urgency of your response."

"I'm always concerned about the custodian services. It even keeps me up some nights. I hope to get some answers today, but it's the same thing over and over. Thankfully, it is nothing like it was back in the days, eh?" Julia leaned against the wall. "What else?"

"I emailed Jose about some staff questions that need his approval but have heard nothing at all. It's going to start being a problem sooner than later, so I wanted to give you a little notice. Also, Jose keeps writing Georgie up for minor things. It seems like he's back to his old tricks."

"Mm," started Julia, "I had a feeling he was doing his best to make her life miserable. She hasn't shared this with me. Forward me the emails, so I know what he's doing. You know the drill. Same shit, different year. He never stops."

Alex moved to his desk as Georgie entered the room with the students; Lilliana trailing in behind. Georgie took the lead at the front of the room. "Find your seats quietly so we can get started." Lilliana shadowed one student, reminding him to place his books on the floor under the desk.

Georgie walked over to Lilliana and whispered, "Let's give our lesson materials to Julia and do a great job. You OK?"

Lilliana nodded, "I am focused. Let's do a great job. Sorry I was running a little late. Can we talk later?"

She winked at Lilliana, hoping to relax her a little. "Sure," she said as she moved back to the front desk. "Boys and girls, we have Mr. Williams here to help us if we need it today. We also have Ms. Bradley in the back today to see our lesson. How about you turn around and welcome her?" All the students turned to Julia, and either waved or said, "Good morning."

Georgie provided Julia with the lesson plans first, then Lilliana handed Julia her students' modifications and accommodations as per their IEP.

Julia responded to Georgie and Lilliana at the same time, "Thank you. Very excited to see your class today!" She looked at the materials and started to type the information on her laptop.

Georgie and Lilliana moved immediately to the students. Georgie's neck was covered with red blotches as she began, "OK, let's get started! We have a lot to do today."

For the next forty-five minutes, Georgie walked around nonstop, rephrasing directions as needed for the project. She was pleased that the students she had carefully put together were fully engaged. However, she was a little concerned as Lilliana did not appear to be as in sync with her as she needed to be. There were several occasions where Georgie would have generally met with Lilliana to discuss student progress, but this had not happened. It appeared her co-worker was working individually with students and ignoring Georgie. Some of the students Lilliana would have focused on without any effort, also needed to be covered by Georgie. This was not the best example of their team-teaching approach. She was getting more nervous, even sweating a little. She was baffled by Lilliana's lack of communication, hoping it wasn't evident to Julia.

Alex stayed out of the way so they could shine. He did not see any friction or tension between the two, only teamwork. Instead, he thought they demonstrated high levels of teaching pedagogy. When the bell rang, Julia left with her laptop, saying to Georgie and Lilliana, "Congratulations on your first observation. I will email you about the post-conference discussion. Thank you for inviting me."

Alex winked at Georgie, who was now so blotchy, not only on her neck but her cheeks too. Georgie had read about flushing being a symptom of her disease, so was hoping it would subside once she started the shots next week. The students left the classroom. Lilliana also walked out of the room as quickly, without any acknowledgement to either Georgie or Alex. It was odd, but then again, she was acting off. That left Georgie alone with Alex for a few minutes.

Alex cheered. "Are you relieved?"

"I think so. The kids were terrific. Did you see Lilliana, though? Weird, right?"

Alex shrugged. "You know her better than me, but you both seemed in sync with the lesson. Maybe she was as nervous as you. Everyone is different. You get purple, maybe she runs!" And he laughed.

Georgie giggled. "I deserve that. Yes, my blotches have blotches today. I better run to the next period. You were right. Great advice."

"You are well on your way to your tenure," Alex called as he welcomed the next group of students who were running into the lab.

Georgie touched her cheeks with her cold hands, hoping to cool them a little as she moved on to her next classroom. Walking in, she saw some of the students already sitting, getting ready for their activities. She did not see Lilliana. Georgie was talking to some of the students at the front of the room when the bell rang. Lilliana appeared at the back of the room.

"Students let's open with your journal entry for the next ten minutes of freewriting. You know the routine already," Georgie told them before moving closer to Lilliana.

She leaned close to her ear, "Lilliana, what's wrong? You've been crying."

Lilliana shook her head emphatically. "I'm fine. Let's get through this period, please. I have to keep it together for the kids. Can we talk later?"

"Do you want to go to the nurse or take a break? I have this class under control. I'm worried about you."

Lilliana shook her head. "No, let me do my job. We can talk later."

"Listen, we did a pretty nice job last period," Georgie lied as she tried to keep Lilliana calm. "Don't worry about anything," she whispered.

"If only it were that simple. Can we meet after school? Someplace new, safe, out of the way, like the diner near the highway? I don't even want to talk in this building."

"Sure. Text me a time to meet. Whatever you need," Georgie reassured Lilliana. Then turning to the class, she continued with the primary objective of the lesson. When she next looked at Lilliana, she was leaning over a student, re-reading directions for her like a professional.

✄┼┼✄

The diner near the highway was empty. Georgie briefly closed her eyes, her muscles felt weak. She and Lilliana needed to air things out. Was it the lesson? Was she still upset over Bob? Overall, Georgie was baffled. Sitting in a corner booth, she sipped a cup of tea and waited.

Lilliana came into the diner, looking around suspiciously to see if she recognized anyone. Catching the eye of the waitress, she ordered some tea before joining Georgie.

Georgie's pulse was racing. "What's going on, Lilliana?"

Lilliana appeared to hyperventilate. "I owe you an apology. I am so, so sorry."

"What are you sorry for? We did well today! I thought you were fine with me emailing Julia for the observation. I'm sorry if it was uncomfortable or wrong. I didn't mean to overstep my bounds."

"Stop apologizing! It's me that needs to say something. I didn't tell you everything that happened while you were out." She gripped her neck. "Now, I'm caught in the middle."

"Middle of what?" Georgie started to feel a fluttering in her stomach.

"Jose and you." Lilliana bit her lip.

"What about Jose and me? If anything, he hates me. Writes me up all the time. I have had several nasty emails from him. It's upsetting." Her face started to flush, stinging a little.

The waitress placed the tea with milk in front of Lilliana. "Anything else, ladies?"

"Not yet, thanks," replied Lilliana, barely able to look Georgie in the eye. "I know. While you were out, Jose did an observation of me with Angelina. It was outstanding, all fives. He told me he would do another one as long as I helped him."

"Helped him with what?" Georgie's eyebrows squished together.

Lilliana started to cry. "Tell him where you are when he asks."

Georgie blinked rapidly. "What do you mean?"

Lilliana looked down. "I had to text him. Tell him where you were for the write-ups. He was not coincidentally around; he told me to text him when you were not where you were supposed to be. He's out to get you."

Georgie's mouth dropped. Her tone deepened. "Why the hell would you do that? I've done nothing wrong to you! Shit, I trusted you."

Lilliana confessed, "That's why I'm coming clean. I can't do it anymore. *You are a fantastic teacher.* Head and shoulders above Angelina, trust me. The kids love you! Today with the observation, he wanted me to tank it on you, but I couldn't do it. Since Angelina started seeing Bob, I have distanced myself from her. I don't want to be involved with her, Bob, or any of this. How do I get out of this mess? I am seeing someone else now anyway. I'm so sorry."

Georgie rubbed her forehead. "I don't know what to say. Other than that I am disappointed. But if you want to make amends, then for God's sake, let him know where I am when I'm doing things right! I'm where I need to be ninety percent of the time. Let him know, so he only sees me doing the right thing. That's a start!"

"Do you think that will work?" Lilliana bit her nail.

"It can't be any worse than what the hell has been happening. Lilliana, he has written me letters of reprimand at least three times! The only saving grace is Julia did our observation today, and we did a decent job. It would have been outstanding had we been on the same page the whole time! I felt like we were not in sync as much as we have been, but Alex thought we did a great job, thank God."

Lilliana popped a white pill from her bag. "I know. I froze. I didn't know what to do at first. After we started working with the kids, I realized the only way to do the best job for them is to work with you. You have to know that!"

Georgie shook her head. "We were not an effective team today as much as we have been. It's disappointing we did not show Julia how well we work together. I think we were fine, but I wanted to kick ass! Show her why we deserve these jobs." Georgie looked outside the window, holding back her tears.

Lilliana's pulse raced. "I am truly sorry. It will never happen again, I promise. You have to understand how much I need this job with all the debt I have from college. I will never be able to afford graduate school if I don't keep it. I cannot disappoint my family, either. It's a lot of pressure."

Georgie cracked her knuckles. All this stress was not good. She sipped a little tea and regrouped. "In the grand scheme of things, it's no big deal. Julia is pleased with both of us. The kids' writing is slowly improving, so we have to stay away from Jose. Stay clear of him, both of us. What do you think?"

"Is there nothing more we can do about him?" Lilliana was jumpy.

"I can't think of anything other than we do our jobs. Keep our noses clean. Maybe you should stay away from Angelina; stop going to Rosie's. She is here in the building subbing all the time. Avoid her. Who cares that you grew up with her? Stay clear away from drama. Cut the crap dating people in the district. Hopefully, Jose will leave us alone. What do you think?"

"I agree. Maybe Jose is losing it with his wife leaving him. I hear he's not on speaking terms with Dr. Salva."

"I didn't know any of this." Georgie's head was swimming with new information that had nothing to do with her performance with kids. "I guess it is good to know. Information is power, so thanks for letting me know."

"I'm sorry you didn't make it to Rosie's. You missed a lot. A few other new hires mentioned some things about Jose. Some are concerned about him, others like him. One thing is clear. Everyone admires Julia." Holding her cup to toast Georgie, "I'm sorry it was not the best lesson, but I do think we did a great job."

Georgie lifted her cup and clinked it with Lilliana's cup. She shrugged, "I think we did well overall too."

Lilliana patted Georgie's hand. "I am firmly on the same page as you. I swear this will never happen again, *mi amiga*. It's been eating at me for some time."

"I hope so, Lilliana. Remember, we are here for the kids, not all this bullshit!" Georgie was well used to backstabbing from her previous job. Considering she had her first oncologist appointment for the medication in a few days, she had bigger things to worry about.

CHAPTER 20

Georgie knocked on Renata's door the day after her oncologist appointment. They agreed to meet early in the office, so Renata could show her how to use a syringe. The door was open. She found Renata on the ground, taking photos of the lock on her cabinet. "What's going on, Renata?"

"I have been taking daily photos of the lock to see if there are any changes. I am positive something alarming is going on. So many people are in and out of this office all day, who can tell? Give me a hand please." Georgie held out her hand to help Renata up off the ground.

"So you need to self-inject the medicine for the next week three times a day. I suggest you come here to do it or in the ladies' room near your classroom, somewhere private."

"The nurse showed me yesterday, but I've forgotten already." Georgie shrugged her shoulders.

"Not a problem. You'll get the hang of it. Follow me to the bathroom. We don't need anyone walking in on you."

Georgie took a prefilled syringe and alcohol wipes out of her bag. She followed Renata into the bathroom. Renata reminded her, "Be sure to always wash your hands before doing this." Renata washed her hands and dried them. Georgie placed the syringe and alcohol wipe on the sink, then washed and dried her hands.

Renata explained, "You want to inject the needle in some fleshy areas of your body and alternate locations, so you don't bruise. Legs, arms, and stomach are the key places." She lifted Georgie's skirt and pinched some skin on the outer layer of Georgie's upper thigh. "This can be one place that will not hurt. Same on the other leg."

Renata dropped Georgie's skirt. "Please lift your shirt and if you can, lower the waist of your skirt." Georgie was able to lower her skirt with ease due to weight loss. Georgie revealed her stomach. Renata pinched some flesh to the right of Georgie's belly button. "See, here is some nice flesh on your stomach. You can pinch some flesh on either side of your belly button." Renata then pinched some flesh on the left side as Georgie watched. "To me, these are the best places to alternate locations since you are to stick yourself three times a day. No one will see any marks too. Which are you most comfortable starting with?"

Georgie nodded. "I think my stomach so I can see what I am doing, rather than on the side of my leg. Plus, there seems to be more skin to work with."

Renata agreed. "The first thing you do is rub the alcohol pad on the area to disinfect it." She watched as Georgie rubbed the left side of her stomach in a small, circular motion. Georgie threw the pad out along with the wrapper.

Then Renata instructed, "Now take the cap off the needle." Georgie removed the top, placing it on the sink. Renata continued, "Find a little area to pinch your stomach." Georgie pinched about an inch of flesh with her thumb and index finger. Renata cheered, "Great job, now insert the needle, Georgie. It won't hurt since you have flesh." Slowly, Georgie inserted the needle into the pinched skin and pushed the plunger into the barrel filled with medicine until it could no longer move. Renata cheered, "Perfect!"

Removing the needle, Georgie sighed with relief. She replaced the cap on the syringe, asking, "Where do I dispose of the needles? Any suggestions?"

Renata moved to the bathroom door and opened it. "You can return them to your doctor or purchase a needle container so you can dispose of them safely. Don't throw them away in the garbage."

Georgie was a little flushed in the cheeks but was smiling. "That was much easier than I thought. It didn't hurt at all."

Renata clapped. "It's because you did it perfectly! Now continue to switch locations. If you need my help again, don't hesitate to call me. We can Facetime, or I can talk you through it. How are you feeling? Any results yet?"

Georgie put the empty needle carefully in a separate bag in her pocketbook. "Yes, the markers are elevated, so Dr. Hendi believes this shot will help me feel better. Truth be told, I had two shots yesterday. Definitely feel a difference for the better today. I have modified my diet and am sleeping as much as I can, considering. The support groups online have been wonderful. So many smart people are reassuring me that I am not nuts.

Last night I was online with someone from Michigan who repeated a lot of what I read, but I needed it. Too much information. One person from New York gave me some references for nutritionists, so I will make an appointment over the next holiday break to learn more about the diet I need to have. I feel like I have a head start since Alex cooked so healthy for me."

"Well, that's great! I have a folder on my desk but didn't want to overwhelm you. Daisy and I are bonding over reading about neuroendocrine cancer. It's a complex disease. Try to read a little about it when you have some time. Your health is a priority."

"You sound like the doctor. Whoops, must go. Only have ten minutes until I meet with Julia for my post-conference."

⟫⟩+⟨⟪

On-time, Julia called Georgie into her office for her post-conference observation meeting. Georgie was nervous, but with thoughts of the medication, needles, and blood work, her mind was befuddled, so she was having a tough time focusing.

"Come on in, Georgie. Thanks for your patience. Sorry I couldn't get to see you any sooner. In case you hadn't noticed, we've had some fallen ceiling tiles in some of the classrooms needing attention. This place keeps me on my toes, that's for certain. If you want to get into administration, I think you would be good at it, if you have any interest – remember, you can't learn it all from books! Your observation. How do you think it went?"

139

"Well, we accomplished our goals for the lesson. The students were on task and focused, including the two students with ADHD. Working with Lilliana has opened my eyes to students with disabilities. I never had training in this at all. She taught me how to modify my lessons to accommodate their specific needs. The learning curve with Lilliana has helped me grow tremendously."

"Do you have enough support with the curriculum to utilize technology?"

"Absolutely. When we get into the lab, the students have high levels of engagement. Alex is a dream to work with, giving us as much access as possible. He has been outstanding."

"Where do you think you can improve?" Julia wrote some notes as Georgie spoke.

"Maintaining the rigor with the numbers of students. Classes are large, but I'm making it work. Without Lilliana, I fear the students with disabilities would be shortchanged."

"I agree. How about the parents?"

"Not as much interaction as I thought. Some emails, but it seems as if many are logging into the grading program to see homework, tests, essay grades, but after that, not a lot of communication."

"Have you seen improvements with the students?"

Georgie had a gleam in her eye. "Student growth is slow. We have high expectations, but the baseline essays had poor sentence structure. I'm using other resources to strengthen individual students who need more help, provide remediation. Some stay after the day ends, which is a help."

Julia gave a crisp nod. "Well, I think you have a handle on things, that's for sure. The data you input is plentiful, more so than most other teachers. I have to thank you for doing the work so efficiently! How are you doing it?"

"I grade the homework and get it back to them quickly. It makes it easier for feedback."

Julia tilted her head. "Parent-teacher conferences will be here before you know it. How will you prepare?"

Georgie steered the conversation. "I will access my student data, speak to the parents about strengths and weaknesses unless it is Jason Rollins, whose assignments I give to Lilliana. She works with him at home as he recovers from surgery. What an amazing kid. Even with the health complications with his heart, he has a great drive to achieve."

"I hear he will be back in a few months. Keep me in the loop with Jason, please." Julia cleared her throat.

"Yes. The parents and social worker would like to do some teleconferencing lessons in school, so he feels more a part of the classroom. That would mean setting up a webcam. Is that acceptable?"

Julia nodded. "Yes, we have done that in the past with students who cannot get into school for medical reasons. Move ahead, but there are some parameters we need to go over before it starts. I will send you an email on the policy." She wrote the word 'camera,' and Julia's eyes popped. "A camera? Of course."

"Sorry?" Georgie blinked rapidly.

Julia chuckled. "Nothing. I have a big issue. Thanks to you, I have just figured out what to do. Final question, how are things going with Jose?"

"I hardly see him," she lied.

"Is there anything you want to tell me or want me to know? You can say it now." Julia looked Georgie straight in the eye.

Although Georgie hesitated a moment she bounced right back with a fake smile. "I have nothing to say. I look forward to him observing me. I want him to see how hard I work."

Julia put her pen down. "Great observation, great post-conference. Here," and she printed out a copy of the observation report from her computer, handing it to Georgie.

Georgie skimmed the document, her heart raced. "Julia, I am so pleased. All fives and fours! I can't ask for anything more."

"No… thank you. Keep doing what you are doing… Georgie, feel good. I know you had a scary start with your health. Sometimes it makes us realize we have to enjoy every moment." Julia reached out to shake Georgie's hand.

Georgie could not help containing her broad smile while shaking Julia's hand. "I love Eden Hills. This is my true calling, my vocation, I know it. I hope to be here for a long time." Georgie hoped this observation had saved her job.

"If I have my say, you will easily get your wish." Julia saw her phone light on.

Georgie gathered her things. "Julia, how is your dissertation research going?"

Julia's face had a wide grin. "Thanks to your data input, remarkable! Moving right along the way, it needs to go. You might want to consider it yourself, down the road. You have a gift." Julia's phone rang. "Sorry I have to take this."

Georgie waved to Julia as she took the call from Tiffany. Covering the phone piece, she called out, "Don't forget to keep Jason's return to school on my radar." Georgie nodded as she slipped out.

After Georgie had gone, Julia spoke to Tiffany, "I noticed my phone light blinking the whole post-observation. What's the emergency?"

Tiffany rubbed her chin, "I followed up on Alex. He's out again for the third day in a row. Not sure what's going on."

Julia sat back. "That is weird. Not like him. Third day in a row? Thanks for staying on top of that. Also, do me a favor. I want a meeting with the custodians again as soon as possible. There are ceiling tiles in a few rooms that are soaking wet from the rain over the last few days. A few teacher complaints again. I have to nip it in the bud. If you get wind of anything, I need to know." She drilled her fingers on the table then grabbed her cell phone to text Alex. *I hope all is well.*

Tiffany flew in the door, the vein in her neck pulsing. "You have a meeting with the custodial staff tomorrow afternoon. Is that soon enough? I can't believe I found two of them having coffee outside the main office in front of kids! Hot coffee, Julia! Anyway, I told them about the complaint on the top floor. Thought you would be pleased." Tiffany's eyes narrowed.

Julia took a sip of water, "You read my mind. Perfect!" Shaking her head, "Enough is enough." She grabbed a pencil and listed a few other items she needed to address. Glancing at her cell, she hoped to see a message from Alex, but no response yet again. The bell rang, so she grabbed her laptop and set off for another observation. Hopefully, she would hear from him soon.

In Renata's office, Georgie walked out of the bathroom, waving the empty syringe. "Number two is a success. Not bad at all. I did what you told me and put it on the other side of my stomach. Yay!" She placed the empty syringe into the particular spot in her bag with the first one from the morning. "I have to say I am feeling much better with the medicine."

Renata was documenting student medicine logs on the computer. "I'm glad to hear you're on the mend." She sat back in her chair and tilted her head. "Hey, any more consideration on sharing your diagnosis with Julia? It might be good for her to know in case you need some time out, or your schedule needs to be altered."

Georgie gripped her bag tightly. "No! Absolutely not, Renata. No one can know here." Shaking her head, she looked at her feet. "I will not be pitied."

Renata jumped to her feet. "It's not pity! It's understanding, having compassion. This is a big deal! Just think about it. Maybe not now, but at some point when you feel the time is right." A student stormed into the office with a bloody tissue on her nose followed by Jose.

Georgie whispered, "Renata, let it be. I have to go." She moved in silence to the door, but Jose blocked it.

Renata clamored loudly enough for Jose to hear, "Feel better, Ms. Nelson." Putting her gloves on, she moved closer to the child. "What do we have here?"

Jose stayed in the doorway as Georgie tried to leave. "Not well, Ms. Nelson?"

Georgie was a little flush. "Much better now. It's my prep time, so I wanted to check with Renata about something. Heading to the computer lab now."

He moved, walking out of the office with her into the hallway.

"Ms. Nelson." Jose walked at the same pace as Georgie. "Don't make it a habit of using the nurse's room. Renata is busy with students, unless it's an emergency, of course. Was today an emergency?" They both stopped.

Georgie was not sure what the best way to answer the question was. "I suppose I could have emailed her instead. It will not happen again." Her heart was racing, but she was careful to change the subject. "Jose, I had my first observation post-conference with Julia. It went well. If you would like, I can email you a date and time in a few weeks for a special lesson. There are some exciting activities infused with technology if you would like to see?" Being fake with Jose was exhausting.

Jose took his glasses off and bit the arm of the frame hard. "Sounds perfect." Georgie swore he had spoken through gritted teeth. Maybe not. While his voice may have sounded pleasant, his eyes glowered at her, giving her a chill.

"I will let you know." Shoulders back and chin high, she turned and walked in the direction of the second floor. She pretended not to be afraid of him, at least not today.

He stood and watched her chat with some students who were heading in the same direction to the second floor. He bellowed loudly enough for her to hear. "Remember, Ms. Nelson, the nurse's office is emergency only!"

Georgie ignored him as she went as quickly as she could to the second-floor computer room. Stopping at Alex's classroom, she stuck her head inside to see yet again an empty room. No Alex. She decided to text him. *The observation went great! I owe you.* Sitting in his chair, she closed her eyes. The meditation app he had given her helped her with some new relaxation strategies. Georgie felt as if she was floating on a cloud. So much so, she decided to visit those she loved the most. It was a long time coming.

⇥ ⇤

Arriving at the cemetery, Georgie stood, grasping the corner of the granite headstone by the grave her brother and mother shared. In the other hand, she tightly held two bouquets of red roses. This was the first time she had visited since she started at Eden Hills.

"Hey, guys, I'm sorry it's been so long. I brought you special red roses today! Very fancy." Smiling, she bent over, placing them in the center of the grave on the hard dirt. "Seems the grass is growing a bit, which is nice."

She stood staring at the roses as the strong gusts of the fall wind blew through her hair. "I'm teaching, and it's been terrific! I mean, hard, yet awesome. Love the kids, most of my colleagues are great to work with."

She raised her eyebrows. "At least some of them. One is a huge pain, but I'm sure you would both tell me there is one in every bunch."

Biting her lip, Georgie's face flushed. "He does hate me, though. It makes it hard. I have a lot more to prove there, so I won't let myself focus on him and his stupid, *petty* game. Good news! I had an awesome post-observation conference today, so I am here to celebrate with you! Yay! Julia, my boss, was impressed with me. Her comments made me feel as if I made the right career choice. I've finally found my way!"

Her facial features downturned. "Anyhow, I tried to see dad, but he was too tired. Sleeping as always, so I didn't want to wake him. I'll go back another time. They told me better times to visit him." She paced back and forth in silence to muster the courage. "Had to tell you, had to tell someone, well, I'm sick. It seems like it's been with me for a while. Lucky, they found it early, but it is a lifelong thing." She continued to pace again. "I'm taking medicine and feel so much better. I have to change my diet and so far, so good, but it's hard." She laughed, "No red wine, hard cheese, some other stuff too. It's been an adjustment, but I'm lucky, I think. I'm in good company at least. Steve Jobs, Aretha Franklin, they both have it. Well, actually they died of it. The type of cancer. *Neuroendocrine cancer.*" She wiped a tear as it fell down her cheek. "But don't worry, I have a good friend at work, Renata, who I can talk to, you know, confide in. Also, Alex, well, I can't put into words how much he means to me. Maybe something more, too." Georgie found her cheeks sting.

Brushing her hand along the blades of grass, "I am *lucky* to have found a good place to call my home away from home. Speaking of," and here she stifled a yawn. "I'm wiped. That's part of this disease, cancer, whatever you want to call it." Taking out a tissue, she blew her nose and blotted her eyes again.

"I better go, but you know me, I'll be back again soon. Take good care of each other." She kissed the granite and whispered, "I love you both with all my heart. Please watch over me. I could use some help here at times." Standing, she rubbed the bleak granite once more, bent to check the roses to make sure they were perfectly straight, and then closed her eyes, to say a silent prayer.

Just as she opened her eyes, another abrupt gust of wind blew past her, so strong her sunglasses almost toppled off her head. "Wow! That was some sign from you guys!" She shivered. "I'm leaving. Don't worry; I got this!"

She walked languidly to her car, turned around to glance at their resting place one more time, and with her left hand, blew a kiss through the air, hoping it would find its way to them.

CHAPTER 21

Jose stormed out of his office. "Tiffany, email the non tenured staff. I want to meet with them today at 3.00 p.m. How many kids are they sending daily?"

Tiffany nodded so many times that a pencil fell out of her hair. "It *is* a lot. How bad can they be? I'll get right on it." She started typing immediately. "But today? It's already after lunch. They can file a grievance; you know for last-minute meetings. You are supposed to give them forty-eight hours."

His face was purple. "I don't care. I got a scolding from Dr. Salva, who got an earful from parents complaining that their kids are being sent too many times to my office. It has to stop!"

He walked back into his office and closed the door. Clicking on his calendar, he cursed under his breath. "Damnit, I forgot about the coaches. I'll knock two birds with one stone."

Georgie and Lilliana were two of the first to arrive in the dark, dusty auditorium. Georgie glanced around at the ample space. "Let's sit at the back. I don't want to be in the line of fire, whatever he's going to say." Georgie moved into the middle of the last row, threw her pocketbook on the floor and plopped down. "I locked the room, right? I have to go back after this. Can't carry all my stuff all over the place."

"Yes, you did. I have to leave after this." Lilliana sat, crossed her legs, and bit her nails. "Not sure what he wants. I hope we did nothing wrong."

Teachers started to fill the auditorium, choosing seats around the two of them, like they were the cool kids in the class. Carl sat next to Lilliana, arm to arm. "Hey, you guys want to go to Rosie's after this?"

Lilliana bit her lip. "It depends on what we hear today and how long I work with Jason. Text me. Nice haircut!"

Jose walked in the front door of the auditorium carrying some papers. "Come, sign in to the meeting." He placed a piece of paper on the stage. "I need you all to move to the front."

Carl mumbled, "Oh boy, this can't be good."

The teachers all took their things and formed a line to sign in. Jose approached Georgie. "I need to speak to you for a moment in private." He walked her to a quiet corner of the room. "I got a message from the superintendent's office. You need to go over now. This meeting will be about half-hour, and you need to hear what I have to say, so you better hustle. You can sign in when you return." He glared at her.

Georgie's stomach churned. "OK. I'll be back as soon as possible." Turning, she darted to her pocketbook; her face was flushing a little bit already. She stopped and whispered to Lilliana, "I have to go to the central office."

Lilliana touched her arm, "Leave your stuff with me. I'll watch it. Better hurry."

"You're a life-saver."

Walking briskly to her car, Georgie drove to the board office across town. Since she was behind a school bus the entire way, the minutes seemed to crawl. Nervous, she put on a little lipstick while she waited for the bus to unload students block after block. The last time she was in the converted mansion on top of a hill, far from anything in town, she completed all her district paperwork. *What could they want? What did I do now?*

As she finally entered the site of Eden Hills educational leadership, she was met with blank looks and disinterested shrugs. Georgie's last resort was to ask one secretary to call the school and find Jose, but was told he could not be interrupted. Her stomach cramped as time ticked. Storming into the first restroom she could find in the building, Georgie walked to the sink, looked at her stinging flushed face. She turned on the cold water, splashing it on her face and neck several times. It helped reduce the red a little, but she realized she forgot to take her noon shot and had left it at school. She was a bit nauseous, so she took out a small lemon drop candy and popped it in her mouth. Sucking on it, Georgie held her stomach for a few moments at a loss as to what more to do. Defeated, she rushed back to school, even running a red light.

"What happened? You missed the whole meeting!" Lilliana clasped Georgie's hands.

Georgie swallowed hard. "I have no clue, maybe a misunderstanding." She needed to rest a second. "What did I miss?"

Lilliana's babbled. "He yelled at everyone for sending too many kids to his office. He wants everyone to handle discipline more in the classroom." She shook her head. "It didn't pertain to us, thankfully. But one teacher almost cried. Carl was livid. Jose called him out for doing it this morning. I guess the kids texted their parents and went all the way to Dr. Salva."

Georgie rubbed the back of her neck. "Well, at least it was not us. Anything else?"

Lilliana shook her head. "He's going to email us some tips, and we need to meet with the guidance department first, instead of sending kids to him." Lilliana handed Georgie a folder, "Oh, and here. You are *not* going to be happy. I peeked since he gave me one too. Jose told me to give it to you."

Georgie did a double-take. "This form says I am the new assistant volleyball coach, signed off by Jose Gonzalez." Shooting Lilliana a look, "What? How am I supposed to do this on top of everything else?" She shook her head.

"If it makes you feel better, most of the group was assigned a coaching job. Volleyball is in the spring, so we have a few months." Lilliana took her laptop and clapped, "We are coaching together, so we'll have to figure it out somehow. Must run to Jason for an hour, then maybe Rosie's. Do you want to meet later?"

"No, good luck with that. I still have to get my things in the room before I go home." Georgie sat still, grasping the paper tighter and tighter.

"*Adios.* See you tomorrow," and Lilliana scurried out the door.

Georgie slowly stood, holding the folder while her head was spinning. *What have I gotten myself into?*

═╡╞ ╡╞═

Jose powered off his computer for the day. His blood was still boiling from Dr. Salva reprimanding him about the disciplinary issues in the building. Glancing at the sign-in sheet, he decided he would make a photocopy and send it to Dr. Salva to show proof he was responsive.

Julia stuck her head into the office. "You're here late. How did the meeting go? I heard you ripped into them." She stood at his doorway.

He waved the sign-in sheet. "Had a quick discussion with the newbies. I think they heard me loud and clear and how it runs around here. I'll keep a closer eye on them."

Julia nodded. "Let me know if I need to call anyone. We can't have this office so packed with kids for senseless behavioral issues. Thanks for handling it so fast. Was the union upset you pulled it together so fast?"

He shook his head. "Not at all. Alex is not around, so it all worked out. Hey, speaking of not being here, Georgie missed the whole meeting. So that you know, you may be wrong about her. I don't know if she is cut-out for this place."

Julia folded her arms. "Where was she?"

He shrugged his shoulders. "No clue. Can't have her doing what she wants."

"Do me a favor and leave her be. She had a rough start with her health. I'll speak to her." Julia turned to leave. "Night."

Jose rubbed his hands together as he thought about composing the email he was sending to Georgie regardless of what Julia said. He took his keys and glanced out the window at the parking lot. Only a few cars were left, when he saw Georgie's car. He stared like a lion ready to pounce. Raising one eyebrow higher than another, Jose took a copy of the sign-in sheet, highlighted the name of the *only* missing teacher, and then wrote the word *insubordinate,* before putting it in the mail attention: Dr. Salva.

CHAPTER 22

After the full week, Georgie's phone buzzed as she swept her kitchen floor after dropping gluten-free flour in an unsuccessful attempt to bake scones. It was Alex. *Could I stop by in a little while?*

Georgie texted back immediately. *Sure. I'm at home.*

Looking at her disheveled image in the mirror, Georgie took a long, hot, relaxing shower. Carefully picking out a casual sweatshirt to go with her jeans, she sprayed on her favorite perfume for good measure. She was sweating, yet not sure why. Or maybe she did. She had missed seeing Alex the last week, not hearing a word from him at all.

Timely as usual, Alex rang the doorbell. Georgie's pulse raced as she opened the door with a sigh to find Alex holding a bouquet of sunflowers. Looking at the gorgeous arrangement, she blushed as Alex smiled back at her.

Taking the flowers, Georgie hugged him, saying, "You didn't have to, Alex. These are my favorite flowers." Smiling, her voice was bubbly

Alex responded, "Good! Glad they make you happy. Week go well?" Alex followed her into the house.

"Ended up being fantastic. I had an encouraging post-conference with higher than expected scores, thanks to you. I should be bringing *you* flowers."

Alex made his way to the couch and slowly, painfully sat down. He was huffing and puffing from the walk to the house but hoped Georgie wouldn't notice. But Georgie had, although she chose to ignore his pale complexion, slight frame, and the gaunt look in his eyes. She braced herself for a tough conversation.

Sensing it, her eyes glistened, "Well, these flowers have perked me up. Would you like dinner? I have Leo's Organic Garden on speed dial these days."

Alex was gasping for some air. "You read my mind. I need some food!"

Georgie rang the restaurant. "Ah, don't worry, they make organic salads and healthy smoothies. Hi, Leo, yes, it's me again. The regular, with salad. Yes, I have company." Covering the phone, she told Alex, "I never get a salad when I am alone, ha!" Then she continued, "Sure, Leo, throw in a gluten-free cookie for my friend. Well done. Put it on my tab. No, I have no interest in owning your restaurant. Yes, I will talk to you tomorrow night at about the same time. Be well." She giggled as she tossed the phone on the chair. "I guess I am pretty predictable these days. No secrets!"

Alex laughed a little, closing his eyes tight. "Listen, Georgie, can we talk a little, please? I need to talk. Friend to friend. I need a friend."

Georgie stayed quiet, fists clenched, as he continued. "I have some things to tell you. No one knows this. I need to talk. Otherwise, I think it's going to get worse." She moved closer, next to him on the couch, grabbing his hand as if in doing so, she could infuse him with extra strength.

After a short pause, he took out a small piece of paper, looking at it instead of her face. "I went to a new doctor, and I have been diagnosed with… well, it's not good! I have to see an oncologist later this week about the next steps."

Looking into her eyes, he saw her face flush as she patted his hand. "I imagine you knew something was wrong. I look like shit. I think everyone knows I look like shit." Georgie sat still, holding his hand, but now she was rubbing his back with her free hand too.

He continued, "I've been sick for so many years, been to a bunch of doctors who gave me the runaround, wrong medications, wrong diagnoses. When Rebecca, my ex, left me, I blew off the doctor's appointments, biopsies, scans - pretending I was fine. I use the inhalers because they work, sort of. But I'm tired all the time; my lung capacity is horrific. I don't think they can remove the mass or tumor or whatever they call it, but truthfully, I only wrote a few notes on the paper." He handed her a scrap of paper with his barely legible writing. She read the scribbled words.

Silence. She held the paper, wishing she could tear it to shreds as if it did not exist, but it did.

Alex sat back on the couch. She could hear him wheeze. "Do you mind if I close my eyes for a little while? I'm exhausted."

"Whatever you need, Alex. Sleep for a bit. No worries."

Gently she helped him lie on the couch, took off his sneakers, and placed a blanket over him. By the time she had done so, he was already asleep. Sitting in the chair, she looked at her friend for several minutes, barely able to breathe herself. She was in turmoil - a mixture of fear, concern, and dare she say it - love for him.

After a while, she decided to leave him to rest, going to sit on the front porch to wait for the delivery man. As she held his little piece of paper with the doctor's name on, she realized it was one of the doctors from the same practice as her oncologist in New York City. *What a small world.*

Continuing to stare at nothing particular, Georgie waited for something inspired to come into her mind, something she could say to Alex.

⇒+ +⇐

It was nearly two hours later when Alex's eyes opened. He found himself lying on an unfamiliar couch. As he slowly woke, he saw Georgie at the kitchen counter typing on her laptop. He watched her for a moment, his heart beating a little uncontrollably. She looked intensely immersed in her work, beautifully focused.

"Georgie, I am so, so sorry!"

Georgie walked over to the chair next to the couch carrying two cups of chamomile tea. "You were wiped out. There was no moving you. I can heat some food for you if you want."

He slowly shook his head. "I have no appetite. Sorry to unload all of this on you. I don't remember if I asked how you were feeling. How are you? You look good - always do to me."

"I'm stuffed from dinner, but I appreciate the compliment. I'm back on track." She could never burden him with her health issues, now especially.

She watched him sipping some tea before she broached the subject. "Did you think about what you are going to do?"

He paused before answering, "Well, I have this new doctor to see next week, so I'll take it from there. I'm not sure about anything."

"Do you have someone to go with you?" She wanted to say she'd go with him, but it would be too risky going to the same doctor's office. Inevitably, someone would say something, or would recognize her. She tried hard to keep her composure as her heart raced. Lying was not something natural for her.

"I guess I could call my brother, Charles, but we're not close. Typical sibling rivalry stuff. Not in the mood to share all this with him until I know what the deal is."

Plucking up the courage, she took a chance. "I can go with you if you like."

"No, no, no." He shook his head and tried to stand, but immediately stayed put. "I have to tell you. I'm so exhausted I can't even think straight anymore. They gave me some new medication. I'm not even sure I should be taking it. So many prescriptions, so many different doctors. So confused." Alex yawned.

"Why don't you confide in Renata? You can trust her - I do! She is worried."

"Renata's marriage has been rocky since she started in the district. I can't add more to her. She already gets way too involved in situations. No, no-one can know, Georgie."

"I understand what you are saying; trust me. But this is a lot for you to handle on your own." She looked at her watch. "It's almost 8.00 p.m. Would you like me to call your brother for you from here?"

Alex pursed his lips. "What do I say? We barely talk. I don't know much yet."

"Tell him what you know. You are family. Trust me, my cousin Clare is texting me practically every hour. I didn't want to tell her anything about my operation either, but she cares. She wants to know. Your brother will too," she explained gently.

Alex rubbed his eyes. "I'm too tired to argue with you. I'll call, I promise."

Georgie stood. "I'll give you some privacy, heat some food for you. Take your time. I'll be in the other room. If you need me, call me."

He found Charles's number as he scrolled his cell phone. "Err... I think I'll eat something first. Need the energy."

Georgie was already putting the stove on when she turned around, surprised to see Alex standing in the kitchen doorway. He stared at her as she poured him some water and took the other half of the salad out of the refrigerator. "How are you feeling?" He sat back in his chair. "Major surgery is no joke."

"It's been a shock to my system, but I'll be fine."

She placed the food in front of him. He started to dish out some salad onto his plate while she realized she needed another shot of her medicine. Starting to clean, she said, "Do you want to call your brother?"

Alex sighed. "I am going to call him when I get home. I need to think about what to say. Maybe I'll come by again when I'm feeling a bit better. If that's OK?"

As Georgie walked him to the front door, she had the urge to hug him, touch him, console him. "I would like that. I did take a rain check from Rosie's, so I owe you, Alex, for so much."

He started to walk down the front steps but stopped, turning around, he took her hand, and rubbed her palm while looking at the floor, he regretted meeting her at this time of his life. "Let me talk to Charles. I need to get things organized in my head a bit more. I'll keep in touch. Sorry I have been distant with your texts, phone calls. I apologize. It's not like me to be so... unreliable."

"Are you kidding? I feel bad for bothering you. Whatever you need from me, any time, you can trust me. School is not the same without you. We need you there, so keep fighting. The kids are always asking where you are. Kids, staff, we all need you!"

With a lump in his throat, he sighed, "I needed to hear that. The kids are why I have been doing what I have been doing since day one. Have tons more stories to share with you about them. You'll see, they'll keep you going; on the good and bad days too! Tell them I said hello. Jeez, I really miss their stories. See you again soon. Night."

She watched his car drive off until it was no longer in view. She felt worse for him than herself but realized she, too, had to put her health first. Time for her shot, then to bed. As she closed the door, she looked at her bouquet. Bringing the vase with her to her bedroom, she placed them carefully on the nightstand. She collapsed on the mattress, letting out a heaving sob that had been just under the surface since what seemed forever. Georgie was infuriated, having to hear bad news after bad news for years. Today was no different. When would it stop? It was almost too much to bear.

CHAPTER 23

It had been a quiet week at Eden Hills. Georgie, feeling better daily due to her shots, had more energy than in many months. Her lesson plans were coming to life with steady success. The grading program helped her analyze when students were falling behind with assignments. Although nervous at first to call parents, it soon became more manageable thanks to Lilliana's encouragement.

Lilliana's voice softened, "Georgie, my professors suggested calling parents immediately to let them know of any concerns and what is going on. Not just notifying them about things via email. I am always anxious to call them, so I practice a few times with my therapist. Oh, you should also call them with good news too; like when the students do something special! During student teaching, my teacher made me call parents with her because she understood how hard it is for me. It helped me a lot."

Georgie nodded. "It would be great if you helped me with the first few. I didn't have those experiences. Also, would you mind translating for a few of them? I would like to learn some Spanish from you, too."

Lilliana smiled. "Funny, you should ask. My student teacher asked me to translate all the time. It forced me to engage with others more. I swear she was conniving with my therapist. Let's go use the teachers' room phone, so they don't see our cell numbers."

Georgie followed her lead, impressed at her co-worker's maturity. Entering the nearest teachers' room, they discovered the floor heavily covered in dust. Both of them sneezed at the same time. "Wow, this place is dirty," said Georgie in surprise.

"I haven't seen anywhere this bad since we started," said Lilliana looking closely at the table, before wiping her finger along the top. It was so dusty they could see her finger-mark. "Should we let Julia know? She's always sending emails about keeping an eye on the custodians. Don't want to make trouble, but considering Jason is back soon, we have no choice! He needs to be in a clean environment!"

Georgie emailed Julia from her cell phone and cc'd Lilliana. "You're right. This is outrageous."

Julia was in her office when she received the email. *Damnit, not again. Same floor. What the hell?* Yelling to Tiffany, she said, "Get the custodians in here NOW. It seems as if all I do these days is meet with them. No excuses, please!"

Tiffany walked in. "They're on their way. Want me to log the complaint?"

"You know the drill." Handing Tiffany the email, her cheeks were a shade of plum. "File this with it. I'm so sick of this. At my next meeting with Dr. Salva, remind me to bring the log again."

"I will. Let's hope this time you make a dent." Tiffany shrugged her shoulders, holding the email.

⚜

After the last period bell rang for the weekend, Georgie turned to see Lilliana back in the classroom; this time smiling ear to ear. "Hey, what is going on?"

"Julia did my post-observation conference. Turned out, it was better than expected! I'm so thrilled. She was also thankful we alerted her about the dirty mess in the teachers' room. She appreciated the information."

"Wow, glad to hear." She raised her eyebrows. "Now, on to the progress reports. When are they due? I need to get prepared, but I can't find the email with the dates!"

"The last email changed the date to next Friday. You should have plenty of time. Luckily, I did mine over the last few days. Did you decide what professional development program you were going to attend? We have to decide, then email administration."

Georgie sighed. "There is a never-ending list of things to do. I was thinking about taking the behavioral management workshop. Still, I don't know anything about what they are offering. What about you?"

Lilliana read from the list on the email. "Restraint training we don't need. CPR training might be helpful, especially since we have lunch duty. Suicide prevention is important, but behavioral management pertains to us daily in class. I don't know what to do. Feel like I could use all these workshops. How about we go to different workshops so we can share resources?"

"Sounds great. I think I'll stick with behavioral management. We have some challenging kids, especially in our last period class. Might learn a few new tricks too."

Georgie realized she needed her medicine soon.

"Right. Then I will do the suicide prevention workshop. With the suicide rate rising, it would be good for us to know the signs." Lilliana fished the paper forms from her bag, handing a copy to Georgie to complete. "I'll take both forms to Tiffany."

Having filled in the form, Georgie handed it to Lilliana. "Sounds like a plan. Are you done with your grades? I have a lot more to do. Maybe afterwards, I can finally take you to Rosie's?"

"*Sí*. I will drop these off in the main office. Meet you there in an hour. Sound good?"

Georgie clapped her hands. "Sounds ideal. An hour. We deserve to celebrate your observation!"

On her way out of the building, Georgie decided to take her shot before meeting Lilliana, so she went to Renata's office. "May I use your bathroom?"

"Sure. How are you feeling?" Renata was writing in her logs.

Georgie walked to the bathroom with her pocketbook. "These shots help me feel better. It's unbelievable. I have an appointment in a few weeks."

Renata stopped what she was doing for a moment, asking, "Hey, do you know anything about Alex? He seems to be out a lot."

She was afraid to betray Alex's trust. "No. We text about work, but nothing too personal. Why?"

Renata crossed her arms, biting her lip. "He's out more than he's in at the moment. It's not like him at all. Which reminds me, let me call Julia a second." Renata called Julia. "Julia, we need the custodians downstairs. Remember the room I told you about? It's still filthy dirty. You have to see it. I wanted to move the file cabinet back to cover the door but figured I better check there first. Nothing has been done yet. I wanted you to know."

"What is that all about?" Georgie glanced around.

Renata's eyes bulged. "Oh boy, get ready for Julia. She is *not* happy!"

Georgie put her medication away as Julia marched in, carrying a walkie-talkie. "Renata, what are you talking about? I sent an email weeks ago. I even made copies and handed the keys directly to the head custodian! May I have your keys, please? Must I do everything around here? Jeez!"

Renata handed Julia her keys, who quickly snatched them, muttering a curse. She opened the back-door to go downstairs. As she descended each step, her heels made a loud clicking noise.

Georgie told Renata quietly, "Yikes. I have never seen her so mad."

Renata nodded and whispered, "This is how she gets when things don't get done. I'll fill you in later." She put her finger to her lips.

Georgie bounced on her toes. "Do you have a little time for Rosie's? I'm meeting Lilliana there, my treat."

Renata turned off the computer. "Sounds good to me. I can go for an hour. It has been too long since I had a little fun - perfect timing to celebrate. I just wrote my monthly report for the building, which took me twice as long as usual." She stretched. "Between the medical update information and the dirty room downstairs, Julia is going to go ballistic."

Julia stomped up the stairs. "I'm shocked! That room... well... It has not seen a broom in years. I don't want anyone exposed to the area. Make sure you wash carefully, Renata. I need a shower now too!" Julia announced as she started to use her walkie-talkie. "Gary, come to the nurse's office now! I need a major cleanup over the weekend. No exceptions." She turned the walkie-talkie off and slipped it into her pocket. "Renata, no one goes near that place again. I will check it on Monday to make sure it has been cleaned. We can't have this again!" She stormed off, texting someone furiously.

"My job is done for the day. Let's go! Now I need a drink." Renata, neglecting to lock the door, followed Georgie out the door.

Rosie's was packed, but luckily Lilliana had gotten there earlier, saving seats for Renata and Georgie at a table in the corner. Cyndi Lauper's music played loudly, and the smell of greasy, fried food was in the air. Georgie took a position with the view of nearly fifty district staff members chatting, picking on food, and sipping cocktails.

She could not help but stare. "Lilliana, now I understand why you said I was missing out. This place is packed! How long does this go on for?"

Lilliana laughed. "Happy hour? Until it's time to go home, *mi amiga*. Sometimes early, sometimes late. You never can tell. Can I get you guys a drink - everything is half price - or order some food? Free apps until eight!"

Renata swayed to the music. "Whatever you can carry back with you, I will eat. I would love a gin and tonic with lime, please. Here are two twenties. Buy a round for the table here."

Georgie rubbed her hands. "I am sticking with a glass of ginger ale and some water for now." She had a long drive home and was already feeling tired.

Lilliana laughed, "Forty dollars will last us a while. *Un momento.* I'll be right back."

Renata whispered, "Poor Lilliana, she thinks no one knows about her and Bob, but I have to tell you the cat's out of the bag. He got caught by his wife last week with Angelina, so everything is a nightmare. Last week Bob's wife threw a glass of wine in Angelina's face. Big confrontation. Anyway, I heard Bob is now at his parents' house, and that he's confessed to everything, including his short-term fling with Lilliana."

Georgie covered her mouth. "Are you going to tell her?"

Renata shook her head. "No way… I am butting out! I think that is why it's so crowded tonight. Everyone is waiting for more drama, but it won't happen. Jose is on top of Angelina these days, so she is practically a prisoner in her own house."

"Trust me, I avoid Angelina at all costs. Should I say something to Lilliana?" Georgie cringed.

They watched as Lilliana carried back their drinks.

Renata wiggled her index finger, "Let's see how it plays out." Lilliana put the drinks on the table. "Thanks, Lilliana. Any problems?"

"*No hay un problema.* Food is on its way. A toast to good observations!" Lilliana smiled and toasted Renata and Georgie. The three cheered.

Renata's sip of gin and tonic was more like a chug. "Great to hear you guys are in good standing so far."

Lilliana smiled, "Julia's so supportive! Even when we told her about the dirty teachers' room, she made it her business to thank me for letting her know."

Renata rolled her eyes. "Dirty teachers' room? *Not again.* Julia is going to lose her mind with those custodians."

Georgie's eyes tightened, "Does this happen a lot?"

Renata leaned in closer to Georgie and Lilliana. "You saw Julia today in my office, Georgie. She was furious. There were health issues a long time ago. Alex told me about it when I started. He was sick with breathing problems, and a rash. Poor construction or something. The cleaning was not done properly, either. Every time he coughs, I can't help but think... I don't want to think about it. He gave us a scare last year, but it seems like he's a bit better now." Renata took another chug of her drink as a waitress dropped off small plates of chicken fingers, stuffed mushrooms, and nachos.

Lilliana handed everyone plates. "Alex has not even been in school lately."

Georgie sipped her ginger ale and veered the topic away from Alex. "Well, Julia was responsive to us a little while ago upstairs, too. It sounds like she is on top of things or tries to be."

Renata piled as much as she could fit on her little plate and started eating a chicken wing. "She is one fierce lady when it comes to the building. Keeping it clean is a passion for her; she does not tolerate any issues at all. I'll give her credit. Always responsive."

Lilliana and Renata ate in silence as Georgie watched. There was no way she could attempt to eat that kind of food. She would be sick from pretty much everything on the plates.

Lilliana put her arm around Georgie, "You are not eating or drinking. Are you OK? Can I get you something else? They have salad or pretzels."

Georgie smiled and shook her head. "Don't worry about me." Georgie sipped some water, causing her stomach to flutter. "What about the kids? Were they sick, too, in the past?"

Renata was licking her fingers. "I'm not sure about before me, but the medical needs are the highest in my three years at Eden Hills. Between students with allergies, diabetes, asthma, cancer, sickle cell, you name it. The numbers of sick kids are through the roof. No wonder I'm freaking worn out. Talked to the other nurses in the district." She licked her fingers. "Seems worse in our building than the others. I just emailed Julia today. Bad news!"

⌗ ⌗

Julia stormed into her office, gripping the phone. "Jose, I need to see you now."

Julia emailed Alex, as she always did over the years, when there were problems with the building. It was still necessary for both of them to be in the same room as she talked to Dr. Salva, so everyone was on the same page. She was surprised when Jose entered her office in no time. She would have to fill Alex in on the issue later. "We have another major issue in the building."

Calling Dr. Salva's number, she put him on speakerphone. "Dr. Salva, I am here with Jose. It came to my attention that there is a room downstairs, below the nurse's office, that has been untouched by the custodians for what appears to be years. We need major cleaning NOW. I have spoken with Gary, but this is unacceptable. Yet again, another issue which should have been resolved a long time ago."

Swallowing to control her temper, Julia continued, "I guaranteed a clean environment for everyone in this building, but here I am, yet again,

163

concerned. I would ask you again to reconsider another custodial company. We cannot risk a repeat of the health issues from years ago." Her nostrils were flaring, her fists clenched. "I really would appreciate your support."

Dr. Salva's voice was calm. "Julia, we have gone over this for years. We are fine with the group we have. I'll find money in the budget to get it cleaned out over the weekend. Give the guys overtime for a full clean up."

Julia demanded. "Air ducts as well, and air quality testing afterwards, Dr. Salva? We need a full building cleaning! The child with the heart transplant - Jason Rollins; he will be back in school at some point. I gave his parents *my word* that everything is fine here. You know how I feel about this." And she pounded her hands on her desk to make her point felt.

"Yup, concerns heard. Glad you found the issue so we can address it. I'm confident with who we have. We'll get this rectified." And with that Dr. Salva ended the call.

Jose stared at the floor, rubbing his hands. "What do you want from me? What can I do?"

She leaned toward Jose. "Help me check the room on Monday first thing. Maybe even on an ongoing basis."

He shuddered. "Julia, same shit, different day with this place. You will have a heart attack worrying about this stuff. Not worth it. I'll continue to monitor as usual. I didn't even know there was a room there." And with that, he too headed out for the day.

As soon as he was outside the building, Jose called Dr. Salva on his cell phone. "Thank you for taking my call."

Dr. Salva answered on the first ring. "What is it?"

Rolling his eyes, Jose gritted his teeth. "Do you want me to keep an eye on things as usual? I wasn't sure what you wanted me to do, considering the circumstances. I have not heard from Maritza for weeks; neither have the kids."

Dr. Salva's voice was icy. "Don't expect to. Maritza is done with all of you. Let the lawyers handle things. I'm not getting involved."

Jose picked up a loose rock off the ground, throwing it into the woods in anger. "What about this situation, the new development?"

"They will clean as usual. No difference because Maritza is divorcing you. Do your job," and Dr. Salva ended the call.

Jose continued to pick up some loose rocks, throwing them further and further away from his car. He took some deep breaths, the beads of sweat running along his brow. "Three more years of this shit does not work for me. Not at all."

⚓

A short time later, Marko Medrano walked into the expensive five-star Italian restaurant fifteen minutes from Julia's office. The one they had always frequented before she had met Brendan. He saw her sitting at the table, with a glass of wine, and a massive grin. She could not believe he was still as gorgeous as the day they'd first met; her first year of teaching at Eden Hills. They found eating at Morella's brought them back to simpler days.

"Julia, nice to see you. This place brings back memories." Bending, he kissed her on the cheek then he sat down.

She could not help but smile, "Seems like a lifetime ago. Twice in one month, I am honored. What happened to the wife, if you don't mind me asking? I thought she was *the one?*"

He chuckled, looking sheepish. "Well, for a start, she depleted her expense account." He ran his hand through his hair. "Then she managed to find a hot trainer at the gym who was, let's say, more her type. You know how it is, Julia. My hours suck. Long hours don't lead to happy marriages."

She rolled her eyes. "Oh please, plenty of lawyers have great marriages. You haven't yet met anyone worthy of you."

His eyes glistened. "Sure, I have, but you won't have me. How many times can I ask? How long should I have to wait?"

Julia sucked down the rest of her wine. This was going to be a two-bottle type of meal. "Old news, Marko. Let's move on." She gave a casual glance around the room before continuing, "I need a favor; I need your brilliant mind."

He chugged his full glass of wine, then called the waiter over. "We will have the house Chianti. And keep it coming. She is a dangerous dinner companion," and he laughed lightly at his own joke.

Julia blushed a little. They stared a little too long at one another before, licking her lips, she leaned in very close to him. "Seriously, let me get this out, a little business before pleasure, please." Marko raised his eyebrows. "Can we talk about the district? I never knew why Salva got rid of you."

He tugged on his ear and paused before answering, "How can I forget those years so long ago? That's when I met you." He glanced around the room, clearing his throat. "It was a mutual separation. Why do you think he got rid of me?"

Julia shook her head. "Cut the shit. I know you. As smooth an operator as you are, you are an ethical son of a bitch too. That's why we always got along so well for so long. Tell me. Why did he get rid of you?"

He puffed his chest out, smoothing the tablecloth in front of him. "He stopped following my recommendations. It became a fractured relationship. His compass was off. Salva's ego ruled, no matter what. I told you never to forget that. Why do you think there has always been a revolving door of board attorneys during his tenure? Let me guess - people are sick again? That situation was pretty bad."

Her eyebrows raised. "The truth is, I'm not sure at all anymore. I'm on it all the time; both Alex Williams and I are, but is it enough?"

He rubbed his jaw. "Wow, Alex Williams. I have not heard his name in a long time. Is he still the union representative? I liked him a lot. Exceptional reputation with everyone, kids, parents. Nice guy, fair."

Julia was not to be diverted. "Yes, he is. But that isn't why I asked to see you. I found some old records today in a filthy, potentially toxic basement closet. I spent some time looking at them. Even with all the shit that happened, we're still using the same companies to this day. Don't get me wrong, there have been no major issues. I'm on the custodians *all the time*. My colleagues are too. We continue to build using the same construction companies, same custodial companies - nothing is changing! I heard Salva is putting together another referendum this year for more space. The numbers of kids per classroom is appalling. It's a disgrace. Teachers are stretched so much, and jeez, the turnover is high. I'm doing my best but… You know, he's not retiring as planned? The board offered him another three-year contract."

"Why would he retire? He's got them wrapped around his fingers. Salva will continue to approve the same companies' bids for the work too. Bet you a million dollars! It's easy for him to do the same thing over and over," quipped Marko.

The waiter came over and poured the expensive house Chianti for Marko to try. He swirled the wine in his glass, then held it momentarily in his mouth and signaled the waiter. "Excellent." After the man had refilled both glasses, he left them alone. Marko moved closer to Julia, continuing in hushed tones, "Let's say things don't change. People don't change. It's been a problem for a long time. Tell me, why are you so upset? Are you sick? You were one of them."

"I haven't had any health issues since then. Jose seems fine too. Alex is sick. He hasn't told me to my face, but I know it. The rest of the group, well, it's been a long time. No one else is in the district, that I know of. Life happens - what can I say? Alex, Jose, and I are the only three left in the building. Jose does not help at all." Julia shook her head, feeling some despair.

Marko sat back in the chair, crossed his arms, then rubbed his face hard. "I'm sorry to hear that. It seems like you needed to talk. You should have called me sooner."

Carefully, Julia composed herself. "I don't know why I'm upset. But the last time I saw Alex, I looked at him in a different light. Then running into you a few weeks ago, now these files… Am I rambling too much? It has made me wonder. Why did you leave the district?" Julia's lip had started to quiver once more.

Marko spoke softly, "Listen, I resigned because Salva wouldn't listen to me. End of story. I did warn you. How many times? Because Alex is sick, it does not mean it has happened because of the building. There could be many factors, you know." He sipped some wine before asking, "How's he doing anyway?"

Julia bit the inside of her cheek. "He is retiring at the end of this year. One minute I thought he would be a colleague, you know, a fellow administrator. I was shocked. It's put a bad taste in my mouth. I mean, he has the years, barely takes any sick days… until now. I think I need to do my due diligence!"

Marko lowered his voice again, "Well, I am sure all those documents have my name written all over them." He held her hand. "Listen, you had an awful few years after Brendan's death. And now, who knows?" He shook his head.

Julia gulped her wine. "Don't you worry. I'm upset now, but underneath, *I am furious.* I did not take a leadership position to sit back and do nothing for anyone or anything."

Marko grinned as he gazed at her. "Atta girl! Get angry." He licked his lips. "I love you mad. When you're mad, you can do anything. Mad is what you need to be to deal with all this. Jonathan Salva had no idea who he hired when he promoted you to be principal."

She was shocked. "What do you mean?"

Marko stared slyly. "I bet he thought you would be compliant. You know, a 'yes' person. Salva loves those types of people. He's screwed because he sized you up wrong. You might be his worst nightmare dressed in a gorgeous red dress with killer legs! I love it! Let's order so we can get outta here. Maybe we can catch up on getting reacquainted." And he shot her a wink as he gently stroked her arm some more.

CHAPTER 24

Over the weekend, Georgie and Alex managed to walk a little on the beach. The unseasonably chilly weather did not hamper them from getting some fresh air. Walking barefoot on the sand, they found they were alone for as far as the eye could see. Occasionally, Alex took hold of Georgie's hand. His excuse was to support her, where the footing was uneven. Often, he held on longer than necessary. She didn't argue the point.

Alex sniffed in the salty air, taking a mental snapshot of tranquility. "You are quiet tonight. What's on your mind?"

Pushing her hair out of her face, Georgie said, "It's just my father's nursing home bills are piling up. On top of that, I still get bills for some of my brother's rehab stints too! It never stops. Believe it or not, I am relieved to have the coaching job later in the year for some extra income. I'm going to need it." She sighed.

His head tilted to one side. "I get it. Teaching is not going to make you a millionaire, that's for sure, but at least we have a good salary guide, considering." Alex took his hands and blew into them.

"The benefits are so much better than my last job. Medical especially." Georgie had been reviewing her hospital bills the night before. She was thankful they were all covered by her medical insurance. "I'm coming to terms with the idea that the house is too big. Just for me, it's way too big." She shivered.

He tapped her shoulder. "You could rent out a couple of rooms in the place, like a bed and breakfast, it's so big. Ever think of doing that?"

Georgie nodded. "Huh, I like the idea a lot. Maybe I'll rent it out in the summer months. The realtors call me weekly." She laughed, "I have emails and messages all the time. Some of the neighbors are not too pleased. I haven't kept the house to their liking. Need to get on with that too, I suppose."

They walked further to the edge of the waves which were breaking minimally, it being low tide. "It would be a lucrative income to help me save for another degree. I'd like to go back to learn more about how to help kids. The more I'm around them, the more I feel as if I need to know more. Lilliana has helped a lot, but there are so many needs in the room."

Alex smiled. "Don't worry, there is summer work in the district. You never know what can happen."

Georgie looked out at the water, closed her eyes, hoping she continued feeling good with her shots before even thinking about any other long-term dreams. Seagulls flew by, dunking their beaks in and out of the water, searching for their next meal.

Alex broke the silence. "Charles is coming this week."

Georgie brushed his arm lightly. "Who? Charles? That is huge! Will you be in this week?"

He shrugged. "Sure. What about you, is Clare coming? You keep telling me, she can't wait to visit you to make sure you're in good health, now you have one less organ."

Nodding her head, Georgie agreed. "No, I told her maybe over the holidays. I have to say, thanks to Eden Hills, I feel like I have made some nice new friends. You, Renata, even Lilliana all feel like family."

"Pretty damn crazy family!" laughed Alex as he tried to catch his breath, before coughing for several seconds.

The sound of him clearing his throat for air made her sniff back tears. She sighed, "Hey, we better get back. Long week ahead again. Good news - I heard Jason's heart surgery was a success! Lilliana told me his family would start live lessons via a computer for him. He is so excited, we all are. You know, she found out Jason had a twin brother who died at birth. Take it from me, when your twin passes away, you feel it. My brother's spirit gives me strength every day. I bet his brother is helping him stay strong too."

Slowly they left the beach so they could go their separate ways. Alex dusted the sand off his feet. "That's a sweet way of looking at things. You have a glass half full mentality, which is what I like about you."

She gazed into his deep brown eyes. "When you have had tough times, it's the only way to look at it."

Bending, he kissed her on the cheek, then they parted ways, both going to their respective homes, to get much-needed rest.

⊰ ⊱

As Georgie pulled into her spot at Eden Hills after what seemed to be a fast weekend, she received a text from Renata asking her to come straight to her office. Gathering her things, she found Renata pacing, wringing her hands, in her office. "I came as fast as I could."

"Georgie, do you remember if I locked my office when we left?" Renata questioned urgently.

"I don't remember. Why?"

"The door was open when I got in this morning. I *always* freaking lock it."

Georgie looked around. "Was anything taken?"

"No, but I always make sure it's locked! No one has a key, except the other nurses in the district. I'm already concerned about the cabinet lock. Now, this. Damnit." She threw her coat on the chair in frustration.

Georgie walked around, checking the cabinets to see they were all locked. "Can you talk to Julia about it? Aren't there cameras in the hallways?"

"Yes, and yes, but I am better than this," said Renata, placing her hands over her face. "I think I'm becoming so distracted with things."

Georgie moved closer, lowering her voice, "Hey, there's a lot going on in your office. You told me so yourself, at Rosie's. We all have a lot on our plates." She waited a moment as Renata double checked all the cabinets and drawers. "And, we know Julia is nothing but supportive. Just call her."

Renata walked to the bathroom and put some cold water on her face. Taking a paper towel, she blotted her cheeks with it. Fixing her hair in the mirror and chucking the paper towel into the garbage can, she said, "Ugh. You're right. I'll speak to Julia."

"Glad to hear." Georgie patted her on the shoulder.

Renata turned her face upwards, "Thanks, Georgie. You're still feeling well?"

"Yeah, feeling good. Saw Alex. I think he might be back today."

Renata squeezed her body tight. "Well, well, fan freaking tastic news!" She sighed, "Let me get this over with." And as she called Julia, she bit her fingernail.

"Hi, Julia, would you mind coming to the office, please?" Renata pointed to a notebook. "Can you sign the nurse's log, Georgie? I started this procedure again. Need to keep track of who the hell is in this office at all times."

≈‖‖≈

The minute Julia walked into her office, Renata blurted out the words she hated the most. "I have to confess. I'm so sorry."

Julia interrupted her. "No need to apologize, the custodial group worked all weekend in the building, cleaning rooms along with the air ducts. I'm sure they left it open. Anything missing?"

Renata rubbed her neck. "Wow, I forgot. No, the lock looks okay too. I'm so relieved. I was losing it for a minute. Did you read my monthly report, by chance? Lots of issues?" Renata rubbed her sweaty hands on her scrubs.

Julia rubbed her head a little from too much Marko over the weekend. "Yes, I sent it to Dr. Salva. Helped my case to get this place cleaned from top to bottom, so perfect timing! Also, we will have air quality testing done soon again to make sure everything is up to code. Having all the health data in the building was more than I could ask. You are a gem! Any issues I need to know ASAP!"

≈‖‖≈

Georgie decided to check her mailbox in the main office. She was shocked to see her professional development form marked in red with a big X on it, along with Jose's initials. Confused, she went to see him.

Knocking on his door, she entered. "Excuse me, Jose. May I ask you about my professional development form? Why am I not allowed to go to this program?"

Jose took off his glasses and ground his teeth on the arm. "Did you not read the directions on the form? The program you registered for was for special education teachers, not general education teachers. Choose again."

Georgie read the form and saw her error. "Oh, my goodness, I missed all that. I will choose the test preparation workshop. No problem. Sorry for the confusion. I will return the form to you later today." She scurried out of his office, grasping the form so tightly as if she needed it for dear life.

⚒

Georgie reread the form in her classroom several times. She could not believe how confused she must have been to complete the form incorrectly. *What am I missing? Was Lilliana involved again?* Anyway, after glancing at her lesson plans, she took a peek at her emails. She expected only a few since she checked them earlier in the morning. Her mouth was wide open when she saw a lengthy email from Jose.

TO: Georgie Nelson
FM: Jose Gonzalez
RE: Concerns

I have many concerns with you following the rules as per the Eden Hills faculty handbook. I have witnessed you using your cell phone for personal use, leaving students unattended after school, missing mandatory faculty meetings, and incorrectly completing professional development forms. These infringements must not continue and must be corrected immediately.

"Shit, shit, shit," she muttered. As Georgie finished reading the email, Lilliana walked in.

"*Buenos dias*! What a great time Rosie's was. *Muchas grac...*!" She saw Georgie's pained expression. "What's happened?"

"Were you behind this again? I got into huge trouble about the PD form *you* handed in for me." Georgie crumpled the form and threw it in the garbage.

Lilliana took it out and examined it closely. "I thought what you chose sounded good. I don't see the problem."

Georgie pointed out the prerequisite was for special education teachers in bold letters on top. "Look, I can't take it. Now I'm in trouble for not following directions - all the other things you were behind. I cannot even look at you. *I am so hurt.*"

Lilliana was shocked. "Wait! I made a copy of the forms on Friday before handing them in. That information *was not* on the form, I swear." She took out her copy to show Georgie. "Look, it lists the options; nothing like the one he gave you back!"

Georgie grunted. "Uh! How can I handle his bullshit, Lilliana? The new one he gave me has last year's date on it."

"Damn right, I know how it looks. I always make copies of things for my records, so there is no confusion. Make a copy of anything you send. Let's write a rebuttal to Jose to knock him on his ass." Lilliana banged on the desk.

"How can we do that?" Georgie's shoulders sagged.

"Simple," Lilliana clapped. "We copy Julia and Dr. Salva. Notice how none of his emails to you are cc'd, which means Julia has no clue what he is doing to you. We'll work on it in our prep time. Rebut his ass off."

"I think I have to do something! If you help me, that would be great." Georgie looked at Lilliana suddenly, feeling terrible for doubting her.

"Georgie, it's on! Screw him! We have five minutes before the kids arrive. Let's draft something now, so you can email him tonight. OK?"

"Lilliana, I'm sorry to admit I thought you were behind this confusion. I feel so bad." Georgie lay her hand on her breastbone.

"Hey, my days of helping Jose are *long gone*. I told you." Lilliana's hands were on her hips.

"I won't doubt you again." Georgie murmured sheepishly.

"I owe you. It is the least I can do. Plus, I am so hungover from watching the Giants lose last night, I need something to put a smile back on my face!"

After lunch duty, Georgie passed Alex's classroom to find him going through his filing cabinet at the back. "May I run a draft of an email by you? Jose isn't going to stop."

Alex rubbed his hands. "Give it to me. I want to see what you are made of." He read it aloud:

TO: Jose Gonzalez
FM: Georgie Nelson
CC: Dr. Jonathan Salva, Ms. Julia Bradley
RE: Professional Development

It has come to my attention that the professional development form that was placed in my mailbox today was not the form I completed, nor the one my colleagues completed last week. My completed form from last week, along with the altered form I found today in my mailbox, are both attached to this email for you to review. Please note there are significant discrepancies since one is from last year. If it confuses me, I am sure the rest of the staff have concerns too. As per my conversation with you this morning, I look forward to taking the test preparation professional development program. I hope to learn about new strategies and techniques to help my students succeed on the state tests in the spring. The program sounds like a fantastic opportunity to enhance my teaching skills to meet the building goals of high student achievement.

"Well done, Ms. Nelson. Bcc me as well. You are finally learning. To be sure, do you want Dr. Salva and Julia in on it? I'm fine with it, but when you put their names on it, it brings it to a whole other level."

Georgie thought for a moment then decided. "I am sure. Alex, this has to stop!"

"Agreed. I'm thrilled you are standing up for yourself. If you don't do it now, it will only get worse."

"I finally understand what you have been saying," she said, holding the paper against her chest.

Alex's eyes danced as he looked at her. "Any interest in celebrating your rebuttal? Get some food? We should eat a meal together, but not at Rosie's, not with work people."

"That would be great." She grinned, turning beet red. "I need to keep busy. I can't tell a lie. I'm feeling deflated." She shrugged her shoulders. "I'm beginning to think teaching is not for me."

After having a brief coughing fit, Alex smiled at her, before focusing on the idea of food. "Enough! That is the last thing you should be thinking about. The bigger question is… should it be Italian or sushi?"

Georgie's smile was faint. "Italian is more comfort food. Rocco's near us is great. Do you know it?"

Alex's heart nearly exploded. "It's my favorite. They cook clean, light food, especially fish. I'll meet you there so we can celebrate you getting a backbone!"

⤜╬╟⤐

Rocco's was nearly empty by the time Alex and Georgie finished their dinner. The candles were flickering, and there was the whisper of jazz in the background. Georgie wiped her mouth, feeling satiated. "Amazing scallops and salmon." Pointing to the container on the chair next to her, she said, "I will be eating the leftovers for a few days, I think."

Alex pointed to his container too. "We are quite a pair. I'm not hungry lately, but why are you eating so little? I would think you would be all set to run around by now. You seem kinda sluggish still."

Georgie swished the water in her mouth and lied. "I'm fine, having smaller meals. Trying to be careful. Sometimes my stomach is upset." At least all that was true.

"You worried about things at school? You're handling Jose the best you can. You should be proud of yourself. No matter what happens, don't back down or submit to him. He preys on weak people."

Georgie nodded as her stomach felt bloated from the few bites of the meal. "Why teach, Alex? You have been in the classroom for a long time. Happy with it? No other dreams or interests?"

Alex's tired countenance glowed under the dim light in the room, a slight wrinkle around the corner of his eyes. "I had some chances to do other things, but the kids keep you young, and on your toes. I've always loved them, and it never gets old, helping them grow. It sounds corny, but it's all I've ever wanted to do since I was a lost kid in middle school. I had a terrific black male teacher who mentored my brother and me when our dad died. Come to think of it, he taught both of us to be ethical, fair, and honest. Charles and I were talking about him last night. He played in a jazz band for extra money, so would practice after school for us, the latch-key kids, while we did our homework." He shrugged. "Pretty open book. I have no regrets in life. How about you? Where do you see yourself in five years?"

Georgie sat back, shaking her head. Before she realized what she was saying, she responded without thinking, "I want to be alive in five years."

Alex struggled to find the right words. "What does *that* mean? You will be alive and kicking. Unless there is something you are not telling me." And he jerked his head back.

Georgie rubbed her hands together. "I mean, everyone wants to be healthy and happy. That's all." She sighed. "Five years? I want to help kids in different ways. I've been learning so much from Lilliana about special education, so maybe I'll go back for another degree. Or maybe even look at administration? Julia mentioned I should consider that."

Alex nodded. "You would be terrific either way. Don't settle. That's my advice."

Georgie bit her lip. "Going back to school after already finishing my first degree in teaching would be expensive and an investment. I'm not really ready yet for the financial commitment. It's a lot to think about. Funny, I'm living in the here and now." She stared at the candlewick flickering, her mind drifting. Five years was another lifetime away. At least for now.

※∔∔⇒

As the next week passed, Georgie continued to struggle with balancing the job and her health. Day after day, as she sat at her desk at lunchtime, she found grading her student classwork was becoming a constant challenge. Lilliana stormed into the classroom, closing the door. "Did you hear Alex is out for a while? Angelina is his substitute indefinitely, so she told me. Bragged about the assignment."

"*Indefinitely*? Let me text him." Georgie sent him a message, but with three-afternoon classes, she was too busy working with the kids to look for a response. By the last bell, her heart raced as she glanced at her phone and reviewed her emails. Radio silence for this length of time was not like Alex at all. She had not heard from him since they had the luscious dinner over a week ago. With report cards due, she had lost track of everything else. She was spending every waking moment trying to complete the grades by the deadline, while squeezing in her oncologist appointment.

Lilliana saw Georgie biting her lip. "Any word?'

"No. But I'm sure Alex is fine." Yet Georgie was confident he was not.

CHAPTER 25

Alex could not move from the bed for several days. Memories of the long chunks of time he had spent with Georgie were a delight. In truth, he was happier than he had ever been. It had almost made him forget his chest pain and sheer exhaustion. That was until it hit him like a brick wall.

He had slept through his alarm, calling Tiffany at noon as he finally grasped how late he was for work. "Tiffany, can you please add me to the faculty sick list? I always leave my room keys in the mailbox anyway. I know it's against protocol, so apologize to Julia for me."

Tiffany responded, "Hey, I'm worried. Julia is too. Do you need anything? What's going on?"

Alex cleared his throat, "No worries. I'll be back soon. I just need a few days to get some things out of the way. The last thing you need to do is to worry about me."

Tiffany tapped a pencil on her desk as she could hear Alex gasping for air. "I'm not trying to pry, Alex. But we go back a long way. Take good care of yourself, you hear? We need you back."

Alex played with the label on the water bottle on his bed, "Thanks for always looking out for me. Hell, for everyone, Tiffany."

Next, he texted Julia, but Alex could hardly see the letters as he typed. *Spoke to Tiffany. Am out but will be back soon. Sorry for any confusion.*

Looking closer, he realized he had several text messages from Georgie, all from different days. He hated to disappoint her, but his next call was the highest priority. Clearing his throat, he propped himself against a pillow in bed. "Hi, I'm a new patient for Dr. Grace Hendi. Yes, I forgot to make an appointment. I was hoping to move my appointment. I'm not feeling great. Tomorrow? What time?" As he ended the call, Georgie called. His lips were pressed together in a slight grimace as he pressed the phone on.

Georgie whispered, "Alex, I'm so sorry to bother you. I heard Angelina is subbing for you. Are you feeling, OK? Can I do anything?"

Alex reclined in bed. "I'm tired, no worries. It's not your fault. I had a great time with you at dinner, Georgie. It flew by. Can't believe how late we stayed too, closing the place," he tried to laugh but coughed instead. "Do me a favor? In my classroom, press the locks in on the cabinets as soon as possible. I want my personal effects locked. Also, I will text you a new password, so no one has access to my computer."

Georgie blushed. "Of course. I promise I will handle it immediately. Do not worry, your computer will be locked. I'm heading there now. No problem. I worry you know." She bit her lip. "I care about you a lot. If you need anything, I can always drop things off for you. Don't hesitate to ask."

Alex held his hand on his heart. "Very sweet, but I'm good. I am going to rest now. I'll be in sooner than later. Hey, any word from Jose in response to your kick-ass rebuttal?"

Georgie laughed. "Not a word. It looks like everything is looking up! Please get some rest. Love to see you back soon!"

Alex sighed. "That is where I want to be. Have a great day, Georgie! I can't think of a better person to spend my time with than you. Getting to know you has made me very happy. I am, I mean Eden Hills, well, we're all lucky to have you."

On that note, he clicked off. Slowly he moved back, laying his head on the pillow. Before he knew it, he had slept away the remainder of the day.

⇥+⇤

Twelve hours later, Alex sat in Dr. Hendi's office in the same seat Georgie had occupied several times before. Too weak to drive, he'd taken a car service to his appointment. Alex was out of breath walking from the car to the first-floor office space. He was dragging-- so much so, that he could barely fill out the pile of forms he needed to complete. His writing was slow and labored. Most words were illegible. When he dropped the pen on the floor for the second time, Francisco, the nurse, looking at him, noted his difficulty.

Francisco walked over to Alex; he opened his arms. With a kind, gentle tone, he helped Alex to the back room. Then taking the incomplete forms, he said, "I can review these with you if you would like?"

"That sounds good to me."

When it was time, Alex put his arm against the wall to steady himself as he followed Francisco into Dr. Hendi's office. Francisco then held Alex's arm, helping to lower him into the chair and pointing to several questions he'd omitted. Finally, Alex signed his name and placed his initials on the lines. Francisco took the forms from him and patted his arm. "I'll be right back. Just going to get the blood pressure machine so I can take your pressure before Dr. Hendi comes in."

Alex's mind was foggy. He couldn't remember the day of the week nor the month. He read, but could not comprehend, Dr. Hendi's degrees on the wall. The photo on the desk facing him of a married couple seemingly blissful, bringing a slight smile to his gaunt cheeks. Looking at his boney hands, he tried to think of a question for the doctor, but his mind was slow, much like a runner hobbling to the finish line. It took all his effort to shift in the chair a little since his bottom hurt to sit on the soft cushion. His legs felt like cement, he was lightheaded, and he physically ached as he breathed. The waiting seemed to go on for a long time, but it was mere seconds. There was a slight knock on the door, and Dr. Hendi walked in. Alex hoped she would help him soon feel better. He had much to live for.

Dr. Hendi shook his hand. "Good morning, Mr. Williams." She placed a thick folder on her desk, purposely leaving it closed. With a nod of the head and a slight smile, her tender-hearted eyes looked into Alex's weary ones. "I have read your file. How can I help you?"

Alex's usual jovial attitude wasn't evident today. "Well, I hope you can make me get better, but to be honest, I'm not sure what you can do for me. I've been to many doctors over a number of years, as you can see."

"Yes. Mr. Williams, I studied your file and contacted your primary physician. Dr. Barry is a close colleague of mine. In fact, we talked at length yesterday. Sometimes we have to rule out a lot of things. Quite frankly, I see some recommendations from several of the doctors who may have given you medication which was not effective."

He shook his head. "Yes. Lots of medications, little help."

She folded her hands on her pristine desk. "You were recommended to get a series of scans last year, correct?"

"Yes."

She spoke calmly. "When I did not get those reports, I discovered you never had the scans, no biopsies. Well, Mr. Williams, without all that information, it's hard for me to help you. I can send you right now to the hospital so we can get all these tests done, go from there. May I do that? When I spoke with Dr. Barry, she told me she offered to do the same thing a few months ago."

"I'm too tired to do a whole lot of things anymore." His fingers were tingling again.

She swallowed hard, "I understand." She repeated, "We can get you in the hospital and go from there."

Silence. Alex rolled his eyes. *Another useless hospital visit.*

"I can help you, but I need more help from you. Do you want help?" Her voice broke a little.

Alex's eyes were lifeless, "Of course! I'm sick of not getting better."

There was a pause. Then Dr. Hendi said, "Mr. Williams, if you want my help, then you have to help yourself. Get these tests done and hopefully, and I say hopefully, we can do something."

There was another short pause as Dr. Hendi became blunter in her approach. "Mr. Williams let me be clearer; we don't have much time."

He shrugged. "What! You mean now?"

Dr. Hendi rubbed her hands together. "Yes, I do."

Alex thought for a moment. "Can it not wait a little longer?"

Swallowing hard Dr. Hendi spoke slowly and quietly. "Mr. Williams, I mean now. If not, then I must ask you. Do you have any family, someone who can help you get things in order?"

He smiled a little. "My brother, Charles, is on his way. I guess the thing I want to know is since I am this sick, can my brother get this as well? Is there a genetic link?"

She was clear, "There is always a possibility of a hereditary component, but we can test for it. Again, we need tests. At the moment I am relying on your old scans and tests. Because we don't have vital information on you in over two years, I don't know what it is exactly right now. There are many new innovative treatments, but I need information."

Alex took two crumpled pieces of paper out of his pocket and handed them to Dr. Hendi.

She flattened the papers on her desk and read the results from an MRI and biopsy he'd had done a few weeks back. She carefully read them, then her head jerked back. "Now, I have the information. Based on this, I can treat you and can give you a little more time. We can try something. It will not cure you. I think you know that, but it will give you time."

"I guess a little more time would be good. Not sure how long I can keep going; breathing is hard. In truth everything is hard," said Alex clearing his throat.

Dr. Hendi leaned in, "As you have read from your tests, you have many issues, more than the lungs… Let's focus on today, please. Don't look back or ahead, only today." She moved toward Alex, squatted to his eye level, and placed her strong hands into his feeble ones. She used all her momentum to help him stand. Eye to eye, face to face, she wrapped her arm around Alex to steady him and whispered, "Let's get started."

⚒

Another week passed with no word from Alex other than a brief text message to Georgie. As much as she wanted to text and call, she knew he was with Charles. She realized more and more she needed to focus on her own health. Her downtime at home involved sleeping extra hours, eating healthy food, and taking her scheduled shots as per Dr. Hendi's instructions. With all that, along with keeping her health journal, she recognized higher levels of energy and fewer neuroendocrine cancer symptoms.

One thing she could not shake was the constant headache of waiting for her next appointment. Her worry led to nausea, which led to sadness then feelings of dread. Renata offered to go, but Georgie decided it was best to get into the routine of visiting the oncologist every four weeks for her medicine by herself. Being busy at work, staying a little longer with less time at home, was becoming the best way she could think of to cope. At least for now.

⚓

Julia, pacing her office, gripped her cell phone so tight she had the phone's indention on the palm of her hand. Alex texted her. *I need to speak to you and Marko Medrano together. Call my cell phone ASAP.*

Julia instructed Marko to slip in the side door of the building. He pushed his hand through his damp, sweaty wind-blown hair while he closed the door to her office. "What's going on? Why wouldn't you tell me anything on the phone?"

Julia grabbed his hand and pulled him next to her. Her lips quivered, "We have to call Alex Williams together. He's texted me after being out for some time. This is not like him at all. I'm worried. Let's call now."

She dialed Alex's number, putting it on speakerphone. He answered on the first ring. "Hi, Julia. Is Marko with you?"

Julia held Marko's hand. "Yes, we are both here, Alex. How are you?"

Alex's voice sounded labored. "Listen. Hate to tell you this on the phone, but I'm in the hospital. My doctor put me in for tests, and I guess it's been a few days already. I'm having surgery tomorrow. My brother Charles has been with me, so it's been good seeing him. What can I say, it is what it is!"

Julia and Marko shot each other a look, not speaking, but listening intently as Alex continued. They could hear how he struggled to breathe. "I won't be able to go back to work for a while, but I hope to see you both when I feel better."

Julia choked back her tears. "Alex, can we come to see you? Help you out?"

A long silence followed. Julia was worried something had happened.

"Hi, this is Charles. He's going to take a nap now. He wanted me to write his last wishes since he does not have a will or any of those types of documents. Give them to Marko, the attorney. Understood? Any problems with this?"

Marko texted his info to Alex's phone number. "I will handle whatever you want. I can come to the hospital now if you text me the address. Just texted you my info."

"That sounds good since he wants this done before his surgery, if possible. I'll text you everything now. See you in a bit." Charles ended the call.

Marko and Julia stared at the phone until Marko's phone buzzed. "I'd better go do what Alex wants. Can I come by to see you later?" He rubbed her arm as she continued to stare at her phone.

Her voice was shaky. "Yes, please do. Tell Alex I can go any time if he wants to see me," Her head fell onto Marko's shoulder.

"If he does, I'll let you know right away." Marko kissed the top of her head, leaving Julia numb to the core of her soul.

CHAPTER 26

Georgie checked her phone once more to see if Alex had responded. She hoped that no news was good news. How she ached to share her successes with him, and right now, she was on a roll with her teaching.

She had another collaborative IEP meeting with Lilliana, feeling calmer, more confident, and more organized as the days went by. Georgie and Lilliana contacted a few thankful parents about student concerns and averted a few student issues. Even her doctor's appointment went fabulously! Some blood work improved, and her response to the shots was successful. Thankfully, she was adjusting to her new life.

As she welcomed students for her last period class, she was surprised Lilliana wasn't there. Her co-worker was definitely in today. This class, more than any other, had several challenging students, one of whom was classified with Tourette's syndrome. It was Lilliana who always did a beautiful job keeping this particular student-focused, having implemented a superb behavioral plan. He was not her biggest concern since two other students were already becoming the bullies of the grade. Leaving them alone for one moment could manifest from a small rainstorm of teasing into a tsunami of insults. She gulped hard as she glanced at her seating chart to check attendance. There was still no Lilliana in sight.

Georgie was startled when Jose walked in behind the students carrying his laptop. Georgie immediately grasped her silver pen extra tight as she thought about what to do first. He walked around, looking closely at each student's desk as the bell rang. Georgie pursed her lips when she realized she was still alone, but she was determined to shine. "Good afternoon, Mr. Gonzalez. Welcome to Grade 8 English." She gathered her class roster along with her plan book and gave it to him for the surprise observation. Other than Lilliana, she had not heard of anyone in the school getting observed so far this year by Jose.

Georgie started the class. "Boys and girls, we will be journaling for the first five minutes, then we'll continue our reading of *Strange Case of Dr. Jekyll and Mr. Hyde.* You all know your groups, along with the comprehension questions, so let's get started!"

The class loved the story as did Georgie's other classes. She paid particularly close attention to her classified students, working double-time to ensure their needs were met. The students who were her biggest concern were helping their groups finish their work, so were fully engaged in discussions. Georgie was shocked to hear herself praise them for their insights since she had never seen them this engaged!

Midway through the lesson, as she monitored all on-task student behavior, she bit her lip holding back a laugh. The kids thought Jose was there to watch them, not her! *They were afraid of him.* Before Georgie knew it, the bell rang, causing her to silently cheer. "Great job, everyone. Have a fabulous weekend!" Most kids replied in unison, with a sing-song response of, "You too, Ms. Nelson." She covered a giggle, for this was *not* how they *usually* responded. Georgie felt they all deserved an A for effort today!

Jose left like the last gust of wind after a hurricane, leaving her materials on the back chair. After all the students had gone, she took out a piece of paper to document the observation. She knew she had done the best job she could do, but also knew he would find fault in everything.

Lilliana rushed in and closed the door fast. "What the hell was that?"

Georgie glared at her. "Thankfully, a solid lesson. Where were you? I followed your guidance with the classified students, how you model working with them. It worked out, but you should have let me know you weren't coming. It was against the law not to have support for the kids you are responsible for!" She slammed the desk with her hand in anger.

Lilliana put her hands on her hips. "Jose told me to go to another class for this period. There was an emergency needing coverage. Trust me; I sat in the library with two kids working on the computer. *Emergency, my ass. What could I do?* I texted you the minute he placed me there."

Georgie grabbed her phone and saw the text from Lilliana precisely as she claimed. Georgie threw the phone in her bag, trying to take in a few breaths to calm herself. Rummaging through her giant backpack, she found a bottle of water, opened it, and gulped down nearly half the bottle. Leaning against the desk, she took in more deep breaths.

Georgie could feel the flush from her neck up to her face. Pouring some water into her hands, she dabbed it on her neck, hoping to calm the heat. Looking at the time, she realized she had missed her afternoon shot since she had been so busy with other things. "Some days, I just can't win."

Lilliana moved toward her with a soft tone. "You want me to document what happened?"

Georgie pondered for a moment then shrugged her shoulders, "It won't do any harm, thanks. I know I'm screwed."

Lilliana took a desk in the corner, opened her laptop, and started to type. Several times she glanced at Georgie but found nothing coming out of her mouth.

Georgie needed to go to the restroom and carried her bag so she could give herself her injection. She hoped it would cool her flush. She was getting better at taking the doses and could do them in no time. Returning to her classroom, Lilliana continued to type cursing in Spanish under her breath. Georgie took another sip of water and clicked on her emails. She found, along with a few parent emails, Jose's request for a post-conference meeting Monday afternoon in his office. She slammed her laptop shut, "Shit!"

═╬ ╬═

Julia was on her way to Alex's classroom to make sure Angelina had control of the kids, which was never easy in the last period of the day on a Friday. Peering in the door, she saw all the students in their seats working. She beamed at the sight when Julia's cell phone buzzed. Frowning at the unknown number, she ducked into the empty stairwell. "Hello, this is Julia Bradley?"

After a slight pause, she heard the soft voice of a stranger, "This is Charles Williams, Alex's brother." There was silence for a few seconds. "I'm sorry to tell you... but... Alex passed away a few minutes ago. We knew the surgery would be difficult for him, but it was much worse than the doctors expected."

Julia gasped for air. She shook her head. "I... I... am so sorry. I have no words to say how sorry I am." And she covered her mouth with her hand.

Charles spoke slowly, his voice breaking. "I know. It was bad. Thankfully, he did not suffer. He doesn't - didn't - want a big funeral or anything. He was clear. We had some time to talk about things, thanks to Marko's help. He wanted to treat everyone to a party at Rosie's - does that make sense? We didn't have a big family. The school, all the kids, you guys, were really his family." Julia could hear him on the other end of the line as he blew his nose.

She grabbed a tissue from her pocket to dab her eyes, asking, "I will share this with everyone, if you don't mind?"

Charles sighed. "Yes. I will text you the details for his wake. Ha! Leave it to him to want a bar party." Charles took some more deep breaths. "Julia, he had some wishes I need to share with you at a later time. He wants Marko to handle things. He trusts you to honor them."

Julia continued to cry, blotting away her tears. "I will... will do whatever he wants. I promise. I will let everyone know when you share his plans with me. Charles, I'm so sorry." She paused to take a few more deep breaths.

"Oh, Julia, he wanted me to talk to a teacher, Georgie Nelson. Would you know where I can find her or what is the best time to contact her? I guess you're still in school."

Julia swallowed hard. "Of course. Give me a few minutes. I'll call you on my number with Georgie. She's with students right now." Ending the call, Julia nearly collapsed. To straighten her mind, she sat on a step, staring ahead at nothing in particular. There had been some bad days at Eden Hills, but this was the worst one for her.

When she walked to her office, she called Tiffany aside. "I need you to make an announcement. We will be having an emergency staff meeting today after school. All are required to attend, but first, page Georgie in her classroom. Tell her to come to see me immediately and to bring her things." Tiffany opened her mouth, but Julia walked away too fast for any further discussion. Julia had to call Dr. Salva, but first, she needed to hear a caring voice, so the minute she had privacy in her office she texted. Her phone rang immediately. Shutting her moist eyes tight, she answered the phone and heard Marko's voice say, "Talk to me."

⚔️

Jose was in his office, working on Georgie's evaluation when he heard her paged to the main office. His body tense, spit flying out of his mouth, he confronted Tiffany, "What's going on with Georgie?"

Tiffany shrugged, "Not sure. Julia wants her to come to her office. I guess she is going home right after the bell."

Jose sneered. *Another perk of being the prized pupil.* His cell phone rang as he glanced at his watch. "Yes, I'm running a few minutes late. Tell them I'll be at my son's IEP meeting. I am well prepared with a list of things we need to discuss as he transitions out of high school. Have some good ideas about what he can do based on his interests. We've talked about it for the past week. I'm leaving school now." He put his computer off and took his keys. "I appreciate all you do for him." His face beamed with joy. "He's thriving! You always know I'm available for his needs. See you in a few."

As Jose walked out of the building to his car, he noticed no one around. Strolling over to Georgie's car, which was closer to his than he liked, Jose walked to the side of her vehicle. He had envisioned this moment for weeks, nearly foaming at the mouth. Gripping his key, Jose pressed the sharp end against the door. He could feel the adrenaline pumping as he started to drag it the length of the driver's side.

"Jose!"

He was startled to hear his name. Jose shoved the car key into his pants pocket, gripping it tightly. Turning, he saw Tiffany waving him back to the building.

"Julia sent me after you! She needs you in the auditorium for an emergency meeting. It's going to last ten minutes." Tiffany stood there, waiting for him to return.

Laughing with an edge, Jose jabbed the key into the side of his leg through the pant pocket. He was furious at being interrupted.

As he stomped back to the building, he snipped, "I have a meeting, Tiffany. It better not be long." And storming past her, he went back inside. If looks could kill, poor Tiffany would have been lying in a pool of blood.

⚔️ ⚔️

As the final bell of the day rang Julia, holding the phone against her chest after hanging up with Dr. Salva, prepared herself for one of the most challenging announcements in her career. Guzzling a bottle of water, she paced the room while waiting for Georgie to appear. Looking in the mirror, she attempted to put on a little lipstick and fix her hair, but instead, she stared into space, praying for strength.

A knock at the door made her jump. She swallowed hard, calling out, "Come in."

Georgie's eyebrows were drawing together. "Julia, you wanted to see me. Is something wrong?"

Julia did not reply so Georgie bit her lip as she made the call. "I have Georgie with me here." She passed her cell over to Georgie. Her head flinched back slightly at Julia's blank stare.

Nodding, Georgie looked at her jumping foot, shaking her head… Then silence, followed by gasps. No air. Julia held her hand as Georgie took in deep breaths.

"Th… thank you… for personally letting me know. I'm deeply touched. I'm so sorry." Georgie pressed the power button off and covered her mouth with her hand. Sitting limply, she swallowed hard, looking away from Julia as the tears fell.

Julia handed her a tissue, rubbing her back. She sipped some water but not too much, otherwise she feared she would be sick. She sat, swishing it around several times.

Finally, Julia knelt to meet Georgie's eyes. Her voice was quivering, "Alex wanted Charles to tell you himself. You had become very special to him in such a short time."

Georgie's gaze was unfocused as she whispered, "I knew he was sick, but... I never got to say goodbye. I texted him over and over. I thought he was, well... I was confused."

"You're not alone." Julia felt as if time was slowing down. "He was a very private person. We go way, way back, Georgie." She rubbed the back of her neck. "He was the first person to appear when we had staff, parents, even student tragedies. I always relied on Alex."

Rising, Julia took out two small bottles of water from her small refrigerator in the corner of her office. Handing one to Georgie, Julia called her name several times before taking hold of her hand and carefully placing the bottle in it, helping her hold it for a moment. Shaking her head side to side as if woken up from a nightmare, Georgie recognized the bottle, nodded, opened it, and sipped a little. Then she poured some water on her hand to rub on her rosy cheeks and neck, hoping for some relief.

Julia's phone buzzed on her desk. She walked over and read the text. "Georgie, I'm sorry, but I need to share this with the rest of the staff. Why don't you sit here for as long as you like? You can use the side door to slip out when you're ready."

"I need some time to gather my thoughts; if that is all right? Thank you... for letting me leave from here. I wouldn't want anyone to see... well, to see how gutted I am." She sobbed into her tissue again.

Julia drank the entire bottle of water, tossing the empty bottle in the garbage can. "Call me if you want to talk, please."

Georgie sniffed, "May I ask a favor? If I come to the building over the weekend, can I still get in?"

Julia stopped, tilted her head. "Yes, your key works for the entrances, but..."

Georgie gathered her things. "Good. That's all I wanted to know. In case I want to keep busy and do some work or something." Her movements lacked energy.

"See how you feel." Julia placed her arm across her body, holding it with her other arm. "We all have to deal with this in our own way."

⫘ ⫘

By the time Georgie got home, she had received at least ten texts from her colleagues, all checking on her, and offering dinner or drinks at Rosie's. As she reviewed them, she knew there was only one place she wanted to be. That was home. Entering the house, she threw her bags on the couch, kicked off her shoes, then walked the two short blocks to the place she had been spending much of her time with Alex - the beach. Georgie sat on the dunes, the wind whipping through her hair, staying there until the moon and stars danced above in the heavens.

Since starting at Eden Hills, Georgie had not had a chance to stop moving or to sit still. Without her friend and mentor, Alex, would she make it through the school year at Eden Hills? *Was teaching the worst decision of her life?* As the evening chill became colder, Georgie staggered back to her house, only to find an enormous box on her doorstep.

She walked up the steps, confident the box had been mistakenly delivered to the wrong house. That was until she saw her name and address on the label. She could barely lift the box, so she kicked it through the door into her living room. Baffled by the delivery, she took a knife from the wooden block on her kitchen counter and slit the package open. She read the name of the sender, tasting stomach acids in her mouth: Alex Williams. With a sigh of relief, she whispered, "He remembered me after all."

Hugging herself, she left the box. Her head was spinning like a tornado. She was not in the mood to go through the box tonight. She needed some rest, so went off to bed, sleeping 'til the crack of dawn.

⫘ ⫘

Saturday morning, Julia was working in her office yet again, desperate to be busy. Being a little hungover from drinking several bottles of wine with Marko, and reminiscing about Alex, had left her feeling empty. This was when she did her most exceptional work. She needed something tedious instead of further dissertation research. For the next few hours, she reviewed videotape surveillance from the camera she had secretly positioned in Renata's office. She was determined to find the culprit trying to break into the medicine cabinet. Since nothing was stolen yet, it was low hanging fruit compared to the countless suspension write-ups monopolizing most of her precious time. Ten minutes into reviewing the videos, her phone buzzed. She grabbed it, recognizing the name, "How are you?"

Georgie's voice was shaky. "Who is Marko Medrano? Where can I find him? I need to speak to him."

Julia ran her hands through her hair. "Say nothing else over the phone. Text me your address. Marko and I will be with you in no time."

CHAPTER 27

"I don't understand why Alex would send these to me," asked Georgie, shrugging as she pointed to the piles of copied documents sat on the kitchen table. "I've skimmed through them, but I have no idea why he kept them for so long or why he sent them to me."

Marko, writing notes on his paper pad, looked up at Georgie with a warm smile. "He trusted you and thought you might be able to do something. Perhaps finish what he started."

"Marko, this is all information about several companies we have used in the district for years," Julia told him. "I would have to check the board minutes. It may take a long time!"

"Well, I can alleviate some of the work for you, so don't worry. I can look at my files to compare the information and go over it with a fine-tooth comb."

Georgie shook her head. "No offense, but if he sent them to me, I don't want them out of my sight. I want to keep them here. He knew both of you much longer than me. But, if he wanted you to have them to keep them safe, then surely he would have sent them to you."

Julia sipped her green tea. "Georgie, you are one hundred percent right. All I can think is that Alex blamed his illness on the poor work conditions from when we first started." She shook her head, "But I didn't think he was obsessed with it to this level!"

Georgie shrugged her shoulders. "Whatever happened to the companies?"

Julia rubbed her eyes. "They never changed. We still use them and will continue using them. I am sure of it. Dr. Salva is putting together another referendum for more construction in the coming year since we need more space. Between Alex and me, we have *tried* to keep the custodians in line, but, if I am honest, there are blips all the time."

Marko tapped his fingers on the table. "We've been at this for hours. Let's take a break. I will review my old records since some of these documents are from when I was the board attorney. I don't want to approach the new board attorney to alert her so this needs to stay between the three of us. Agreed?"

Julia and Georgie spoke at the same time. "Agreed."

Georgie walked them to the door. "I'm thankful to you both for coming. I was at a loss for what to do with this, but I think right now, I will keep them safe in his memory."

Julia rubbed Georgie's arm, "Try to get some rest. If I can think of anything else, I'll let you know."

Marko shook Georgie's hand. "It's a pleasure meeting you. I have your and Julia's best interests at heart, I promise. I spoke to Alex in the hospital. I can assure you he wanted me to follow through with all of these items he sent you."

Georgie watched them drive away before deciding to go for another walk on the beach. Putting her headphones on, and still feeling perplexed about the box, she found her walk unsteady at first. Alex had trusted her with something he considered valuable. While she was lost in thought, listening to the jazz greats Alex had told her about, it drowned out the sound of the mail carrier calling her name. He was holding a thin, flat priority package. With Georgie well on her way to the beach, the mail carrier slipped it into her mail slot.

It was dark by the time Georgie returned to the house. Countless texts from Lilliana as well as Renata's messages were helpful but not what she wanted. Georgie needed to be alone. As she opened her door, she slipped, losing her balance, not seeing the package on the floor.

"Shit, I almost broke my neck!" Grabbing the flat package, she threw it on top of the other mail she had received. "These crappy medical bills will have to wait until another day. Too damn depressing. I can't handle one more thing, I swear."

Sundays were usually lesson planning days for Georgie since she had started working at Eden Hills. Instead, she decided to see her father in the nursing home.

Darryl, the tall, middle-aged aide in a baggy white uniform, escorted Georgie to her father's room. He filled her in on her father. "He had a tough day earlier this week but slept a lot yesterday, so he seems calmer today. Any time there is a medication adjustment, well, you know how it goes by now."

"Yes. I received your texts and emails. I'm sorry I have not been here as much as I used to. New job and all."

Darryl walked with a limp, "How is teaching going? Love it, I hope?"

"Oh, yes. The kids are great."

Daryl stopped at the door. "As I said he's having a pretty good day today. Just watching mass, as usual. Enjoy your visit, honey."

Georgie nodded, "Great to see you again. It's good to be back hanging out with Dad." She winked at Darryl. Walking into his compact room, she carried a dainty bouquet of pink roses. Always looking carefully to make sure the space was clean, she was pleased to see the room perfectly organized and smelling fragrant. She inhaled the scent of her dad's favorite soap as it brought back fun, happy occasions. She saw the older gray-haired male version of herself, only much frailer. Her father's glasses were thicker than she remembered. Wearing a white shirt and black pants with matching slippers, her father almost looked as he had when he was at their house, yet not exactly. As Georgie approached her father, her heart danced, "Hello, Dad. Good to see you."

He rapidly blinked his green, empty eyes. "Hello! Nice to see you. Would you like to watch mass with me?" This was one of the few sentences in her father's repertoire.

Georgie missed his voice. "I would love to. I brought you your favorite flowers. Do you like them?"

Her father repeated the phrase he had told her since she was a little girl, "You shouldn't have, but I am glad you did!" They both laughed with the same giggle as if it was the first time.

Georgie took the empty vase, unwrapped the flowers from the packaging, and placed them inside. She moved the vase to the windowsill in the corner where her father could see it from his chair and his bed. "There you go. Now the place looks much handsomer, just like you!"

Her father beamed and pointed to the chair next to him. "Come sit and watch mass with me. The priest is nice."

Georgie sat and pulled the chair a little closer to her dad. He leaned toward her and smiled, "May I hold your hand while we watch?" Her father held out his tiny wrinkled, boney, cold hand toward Georgie.

"I would love that." Georgie gulped back a tear. She lovingly, and peacefully, watched her father stare at the TV for the duration of the visit, never letting go of his hand.

⚔⚔

As she got into her car to leave the nursing home, her phone rang, jolting her back to reality. Renata was on the other end. "I wanted to see how you were feeling. Been a freaking awful time for you."

Georgie sniffed her hands, which still smelt of her dad's scent. "Exhausted, but I do feel better, so I guess I need the medicine. I have to say, I didn't realize how rotten I felt, until now. How are you doing?"

"Worked a long shift in the ER yesterday. Spending some quality time with my family today. It's times like this we need to appreciate every moment with those we love."

"I feel the same way. I visited my father, and it warmed my heart."

"Good, I'm glad."

Georgie mustered some confidence to ask Renata another favor. "Not wanting to drag you into anything, but I have a post-conference with Jose tomorrow. I know it won't be good. Would you mind coming with me, as a witness?" Her voice broke. "If Alex was here... well, I don't want to meet with Jose alone."

"Sure thing. Do you think you have anything to worry about?"

Starting her car, Georgie said, "I sure do. Not going in there alone, I'm telling you. Getting ready for yet another rebuttal, too. At this point, I'm not even sure teaching is for me."

"*Are you kidding me?* I hear what the kids are saying, who they like, who they avoid, which is why most of them are in my office at certain periods. Georgie, *they love you.* Don't let Jose run you out of town. He has done that to enough good people. You're stronger than he is."

"How many staff members has this happened to?" Georgie's mouth opened and closed.

"Let's see, last year four people left because of him. The prior year, three teachers. It could be more, but those are the staff members who spoke to me personally. This is my tenure year, so I have to be careful. It's not like I could tell Julia everything about the staff - I am *their* peer, and Julia is my boss. I'm not even sure if Julia knows the extent of the bullying, but hey, when you work with the superintendent's son-in-law, you have to be careful. Julia has been sitting on him more this year, but Jose is a tough guy to please."

"Well, at least I know I will not be alone. The post-conference is after school tomorrow at 3:15. You don't have to say a word. Just witness the insanity." Georgie chuckled.

Renata growled, "Fine by me. Try to get some rest so you are fresh for tomorrow. I assume we'll hear more about Alex's memorial this week too. I heard Rosie's is involved, so Alex is getting his way!"

Georgie had only a few more blocks until she was home, which was good as both women were laughing to the point of tears. "No, kidding. It doesn't even feel like he's gone. Renata, you have been a terrific confidante. Without you..."

Renata pleaded, "Hey, I know many people are in your corner, including Lilliana. She has a good heart, but she's young and still green. My humble opinion is she's only making it because of you. Jose gave her a hard time while you were out to make sure Angelina looked good. She did a lot of extra work Angelina should have been doing. She did the best she could."

Georgie's mouth dropped. "She never told me."

"Lilliana didn't want to worry you, but the day you came back, she was like a different person."

"I had no idea." Georgie bit her lip.

Renata's words were garbled, "Hey, have to run. Glad you answered my call. We are all devastated about Alex, so we have to take one day at a time. Until tomorrow."

As Georgie parked her car outside the house, her phone buzzed with a text message. *Please confirm you received two packages. I sent them separately to you by accident. Charles Williams.*

Georgie darted into the house to find the second package.

CHAPTER 28

Lilliana was already pacing the classroom when Georgie walked in Monday morning. "Georgie, you didn't answer my texts or my calls. I am so sorry about Friday. You have to believe me. And Alex... no words..."

Georgie closed the door behind her. She did not make eye contact with Lilliana. "Listen, I needed some time to regroup a bit." She put her things on her desk. "I received your email explaining about being reassigned on Friday, thanks. I'll print that out." She shrugged her shoulders, "It might come in handy when Jose comes after me today at the post-conference."

Lilliana leaned on the desk. "I agree. I've been worried all weekend! I wanted to speak to you." Lilliana adjusted the black belt on her black dress. "I can only imagine how you must be feeling."

Georgie's stomach was cramping, and she was feeling nauseous. She had not felt this bad since she started the shots. "I had a lot to think about this weekend. Everything I learned from Alex was running through my head." Georgie took a hesitant step toward Lilliana. "He and I talked a lot about teaching." Her eyes welled up. "Anyway, we are here for one job only; to educate the kids in the best way possible. You and I have hit some major hurdles but are still doing a pretty damn good job with them. I think we need to focus on the kids and what goes on inside this room. Understand?"

Lilliana's eyes pleaded. "I'm in. You must know that, *por favor.*"

Georgie felt a lightness in her chest. "We have to keep moving forward. Today is a big day for me."

"Do you want to rehearse a little for your post-conference during our prep time? It might help?" Lilliana reached out to touch Georgie's arm.

Georgie shook her head. She had lost a lot of sleep last night mentally preparing for Jose. Taking some materials out of her bag, she put her shoulders back, head high. "I want to focus on the kids. I submitted the plans for the next two weeks already, and we also have an IEP meeting soon. That is what I want to talk about, nothing else today. Got it?"

"*Sí* understood." Lilliana nodded and handed Georgie the IEP paperwork for the meeting. "I made you a copy so we can go over it before the meeting another day." She stood, watching and waiting.

Georgie glanced at Lilliana's work, which was thorough. "You know, this is amazing."

Lilliana bowed her head. "That means a lot coming from you. I learn from you every day, you know. If you don't want to stay in Eden Hills, I understand, but don't let Jose ruin a good thing for you... for us... for the kids. We're doing good work here in Eden Hills, aside from all his bullshit."

Georgie smiled before walking over, pulling out a student's work sample. "See this essay? This was a student who could barely write a paragraph. Now he is writing three paragraphs, on topic! He was a D student last year. Now, with our help, he is meeting with success. That's why I'm here. Is this why you are here?"

"Of course."

Georgie gave Lilliana a wink. "We have five minutes until we have to continue looking mean. How about we greet the kids at the door *together,* so we start the week off on the right foot? It's what Alex would want."

"Let's do this!" announced Lilliana, high fiving her teaching partner.

⟩⟨⟩⟨⟩

During lunch duty, Georgie was usually the one hiding from Jose but not today. She strolled around the cafeteria, holding her hands loosely behind her back. As Jose walked in to monitor the lunchroom, he could not help but notice that Georgie was in the right place at the right time, yet again. He chatted with a few students before approaching her. Adjusting his glasses, "Reminder, today in my office, 3:15."

"3:15 it is," Georgie looked him straight in the eye. Then, spotting a group of girls using loud shrieking voices, she approached them with a low tone, "Hey, guys, what did you do this weekend?" The students' voices dropped to a reasonable decibel level as they took turns sharing their stories. Walking away from the group, she looked around casually for Jose, who was nowhere to be found. Lilliana caught her eye and gave Georgie the thumbs up.

⚔️

Since Georgie had a free period next, she decided to stop by Alex's room. It was empty with the lights off. Putting her hand on the doorknob, she was pleased to see it was open. Leaving the lights off, she sat at Alex's desk, hoping it would channel some of his wisdom. She even sniffed around for a faint smell of his scent. Speaking in a low voice, she choked back a whimper. "Alex, I hope I make you proud this afternoon."

After the last bell rang for the day, Georgie's stomach was cramping, and she was barely able to stand for a few moments. Lilliana was concerned. "Are you alright? Want me to get you anything? Call Renata?"

Shaking her head, Georgie put a mint in her mouth since it sometimes helped. "No, I'm good. Heading to see Renata anyway."

"Text me and let me know how your post-conference goes; if you want to. *Buena suerte*," Lilliana cheered.

Georgie could not even think that far ahead as she walked to the elevator. Her stomach was cramped severely. She was afraid to walk too much. Slowly, she managed to get to Renata's office, finding her getting ready for the post-conference. "Since the kids have gone, may I use your restroom before we meet with Jose?"

Renata pointed to the empty bathroom. Georgie took her bag with her so she could give herself a shot before the meeting. Since stress was a trigger for Georgie, she figured this would be the perfect time to take it.

As she took the cap off the needle, squeezing her left outer leg for some flesh, she heard Julia walk into the office.

Julia stuttered, "Well kinda good news! It took me hours reviewing the camera footage, but I've figured out who is trying to pry the lock open. I'll take care of it *immediately*."

"Good thing you placed a camera there a few weeks ago. It was a big relief, knowing you were watching things when I was not here. That was genius!" Renata bowed to Julia.

"Well, we have cameras all over the building - why not where we have controlled substances? Truthfully, I didn't even realize how many meds you had stored here, Renata. Adderall, Strattera, Concerta; all are no joke! I shared what we did with the other principals. They're all considering adding a camera. Can't be too careful these days." Julia rubbed her hands together.

Georgie added some lipstick, eye shadow, and then tossed her hair as she finished in the bathroom. She hoped her face had stopped flushing for the meeting but felt that was the least of her problems.

As she opened the door, Julia was surprised to see her. "Georgie? How are you?"

"Well, Julia, I'm not sure if I should ask you, but I have my post-conference with Jose. I have asked Renata to be part of it as a witness."

Julia braced herself. "What time is the meeting?"

"In a few minutes."

"I will pop by to see if Jose wants me present as well. Might be best." Let me get a jump on that." And off she went.

Renata looked at Georgie. "You are flushing. Are you doing all right?"

Georgie felt her cheeks were hot. "No, but I want this post-conference thing over with. You ready to go?"

Renata double-checked the locks on the cabinets then rattled her keys. "This time, I want to make sure I lock everything possible! Let's do this!"

※+ +※

At 3:15, the small conference room was full. Renata sat next to Georgie on one side of the table with Julia next to Jose on the other. Georgie placed her lesson plan book and attendance book on the table along with a blank piece of paper, her lucky Cross pen in hand. In her bag, was her phone. Before walking into the room, she had pressed the 'record' button. She most definitely wanted a recording of the meeting. Renata also had a notebook, as requested by Georgie.

Jose had two copies of the observation facing down. He began the meeting. "Before we start, since you have representation, Julia offered, and I invited her to witness the post-conference as well. Do you have any objection?"

Georgie looked at Julia, who slyly winked at her. "No, not at all."

He continued, "Georgie, last Friday, period eight, I observed you during your English class. Why don't you tell me how you think things went?"

Georgie's mouth was bone dry. As much as she prepared for the meeting, she forgot to bring a bottle of water. Licking her lips, desperate to get some sort of moisture, she found a little mint and shoved it under her tongue. "I had thirty-seven students in the class. Five were classified. As you can read from my lesson plans, we accomplished the goals and objectives of the lesson. I began with a journal exercise then transitioned the group to small groups, reading the novel along with students completing the assignment for comprehension questions."

Gasping for air, all eyes remained on her. "The small groups discussed the questions, then wrote responses after they agreed on their answers. This allowed the students to read, review, and synthesize their understanding of the material at a higher comprehension level."

She shifted slightly in her chair, remaining focused on Jose's glaring eyes behind his foggy glasses. "As they worked, I rephrased some of the information to two of the classified students who needed modification as per their IEP." Her posture was tight as she used her hands naturally. She was on a roll. "I think you could see me using gestures to help the students with attentional issues to keep them focused. When I checked their answers to assess their understanding, the groups had done an outstanding job."

Georgie grinned from ear to ear. "I was pleased with the lesson…"

Jose cut her off. "I completely disagree," He crossed his arms. "I saw students with IEPs looking off, not able to keep the pace at all. I *did not* see their work modified. One student with Tourette's syndrome was disruptive. You never corrected him!"

Georgie rubbed her moist palms on her pants. "I work closely with the in-class support teacher every day. First, we purposefully ignore his noises, so as not to embarrass him. Secondly, it's to help him be the role model for the other students as he is an A student. His noises have lessened since the beginning of the year. Since we are not adding to the stress by singling him out or drawing attention to him, he has come a long way. The group we have him working with are wonderful kids. In fact, they were the first group to finish my assignment. I was proud of him, and of his group especially." Georgie flipped her hair back. "I have email correspondences with his parents, who are thrilled with his work this year! Happy to forward them to you."

Jose covered his mouth. "We can agree to disagree with what happened. Classroom management was an issue. Behavioral issues were a problem. The pace of the lesson was too slow." Shaking his head, he shot a look at Julia. "I found there was no individualized differentiation for all levels of students. To boot, assessments were not conducted at all." Jose's brow started to sweat a little.

Georgie calmly opened her plan book. "Here in my lessons, I have the areas highlighted where I differentiate for student needs. See?" She pointed so Jose and Julia could look more closely. "Also, in front of the plan book, I have a behavioral management system for two students who have had a history of disruptive behavior. They met their goals."

She turned to the page with the plans, again showing Jose. "Regarding the pace of the lesson, I segmented the lesson as noted in the plans." Once more, Georgie showed Jose with Julia glancing. "Regarding the assessments, I collected the students' work after we reviewed the answers. Here are the short answers." Georgie spread them out on the table for Jose to see. "Over the weekend, I reviewed the student responses, finding 98 percent of the students were proficient, which I put in the grading database system in a timely fashion."

Jose moved in his seat slightly. "We saw two different lessons. Anything more to add?"

"I have to say how disappointed I was to have Lilliana pulled out of my class to cover another class at the last minute. Leaving the class non-compliant is not fair for the classified students. Lilliana has taught me a great deal about special education. I have already emailed the supervisor of special education with my concerns. The students' needs, as mandated by their IEP, were not met due to administrative decisions."

"Are you saying *I am to blame* for you not meeting the student's needs?" demanded Jose.

Georgie swallowed hard again. "Mr. Gonzalez, you told Lilliana to cover two students in the library instead of servicing her five students in my class. Fortunately, we collaborate on plans so I am well-versed in their individual needs. I believe I achieved this despite the last-minute change to her schedule."

By now, Georgie's neck was purple, and her leg was jumping wildly. No one moved until Jose handed Georgie her observation. Worse than she expected. Her career was in serious jeopardy. Georgie gasped and closed her eyes tight for a moment. "Two's? I expected fours or fives as I received in my first observation."

"We all have bad days, Georgie," Jose laughed sarcastically. "Friday wasn't one of *your* finest days."

Her voice deepened, her pulse speeding. "What can I do to change your mind? To change these scores?"

Jose pushed his chair out, starting to stand. "Write a rebuttal."

Georgie pointed to his empty chair. "I would respectfully ask you to sit back down. I'm not done."

Jose continued to stand. "Well, I am done. This is my meeting."

Georgie glared at him as she took out a folder, placing it in front of him. "I told you *I am not done.*"

Jose grunted. "What, you've written the rebuttal already?"

"Not quite. Take... a look..." And her finger trembled to point to the folder.

Jose opened it, fell into his chair, holding the documents. He read them with his teeth clenching, lips quivering. Julia looked over his shoulder, her eyebrows raised as Jose whispered, "Where did you get these?"

Georgie felt a rushing sound in her ears from her heart beating so fast. "Alex was concerned about Angelina, especially when she attempted to post photos of *my* students on the Internet. I guess when he looked at the multitudes of photos on her social media, he became increasingly concerned."

Julia took the papers from Jose, spreading them out on the table, "What are these, Jose? Police reports? DUI reports? Arrest warrant?"

Jose leaned back in his seat, not responding. Finally, he blurted out, "It's all a lie."

Georgie stood with her hands on her hips. "Is it all a lie, Jose? Look closely at her fingerprints, you will see, as Alex discovered, they are, in fact, your wife's fingerprints. Now, why would that be? Answer - well, since your daughter has two DUIs, received while at college, it makes her ineligible to work here, or in fact, *at any school.*" Georgie placed her hands on the table, leaning closer to his face. "Alex, in doing more investigating, also discovered that her teaching license, and even the transcripts are, in fact, all doctored documents!"

Georgie separated the piles. "Let's look. On the left are your daughter's real documents; on the right the fraudulent ones. *She should never have been allowed to work with any children.* Especially near my students! You," she pointed her finger at Jose's face, "have never given me a chance while I've been here. Never! I didn't know I had been given your daughter's job until weeks after I started." Shaking her head, she had her hands over her heart. "I've done nothing but the best I could do, and you have made me suffer because of it."

Suddenly she slammed her hands on the table. "You will change my observation report or... I will release all of these online! Do you know what will happen if I do? *Your* future, and *your precious daughter's* future will be ruined!"

Julia was speechless. Her body was tense, her nostrils flaring as she first looked at Georgie, then at Jose. "Is all this true, Jose?"

When he did not respond, Julia took a flash drive from her pocket, throwing it on the table in front of Jose. "It seems you have lost your tongue, Jose. Well, let me help you. I also have evidence about Angelina." She sat next to him, trying to make eye contact. However, Jose looked away. "It seems it is she who has been trying to break into Renata's medical cabinet to access the students' medicine! Now, what do you have to say?" Julia demanded, "I want your resignation… immediately!"

Jose's eyes shot daggers at Georgie. Renata was shaking, both hands covering her mouth as she gasped.

Jose pleaded with Julia, "Don't call the police on Angelina. She knows nothing about what I did." Wiping his brow and upper lip with a tissue from his pocket, he took his glasses off. Wiping the grime off them, he placed them back on his face, slightly crooked. With a cocky grin, he laughed, "You'll get my resignation, but I am not going away quietly." He chuckled, "Do you think I did all this on my own? It wasn't my idea. Not in the least."

Then swallowing hard, he tore Georgie's observations with two slow, deliberate crisp rips.

Georgie's eyes went upward, looking heavenward. She bit her lips to keep from smiling.

Wrinkling her nose, Julia's eyes appeared dead. "Jose, we need to meet privately. We have a lot to discuss, and I don't want two non-tenured teachers involved."

Georgie and Renata shuffled out of the room in silence.

Julia slammed her hands on the table. "*You must be kidding me*! All because Angelina did not get the job?" She bared her teeth. "Try to end the career of a promising young woman before it even started? You. Are. Done."

Jose rubbed the back of his neck, glancing at the exit.

✥ ✥

Returning to the nurse's office, Georgie had no option but to run into the bathroom to puke. Renata randomly picked up items from her desk and put them back while taking deep breaths. After a few minutes, she refocused and called out, "You alright in there?"

As Georgie finally left the bathroom, Renata handed her a can of ginger ale. They sat in silence, each lost in their own thoughts until Georgie covered her mouth, "Whoops." She took out her phone and pressed stop on the recorder.

Renata covered her mouth and jumped up, "You taped all that shit?"

"Every... damn... word of it," said Georgie pursing her lips and closing her eyes.

Renata rubbed her temples. "Do you think he will resign?"

Pulling out another copy of the fraudulent documents, Georgie waved them in the air. "Let's say, damn straight, he will resign."

"Georgie, you were amazing. The composure you had in there was freaking unreal."

Georgie's eyes started to tear. "I'm sorry. I didn't want to drag you into anything, but I needed a witness, just in case." Holding the pages to her chest. "Alex sent this to me over the weekend. Well, his brother did." She pursed her lips. "Alex was concerned, big time, about Angelina and boy, was he right to be."

Georgie flinched when her phone buzzed. It read. *See me.*

⚔⚔

Georgie found Julia alone in the conference room and closed the door. "I'm sorry I did not tell you about the second package," Georgie explained.

Julia chewed on a Pepto Bismol for her upset stomach. "Don't worry, Georgie. I wanted to tell you Jose will be delivering his resignation to me tomorrow. I want to reassure you the observation Jose conducted never happened, and the report will never see the light of day." She glanced at the message on her phone. "Also, he's heading over to Marko's office now."

"Marko's office? I don't understand," Georgie tapped her finger to her lips.

Julia leaned in. "Keep the box of Alex's materials locked in your home. This is going to blow up... and fast. You have no idea what you have done! I don't know what more I can say other than I am sorry you have had such a hard time from him. But you don't have to worry about him any longer."

Georgie felt sick to her stomach again. "Will Dr. Salva be upset with me?"

"Don't worry about Dr. Salva." Julia's hands trembled. "Now go home, and please keep things quiet. Renata, too, please. Tomorrow will be an interesting day."

"Oh, and I will email you the audio I took of the meeting." Georgie waved her cell phone. "Never can be too careful!" With a slow smile, Julia nodded.

Instead of heading home, Georgie went back upstairs, carrying her pocketbook. She had one more task to do.

Julia was unsure if she needed water, wine, or what. Maybe Marko could help her decide, but for now, it was imperative she write everything she could remember from the meeting. Just as she held a pen, her phone buzzed. With one glance, she was as happy as a child on Christmas morning! She pressed play, still in disbelief, as she listened to Georgie's audio file while taking notes. Thanks to Georgie, her documentation would be tight.

＝⊰⊱＝

Although exhausted, Georgie turned the door handle to Alex's room, locked the door behind her, and clicked on his computer. She took out an old, tattered manila folder from her pocketbook and list of all of Alex's computer codes. Next, she took out a zip drive from her wallet and plugged it into his computer. As soon as she saw the icon on the screen, she clicked it. Six folders were listed for her to attach to the email: construction contracts, custodial contracts, purchase orders, air quality reports, email correspondences, medical reports. It seemed only fitting that she would send the documents to the list of people Alex had requested of her, from his computer.

She then attached copies of Jose's fraudulent documents to seal the deal. She typed the addresses of the Eden Hills board members, local state news agencies, and Genny Lee, reporter of educational issues. After she double-checked all the addresses and attachments, with one click of the mouse, it was over. With tears in her eyes, she removed the zip drive and shut down the computer, glancing at her watch. It took less than ten minutes.

She swallowed hard as she read the sticky note written in Alex's handwriting: "It is what it is."

CHAPTER 29

On the eve of Alex's memorial service at Rosie's, Georgie accepted Lilliana and Renata's offer to keep her company at her house. While Renata cooked dinner, Lilliana and Georgie were at the dining room table comparing grades before inputting the data into the grading program for Julia's dissertation.

Lilliana sighed, "I can't believe how far behind I feel."

"We have a few more grades, and then we can start discussing the mid-term examination. Don't worry! We're right on schedule," Georgie reassured her.

"I was at Rosie's last night," Lilliana hid a slight grin. "Everyone is gossiping about Jose. I heard he took his kids and headed to Florida, but every day it's something else."

Renata and Georgie exchanged glances, but as per Julia and Marko's direction, they did not share anything about the post-conference with anyone. Georgie changed the subject, saying, "Let's focus on this, please. I outlined the exam last night. I also received some feedback from the other English teachers, even the curriculum supervisor. She even gave me a sample of last year's exam, so I have a format."

"Great. I can create an exam study guide." Lilliana started to write an outline.

Renata stirred the pot of vegetables humming away on the stove top. "Oh, Daisy and the girls will be here in about a half-hour. They're excited to be at the shore in the fall."

Georgie gave a thumbs up. "I can't wait to meet them. So happy you are all staying over, too. It's like family…" They were interrupted by all their cellphones buzzing with text messages.

Renata grabbed her phone first. "Channel 5 News at 5. Wow, this is coming from the district alert service."

Georgie clicked on the TV, cracking her neck. "What the hell is this for?"

Lilliana guessed. "Maybe Jose is going to jail?"

All three watched the commercial, shaking their heads and shrugging their shoulders. Renata tapped her fingers. "The only time this is used is for snowstorms, hurricanes - you know, major alerts." The grandfather clock in Georgie's hallway began to bong five o'clock as they stared at the television.

⚔ ⚔

Genny Lee was warming up her voice five minutes before the five o'clock news. The petite Korean news anchor, with purple glasses frames and a matching purple blouse, stretched her arms. It was something she always did for good luck before a broadcast. Yawning, she had been working on this story since she received the email a few days ago. Then, when she had received the pile of documents in her mailbox a day later, it had connected all the dots. Her heart raced as she read every page and consulted with the network attorney. They gave her the green light to run with the story. Boy, did she. Genny inquired with many anonymous sources, who all seemed willing to talk off the record about Eden Hills. She hoped this story might get her the recognition she deserved nationally. She knew this would be a game-changing story, so here it was! Primetime!

"Good evening, this is Genny Lee, and this is Channel 5 News. We have an exclusive story this evening, an exposé on Eden Hills Township superintendent, Dr. Jonathan Salva. As per my conversation with the board president of Eden Hills right before airing, he confirmed Dr. Salva had been placed on administrative leave pending investigation on a series of allegations. We have learnt that Dr. Salva has allegedly been taking kickbacks from construction companies doing business with the district for more than twenty-five years. Allegedly, he has received hundreds of thousands of dollars, stock options, silent partnerships, and other financial opportunities tied to his position in the district. Bank statements link him directly to construction companies along with custodial groups awarded contracts within the district."

Genny held a pile of papers. "These documents prove that even though he had full knowledge that the construction projects at Eden Hills Middle School were not being done to state standards, Dr. Salva still supported the bids from the same construction company for *every* district project during his tenure."

Genny threw the papers on the desk. "There is still much to be learned about this story. Dr. Salva has been superintendent through four major construction projects at Eden Hills Middle School. He won superintendent of the year awards two years in a row with his creative methods for fiscal savings. Dr. Salva guaranteed the renovations were environmentally sound; however, unearthed documents now prove the contrary. According to state records of air quality testing, the environmental study results made a dozen recommendations for environmental clean-ups which were never conducted. These documents were received by Dr. Salva as far back as when he was building principal of Eden Hills Middle School, but were buried, and never shared with the board of education or the public."

Genny leaned in closer to the camera lens. "Jose Gonzalez, assistant principal of Eden Hills, in a plea deal, has provided documents proving Dr. Salva's payouts were funneled through the bank accounts of Jose Gonzalez's estranged wife, Maritza Gonzalez, for his entire tenure as superintendent. An arrest warrant has been issued for her. We will be back in sixty seconds after a commercial break."

The light went off the camera, and there was a pregnant pause. Genny sighed as she watched the cameraman, anchors, and interns all shaking their heads. Genny swallowed hard then pinched her lips, saying, "I have heard a lot of things lately, but this is beyond disgusting. Thanks to those brave people who sent me the damning files."

Renata shook her head, staring at the television. "I heard gossip but never expected this to come out!" She shot Georgie a look.

Georgie was biting her lip, trying not to smile. "Some news, huh!"

Lilliana jumped so high, she nearly hit her head on the ceiling fan. "I can't believe it!" Her phone was buzzing on the counter. "Do you guys mind if I get this? My mommy wants to talk about all this!" She ran out of the room, saying to her mother, "*Si*, I saw it! I told you he was a jerk. I told you!"

Renata was beaming with pride. "Holy crap, Georgie. Holy crap! I don't even have to ask you how much you knew because I can see it written all over your face."

Georgie put her finger over her lips. "I must stay silent, but the one thing I want you to know…" She stuttered. "It was all Alex. Dear, dear Alex." She walked over to Renata. "May I have a hug, please? I could use a hug."

They embraced in silence until Renata heard Georgie sobbing. Renata's legs were wobbly as she rubbed Georgie's back. "There, there, Georgie. Let it all out." Renata sighed and whispered, "You have been through a lot! Have yourself a good, long cry." And Renata's eyes were moist too.

Georgie slowly moved away from Renata, walked to the sink, turned on the faucet, and splashed cold water on her face. "I think I need my medicine before we go." Drying her face with the towel, Georgie swallowed hard. "How much time do we have?"

Renata looked at the clock on the stove. "We have another hour. Plenty of time to eat something. You do what you need to do. I'll let you know when dinner is ready."

Lilliana walked back into the kitchen. "Wow, everyone is losing their minds over this." She was shaking her head, putting her phone back in her bag. "Enough of all these people contacting me. We are going to see everyone in a few hours. Carl is going to meet us at the service." She blushed. "We're friends. I know, I know! He has been terrific, helping me avoid Bob and that whole mistake."

Georgie shook her head and sipped some ginger ale to calm her stomach. "Hey, thanks for both coming over before we go. It means a lot to me."

Renata rubbed her hands together. "Are you kidding? Any time I can get to the beach it's a bonus. I talked to Daisy about looking at some places around here. Change of scenery would be nice, especially if I get tenure. It's gorgeous!"

Georgie's voice was soft and gentle. "You are welcome to come any time for a trial run. As you can see, I have plenty of room. You too, Lilliana. It would be nice to have some company."

Lilliana's heart beamed with joy. *"Sí, muchas gracias.* How about we do some work here instead of staying at school all the time? I think maybe we would get more done here than at school."

Georgie hugged Lilliana. "That sounds like a fantastic idea! Mix more pleasure with business. I could use more pleasure these days. I have to go upstairs for an errand. Set the table and start without me. I'll be back in a minute."

Georgie ran upstairs to her bathroom and took out an alcohol pad and syringe with medicine from the medicine cabinet. A gust of air from the open window slammed the bathroom door closed. Georgie dropped the alcohol pad and needle into the sink. She turned and walked over to the window to close it. Slamming it closed, she glanced out at the view of the beach right where she and Alex used to sit and talk on those many, many occasions. Nodding with a smile, she whispered, "I know, I know, you're welcome!"

⇒⊢ ⊣⇐

Marko turned the television off in his massive office conference room. He turned to see Julia's eyes shining and Charles letting out a huge breath. "Thank you, Alex."

Julia pushed her hair back and looked at Charles. "You followed through with Alex's wishes. Now we can have closure for him. He suspected the truth all this time."

Charles bowed his head, holding back tears. "He only trusted Georgie with the documents, Julia. He knew she was strong and had nothing to lose. Without you both, we would still be wondering."

Julia hugged Charles. "Jose had no choice but to turn over what he knew. Thankfully he will *never* be allowed to work in a school again!" She hugged herself. "For the sake of his kids, I hope he has a fresh start."

Marko walked over to shake Charles's hand. "Let's go finish the job. We still have things to do."

⚔ ⚔

The crowd at Rosie's was finally dissipating late into the evening after Alex's memorial. Julia, Marko, and Charles sat at the center table surrounded by mourners. Charles' dark brown eyes looked tired. He was unsure of the last time he had slept a good night since arriving in New Jersey. Meeting practically all of Eden Hills today had certainly kept him going, though.

Georgie kept her distance, sitting with Lilliana, Carl, and Renata. She hoped to meet Charles in person without such an audience, but it was getting late, and she still had to drive home. She whispered to Renata, "I have to speak to Charles. I'll be right back." She mustered the courage and walked over to his table. Charles rose to his feet, rubbing his sweaty hands together. With a warm smile, he shook her hand, taking her arm gently before escorting her to a quieter place in the room.

He kept his hand on her arm. "Georgie Nelson, we finally meet."

She could not help but continue to smile. "Charles Williams, a pleasure to meet you in person." She giggled, "I feel like I know you already, though. We've texted so many times. I am so sorry about Alex." She placed her hand on top of his hand as it rested on the bar.

He nodded. "Me too. Alex and I were able to reconnect at the end, but, well, I'm glad we were able to have some quality time." He glanced around the room. "I appreciate all you did for him. He knew you would do what needed to happen."

Her voice cracked, "I tried my best."

Charles moved a little closer to her. "Hey, you didn't just try. You did it! I don't even know how to thank you." His mouth was dry.

She glanced around, then sighed. "It all came out when it was supposed to, I guess. I wish things were different. Alex was such a great friend in such a short time. I feel cheated."

He glanced down at his feet. "We were all cheated."

Georgie's face reddened. "I hope they get what they deserve."

Charles patted her shoulder. "Alex would say, don't worry about them, take care of yourself. And do right by the kids. That's why he taught." Charles' smile lit up his face with the uncanny resemblance of Alex. "Boy, did he love kids!"

She sighed, "The kids are the best part! And meeting amazing educators like Alex. That is what makes it a delight, not all this other stuff." She noticed her friends were putting on their coats.

Charles waved at Julia and Marko, who was watching their interaction. "Hey, stay strong. I better let you go. I see some people are watching us a little too closely."

Georgie nodded. "I understand. Glad we are on the same page. It was a pleasure to meet you, Charles. I'm so sorry for your loss." She rubbed his arm and moved to the door to meet Renata, who was carrying her coat.

Charles watched her leave Rosie's then sauntered with his hands in his pockets over to Julia and Marko. He sighed, "It's been a long, beautiful, tragic day. A fantastic tribute to my brother from start to finish. Guess we better call it a night."

Julia's genuine smile lit up her face. "How did it go with Georgie? Was she what you expected?"

Charles' eyebrows raised. "That and much, much more. No wonder he never stopped talking about her."

<hr />

Meantime, Jose was on Route 95 south, driving with his kids and singing an '80s Milli Vanilli song. It was a fun, lighthearted song sung by two con artists. Very appropriate. Jose chuckled; the irony did not escape him. He had already put the house up for sale and told the kids to get ready for a road trip to see some new homes.

Priority number one was to get them all the hell out of town and not to look back.

CHAPTER 30

Six Months Later

The auditorium was at capacity on the hot, humid June day for eighth-grade graduation. The first ten rows were lined with students in baby-blue gowns, while proud family members sat behind them, holding balloons and flowers. Parents were videotaping with their phones as if it were a Hollywood film production.

Promptly at seven in the evening, Julia Bradley stood at the podium as she had done for the past three years, only this year was different. Completing her doctoral program a month ago, she was proud of what she had accomplished. In the front row, Julia waved to the interim superintendent and Genny Lee, whom she had personally invited for the event. Genny was promised an exclusive report on Eden Hills School District since the significant changes in leadership. It was a brilliant invitation to extend, but more natural for Genny to accept since her nephew was part of the graduating class that night. Personally, and professionally, it mattered to Genny Lee.

Julia began by saying, "Good evening, graduates! This exceptional graduation ceremony is not only for you and your families but also for all of us at Eden Hills Middle School. As you have heard, this is my last day at Eden Hills Middle School after twenty-five years as a teacher, then as principal. I have cherished every moment here. While I will not be here physically, I plan on keeping an eye on this special place as I move to the central office as assistant superintendent of schools. It is an honor to be appointed to the position where I can make a global difference in all the buildings."

The room erupted with applause. Julia acknowledged the roar of the crowd with a wave, gesturing them to re-sit. From the massive smile on her face, it was clear she had never expected all the love.

Julia continued, "While we had a lot of joy this year, we also had immense sadness with the loss of Mr. Alex Williams. There is not a day goes by that we will not remember Alex. Tonight I have invited his brother to make two extraordinary presentations. Please welcome Mr. Charles Williams."

Charles appeared from the back of the stage and walked to the podium to a thunderous standing ovation. Charles waited a few moments until everyone sat back in their seats. He glanced over at Julia, trying to compose himself. His hands and legs were shaking from nervousness.

After the crowd settled, Charles began saying, "Thank you, Dr. Bradley. Alex would find great humor in everyone clapping for me when all I did was walk out, but I guess since we look so much alike, you are clapping for him too." There was a roar of laughter. "I was thankful to spend the last few days with Alex before he passed away. He spoke of his love for this community, the school, faculty, and of course, the students. Part of his request to me before he died was to celebrate life with all of you. He wanted his estate to go to his Eden Hills family, so that is what I am here to do. Alex's wish was to create two scholarship funds in his name this year, and for additional scholarships, to be awarded every year going forward."

There was another round of applause, followed by a standing ovation. It moved many in the room to tears. After several long moments, Charles cleared his throat before continuing. "The first scholarship is for a special student in the building who exemplifies all the qualities Alex loved in his students: perseverance, strength, wisdom. It is my honor, in collaboration with the staff of Eden Hills Middle School, to award the first Alex Williams Student Scholarship for College Tuition to Jason Rollins."

Once again, the crowd stood, applauding as Jason approached the stage. This time, Jason did not have an oxygen tank or a paraprofessional. Now he had his new, healthy heart. His parents hugged each other as they blinked rapidly to try to process what they had heard. Charles shook Jason's hand and pointed him to the microphone to speak, but Jason shied away, quickly strolling back to his chair. Students around him were patting his back along with high-fives as he returned to his seat.

Charles wiped away a tear and put his shoulders back. He wanted to make Alex proud. "The next scholarship is a little different. You see, Alex loved teachers. He was always speaking highly about the staff in this building. We laughed at stories, both personal and professional, that he experienced with so many of you. You were always his first family."

He paused, overwhelmed with emotion. "He knew the value of an education, especially how hard it is to be a teacher today. You see, he knew the only way to learn more was to keep going back to school to gain more knowledge. Alex wanted to create a scholarship fund for the faculty. Each year, one teacher will have the opportunity to further their education without the stress of paying for the coursework. This scholarship, to be awarded every year, will pay for a faculty member's master's degree of their choice in the field of education. With the help of Dr. Bradley, we have chosen the first teacher to receive this scholarship. Alex mentioned this person often and believed this person had the attributes to be, in his eyes, a great teacher: dedication, intelligence, patience, compassion, sense of humor, and heart. In other words, the whole package! The administration and staff were in full agreement that the first Alex Williams Faculty Scholarship for completing a master's degree in education will go to Ms. Georgie Nelson."

Georgie's mouth fell open to another deafening round of applause. As she wobbled toward Charles, just for a moment, all she saw was Alex standing there. The brothers shared the kind, warm smile mirrored in their gentle, peaceful soul. Overwhelmed, Georgie began to cry as she embraced Charles, which in turn brought tears to nearly everyone in the auditorium. She whispered in Charles's ear, "I don't know what to say." It was apparent to those who knew her best how heartbroken Georgie had been since Alex's death. The spark in her eyes had dwindled right until this moment when she had looked like her old joyful self.

Returning to her seat, next to Lilliana, Georgie gripped her friend's hand, holding it tight. Lilliana's support was something Georgie could not put into words, especially after a difficult start. She grasped the envelope Charles had given her, closed her eyes, and whispered a silent prayer of thanks to Alex, as she often did. Georgie was thankful she was to be able to work every day with the help of the great doctors who were treating her. Her shots continued to work, and her blood work improved, as did her symptoms. She didn't take *anything* for granted. Georgie only hoped her health would continue to be stable so she could pursue her dream job of being a teacher.

Renata and Carl patted her on the back in support. The night before, the small group had celebrated the end of the school year at Rosie's. They toasted Renata, with Daisy sitting next to her, for being rehired next year as the school nurse, having earned her well-deserved tenure. Loving Shellview and its proximity to the beach, Renata and Daisy recently moved to the town only a few blocks from Georgie. They began spending quality time as a family, far away from the chaos of Eden Hills. Renata also carpooled with Georgie to work, which forced both of them to have regular school hours. Renata used it as an excuse to help Georgie conserve her energy for teaching. They helped each other survive the roller coaster ride of being an educator. Then, they all signed their contracts for the next year, excited and ready for new adventures in and out of the classroom.

Charles Williams walked away from the podium to find Marko backstage grinning ear to ear. They shook each other's hands and gave each other a heartfelt embrace. After several seconds of silence, both were too emotional to speak. They continued to watch the graduation from the shadows of the stage, as Alex would have wanted.

After the ceremony, Georgie left her peers and was walking towards her car when she heard her name called. She turned around to see Charles walking towards her, along with Julia and Marko hand in hand, following behind. Georgie stood only a few inches from Charles. "I have no words for what you have done and for Alex's generosity. I didn't even know you were back."

They embraced as they had done on several occasions over the past few months. Charles whispered, "Let's just say New Jersey is looking better and better." He squeezed her hand. "Can I drive you home this time? You have a big scan in the morning. You need your rest."

Georgie rubbed his arm. "That sounds perfect. I can't believe you kept the scholarship such a secret from me. All this time? You are exactly like your brother, you know."

With a wink, he opened her car door. "You know what Alex would say."

Under the parking lot lights of Eden Hills Middle School their eyes twinkled and hearts raced as they both chimed in unison, "It is what it is."

ACKNOWLEDGMENTS

Writing this book was a tremendous undertaking of patience and perseverance, which I could not have done alone. Special thanks to the following:

My mother and father are the inspiration for the book. Their unconditional love and support throughout my life gave me the courage to achieve all my dreams.

My brother, Dennis, and sister-in-law Caryn, who are always a fantastic support system. Whenever I have a doubt, concern, question, they are still there for me, and I am forever grateful.

Heartfelt appreciation to my grandparents, aunts, uncles, cousins, godchildren, nephews, extended family members, and friends who send me their good thoughts and prayers daily. Their constant positive reinforcement kept me going even with obstacles.

Ann Brady provided invaluable expert mentoring, including coaching, editing, developmental story guidance, and advice throughout critical points of my writing process. Editor Rebecca Wood provided a thorough critique of my manuscript, which led me to a final product I am very proud of. Elite Authors staff, especially Jenny Chandler and Lydia Bowman, who provided me with continual professional support through the ups and downs of the publishing process. Kerry Kletter for her generous insight in all aspects of writing a novel and publishing, I am forever inspired by her beautiful honesty in her story writing abilities.

My beta readers Dr. Carol Fredericks, Dr. Jacqueline Zarro, Rose McConnell, Susan Kiely, Caryn Edwards, Katie Edwards for honest, thoughtful, time-consuming feedback, which helped formulate the final version of my novel. The comments and suggestions all made the story sharper, more precise, and more organized. Julia Emmanuele, who continues to amaze me with her witty words and brilliant stories.

It Is What It Is could not be complete without the support of a talented, positive group of people who helped me from the first to last step of this novel. The team includes Pam Gordon, Dr. John Muciaccia, Karen Biagioli, Agnieszka Skurka, Kelly O'Toole, Claudine Sullivan, Lori Goldberg, Jackie Hoover, Eileen Cairnie, Diane O'Toole, Rose Vega, Mary Ann Ondish, Tami McLaughlin, Dolores Walsh, Katherine Walsh, Geraldine Walsh, Regina Kilmartin, Irish Business Organization, and Alliance of Independent Authors (ALLi).

I consider teaching a vocation and one I proudly dedicated my career to being part of. Learning from teachers, professors, students, parents, administrators, nurses, and child study team members, provided me with many different experiences in school. I treasured every moment.

The novel discusses an uncommon, rare type of cancer called neuroendocrine cancer (NET). For further information, please refer to the following organizations: Neuroendocrine Tumor Research Foundation (NETRF), the Healing NET Foundation, and the Carcinoid Cancer Foundation. National and local support groups such as the New Jersey Carcinoid Cancer NETwork include brilliant, articulate, and compassionate advocates for patients with neuroendocrine cancer who I consider dear friends. Special thanks to the following physicians for their expertise: Dr. Denise Daub, Dr. Lynn Ratner, Dr. Harry Snady, Dr. Sasan Roayaie, and Dr. Jeffrey Mechanick.

I am a truly blessed and thankful woman! What can I say - "It is what it is!"

ABOUT THE AUTHOR

Maureen Edwards inspiration comes from her extensive experience in education. Edwards served as a teacher, a special education director and supervisor, a learning disability teacher consultant, and an adjunct professor. Her work gave her a keen insight into the delicate relationship between teachers, support staff, administrators, and the communities they serve. She received her bachelor's degree in elementary education, a master's degree in developmental and educational psychology, and a master's degree in special education. She earned her doctor of education from Fordham University and graduated magna cum laude. Born in New York City and raised in Weehawken, New Jersey, she still lives in Hudson County, where she enjoys listening to music, going to the beach, and rooting for the Rangers, Giants, and Yankees.

For more information, please visit:
www.maureenedwardsdr.com
Twitter: @MaureenEdwards_
Instagram: maureenedwards_

Made in the USA
Coppell, TX
21 April 2021